AGONY

MARK BEYER is a self-taught artist who began making comics in 1975. His work has appeared in *The New York Times*, *The Village Voice*, and many other publications, and was a mainstay of *RAW* magazine. He created a series of animated shorts for MTV's *Liquid Television*, designed album covers for John Zorn, and collaborated with Alan Moore. Amy and Jordan, the stars of his graphic novel *Agony*, were also featured in a newspaper strip that ran from 1988 to 1996, and which was collected in *Amy and Jordan* in 2004. His paintings and drawings have been exhibited around the world, including in Europe, Japan, and the United States.

COLSON WHITEHEAD is the author of five novels, including *Zone One*, *Sag Harbor*, and *The Intuitionist*. His latest book is *The Noble Hustle*, a nonfiction account of the 2011 World Series of Poker. He is a recipient of a Guggenheim Fellowship and a MacArthur Fellowship.

THIS IS A NEW YORK REVIEW COMIC
PUBLISHED BY THE NEW YORK REVIEW OF BOOKS
435 Hudson Street, New York, NY 10014
www.nyrb.com

Library of Congress Cataloging-in-Publication Data

Names: Beyer, Mark. | Whitehead, Colson, 1969– writer of introduction.
Title: Agony / by Mark Beyer ; illustrated by Mark Beyer ; introduced by
  Colson Whitehead.
Description: New York : New York Review Books, 2016. | Series: New York
  Review Comics | Description based on print version record and CIP data
  provided by publisher; resource not viewed.
Identifiers: LCCN 2015038146 (print) | LCCN 2015035656 (ebook) | ISBN
  9781590179826 (epub) | ISBN 9781590179819 (paperback)
Subjects: | BISAC: COMICS & GRAPHIC NOVELS / Literary. | COMICS & GRAPHIC
  NOVELS / General. | COMICS & GRAPHIC NOVELS / Crime & Mystery. | GSAFD:
  Comic books, strips, etc.
Classification: LCC PN6728.A36 (print) | LCC PN6728.A36 B49 2016 (ebook) |
  DDC 741.5/973—dc23
LC record available at http://lccn.loc.gov/2015038146

ISBN 978-1-59017-981-9
Available as an electronic book; ISBN 978-1-59017-982-6

Printed in the United States of America on acid-free paper.
10 9 8 7 6 5 4 3 2 1

AGONY

MARK BEYER

Introduction by
COLSON WHITEHEAD

NEW YORK REVIEW COMICS · NEW YORK

INTRODUCTION

AGONY IS A GIFT.

There's *Agony* as a gift received. Thirty years ago, the weekly visit to the comic shop was a liberating adventure for my young self. Who knew what the trucks were going to drop off this week? Maybe an early creator-owned project put out by a traditional publisher, like Frank Miller's *Ronin*, or an oddball deconstruction of an underutilized B-list superhero, as Alan Moore was doing with DC's *Swamp Thing*, his *Watchmen* precursor. Graphic novels were new creatures, discovering their form. Next to the mainstream offerings, magazines like Art Spiegelman and Françoise Mouly's influential comics anthology *RAW* offered an off-kilter view from the alternative underground, one that put my stoner friends' *Fabulous Furry Freak Brothers* to shame. In the spring of '85, I picked up *RAW* #7—*The Village Voice* had run some notices about it—and got my first glimpse of Charles Burns's nutso Dog Boy, Sue Coe's slaughterhouse fantasia, and Spiegelman's fabulist *Maus*. And Mark Beyer's Amy and Jordan. Oddball and overstuffed, *RAW* was an anarchic lesson in the possibilities of being a weirdo, a necessary education for a would-be writer.

Then there's *Agony* as a gift given. Senior year of college, my roommate Tim was struck down by a mysterious virus—a Beyer-esque affliction—and had to spend a week in the hospital. What better present, I thought, than letting him borrow my copy of Beyer's *Agony*? Tim was in bad shape, but how could his torments compare to Amy and Jordan's never-ending stream of misfortunes? They sure had cheered me up over the years. When *Agony* came out in 1987, I xeroxed pages from it and taped them above the desk in my dorm room. Page 39, featuring Amy's exclamation "I'm turning into a human skeleton!" generated a strangely profound identification. In that panel, Amy's face has been reduced to a horrible skull, her skin falls off in strips, and she stands in a puddle of her own flesh while an array of miniature skulls circles her head, taunting her. It's hard to explain: I still had all my flesh, but from time to time felt like a living skeleton. "Why did you give me that?" Tim asked on my next visit. "It's depressing."

Whether you find *Agony* relentlessly downbeat or improbably uplifting depends on how your brain is wired. Beyer obviously shares some DNA with the two characters he abused over the decades. In "Radiator Relationships," an autobiographical effort published in the 1978 anthology *Lemme Outa Here*, oval-faced Jordan is his childhood stand-in, labeled with "HOW I LOOKED AS A KID." The last panel of that strip announces "NOW THAT I'M OLDER I DON'T HAVE ANY FRIENDS EITHER REAL OR IMAGINARY!" but Jordan, at least, had gained a running buddy in Amy by the time of *RAW*'s 1980 debut. (Her first appearance was a few years earlier, in Spiegelman's *Arcade*.) Misery loves company, if only to have someone to drive you to the hospital, or lance your head when it fills with blood like a gigantic grisly balloon.

Agony is one of the most hilarious books I've ever read, but again, your mileage will vary depending on your feelings about the inherent comedy of suicide by acid bath, peanut-loving sea creatures, and forfeiting the security deposit on your apartment because you've saturated every surface with blood. And how you feel about relinquishing the logic of realism in favor of the logic of undying despair, your thoughts about a world whose underlying order rests on the next iteration of suffering.

You may wonder, for example, when *Agony* takes place. According to the newspaper *Mourning Call*, glimpsed midway through the book, some of the action takes place on "FEB 12, 0000." Not much help. The meaningless captions provide no further clues. Events occur "Soon," "Shortly," "Seconds later," and "Suddenly," one after another, with no respect to conventional notions of time. On page 54, Amy makes a remark to Jordan, and when he responds in the next panel it is "Two weeks later."

What happens between those panels? Beyer's editing philosophy is, "If something horrible isn't happening, cut it out." Which leaves only agony.

If we don't know when, how about where? *Agony* starts off in the city, and many of Amy and Jordan's misadventures in other strips take off from the cruelties of metropolitan life. Beyer's "City of Terror" trading cards, which appeared in *RAW* #2, feature our sad protagonists as they are harrowed by The Supermarket Line ("Then she found an aisle where there were only 13 people ahead of her.… Four hours later she finally got out of the store"), Chased By Buildings ("Luckily there was a subway stop nearby. The buildings were unable to get downstairs due to their enormous size"), and Three-Cards Monte ("He screamed 'you bastards, here's your money'"). The capricious injustices of the city are a constant aggressor.

In the extended story of *Agony*, however, Amy and Jordan get into the most trouble during their repeated attempts to leave the evil city for a fresh start. "We could live up there," Amy says, reading of a newly discovered village. "Then we wouldn't have to worry about jobs ever again. We'd live off the land." Of course, "Up North" is just as malevolent as the concrete jungle, as is where they end up after their next excursion into the wild: "Living in this cave is starting to get really claustrophobic," Jordan says. But disappointment won't stop him from suggesting that Amy visit her "aunt who lives in the country," which inevitably brings another round of tribulation. It's not the city that's out to get them, but the universe. Nothing offers comfort or refuge—not the wide-open spaces, not family (as their visit to Jordan's father's squalid abode proves), and not friends ("I'm glad we left that party. That woman had no interest in us other than her grasping desire to dominate us").

Purgatory or Hell is one answer to the question of where Amy and Jordan dwell—certainly their remarkable healing powers, which enable them to endure the next round of abuse, are a feature of eternal damnation. They fit in with other cursed misfits from the late '70s, like Mr. Bill from *Saturday Night Live*, except that Mr. Hands and Sluggo are here embodied by sadistic, disembodied fate. In Amy and Jordan's sneers at the straight life and assorted phonies, we get a dollop of early John Waters, circa *Female Trouble* and *Desperate Living*, and that director's dingy America where freaks and monsters abuse each other in an endless parade of travesties. Hippie idealism has been curdled by reality.

"The small part of my mind that's controlling my life seems tattered and torn," Amy says at one point in her travails. To be aware of your unending sufferings and to keep going: that's the moral idea animating this book. It's not a stretch to bring in Samuel Beckett as another kindred spirit at this point, for many reasons. The flat landscapes of *Agony* evoke Beckett's absurd wastelands. Surely Vladimir and Estragon live in the sublet upstairs, and Nagg and Nell from *Endgame* own the local diner, sans legs and still trapped in their ashcans.

Beyer also shares Beckett's humor and, unlikely as it is, his optimism. *Agony* is about agony, but it's also about the hope that endures despite all that life throws at you. "In the silence you don't know, you must go on, I can't go on, I'll go on," laments the narrator of *The Unnamable*. It's a nice echo of Jordan's encouragement to his partner/roommate/double in *Agony*: "We've just got to keep trying harder. It's a struggle, but what else can we do?" Keep trying harder, and sometimes a big bear will come out of nowhere and throw you to safety, or a winged cave-god deposit you in a nice apartment with pine-veneer furniture.

What can I say—it cheers me up, even now, all these years later.

—COLSON WHITEHEAD

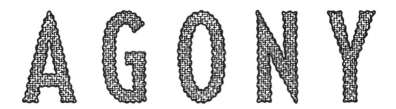

AGONY
BY MARK BEYER

NYRC • NEW YORK

EDITED & DESIGNED BY ART SPIEGELMAN & FRANÇOISE MOULY

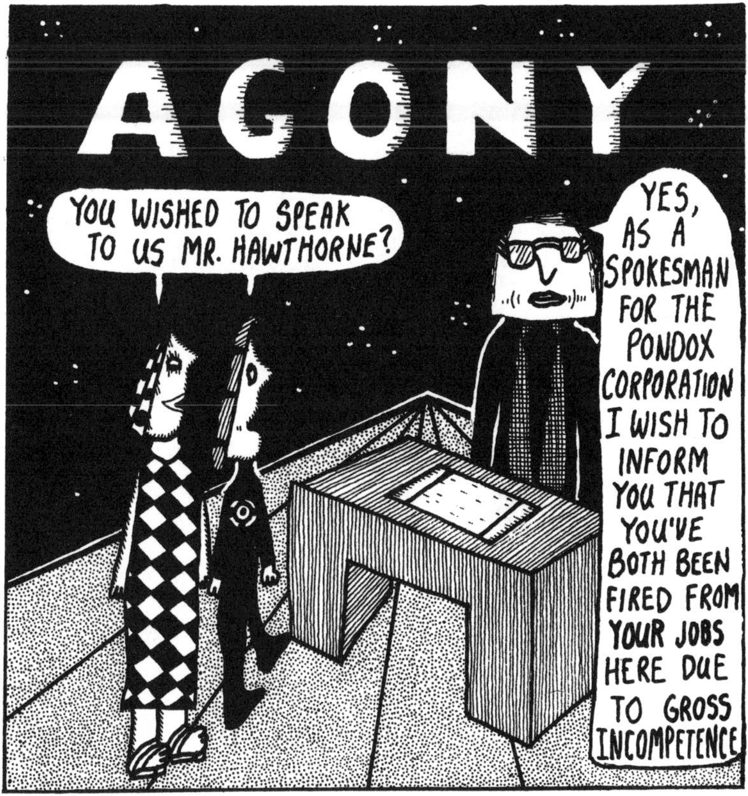
AGONY
YOU WISHED TO SPEAK TO US MR. HAWTHORNE?
YES, AS A SPOKESMAN FOR THE PONDOX CORPORATION I WISH TO INFORM YOU THAT YOU'VE BOTH BEEN FIRED FROM YOUR JOBS HERE DUE TO GROSS INCOMPETENCE

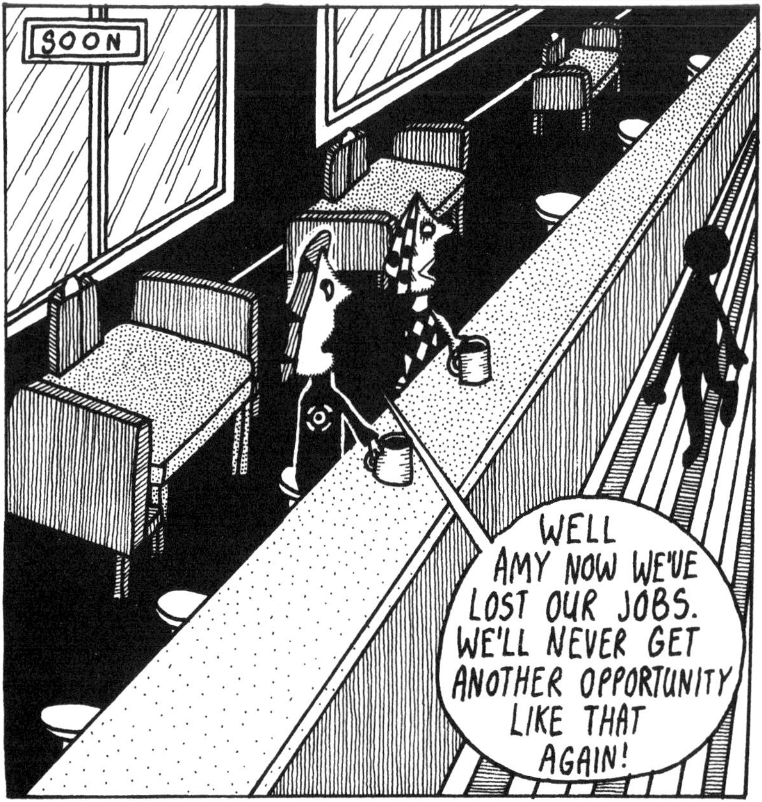
SOON
WELL AMY NOW WE'VE LOST OUR JOBS. WE'LL NEVER GET ANOTHER OPPORTUNITY LIKE THAT AGAIN!

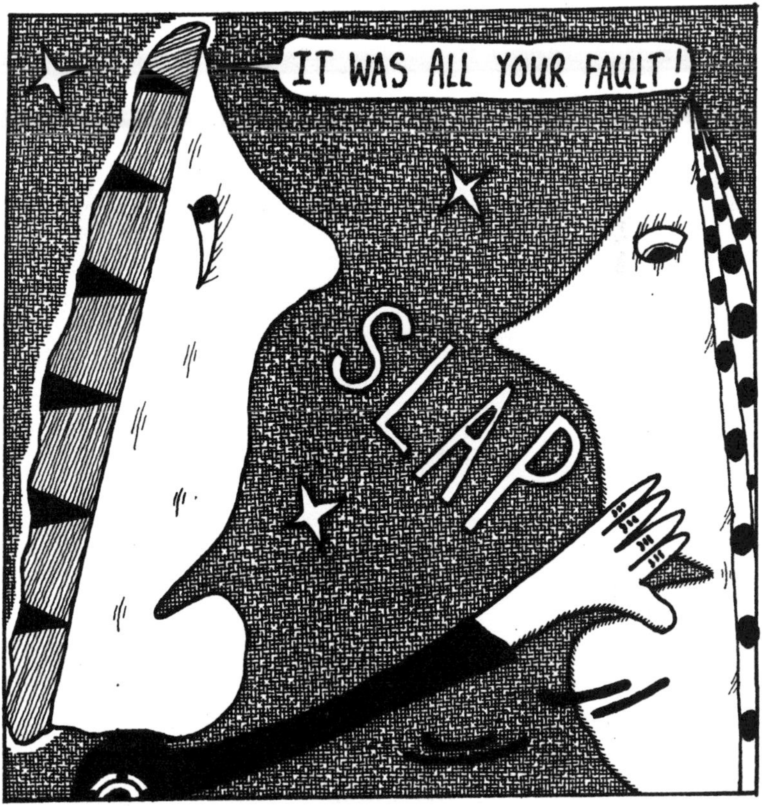
IT WAS ALL YOUR FAULT!
SLAP

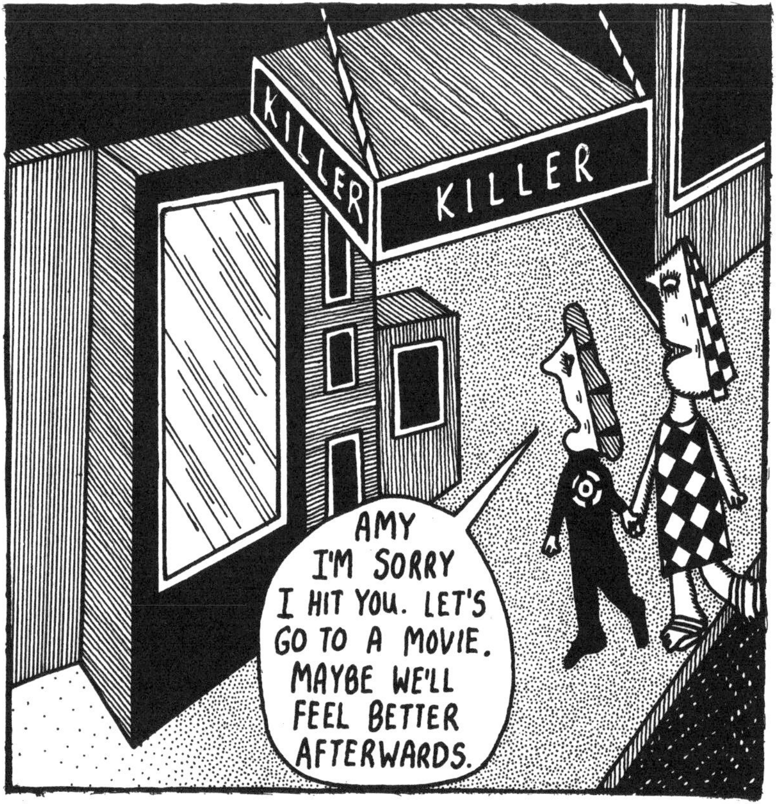
KILLER
KILLER
AMY I'M SORRY I HIT YOU. LET'S GO TO A MOVIE. MAYBE WE'LL FEEL BETTER AFTERWARDS.

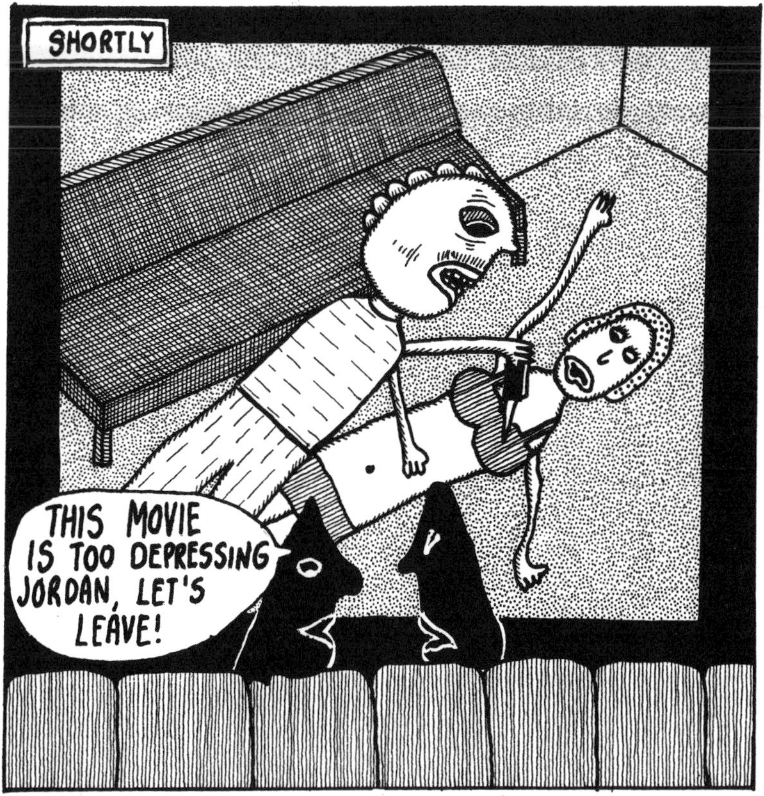
SHORTLY
THIS MOVIE IS TOO DEPRESSING JORDAN, LET'S LEAVE!

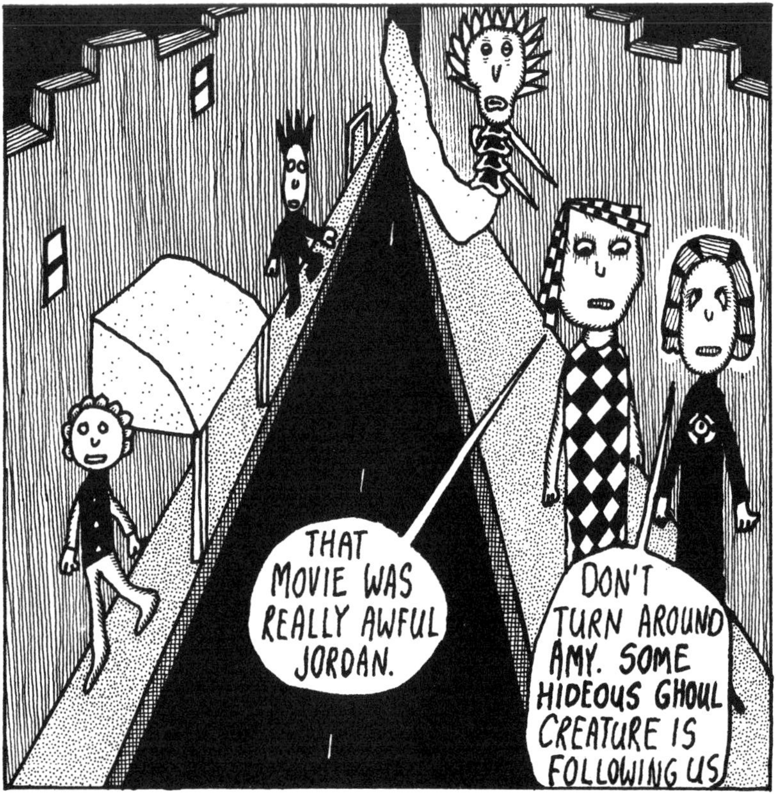
THAT MOVIE WAS REALLY AWFUL JORDAN.
DON'T TURN AROUND AMY. SOME HIDEOUS GHOUL CREATURE IS FOLLOWING US

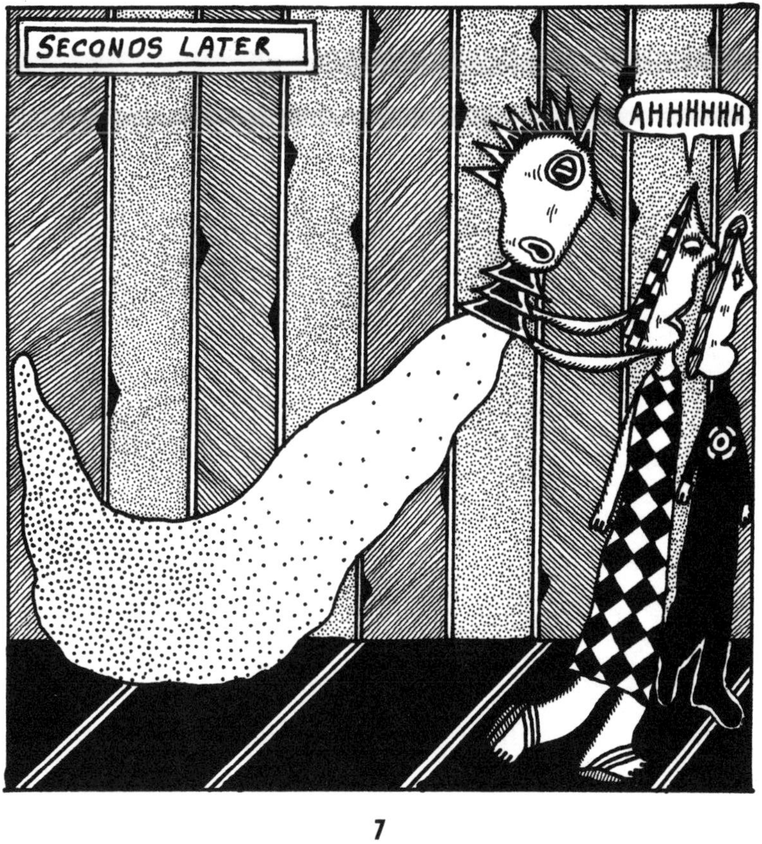
SECONOS LATER
AHHHHHH

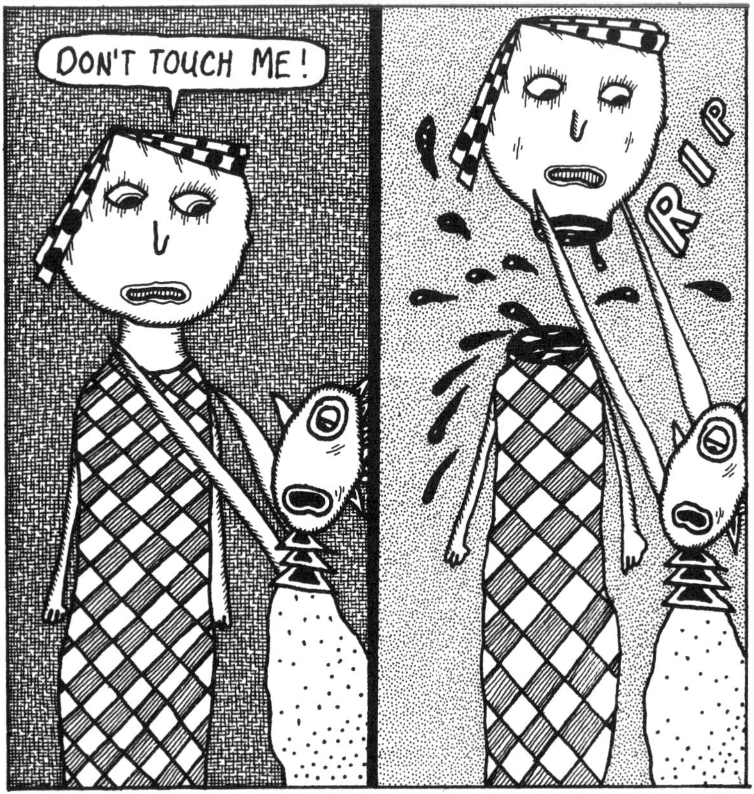
DON'T TOUCH ME!
RIP

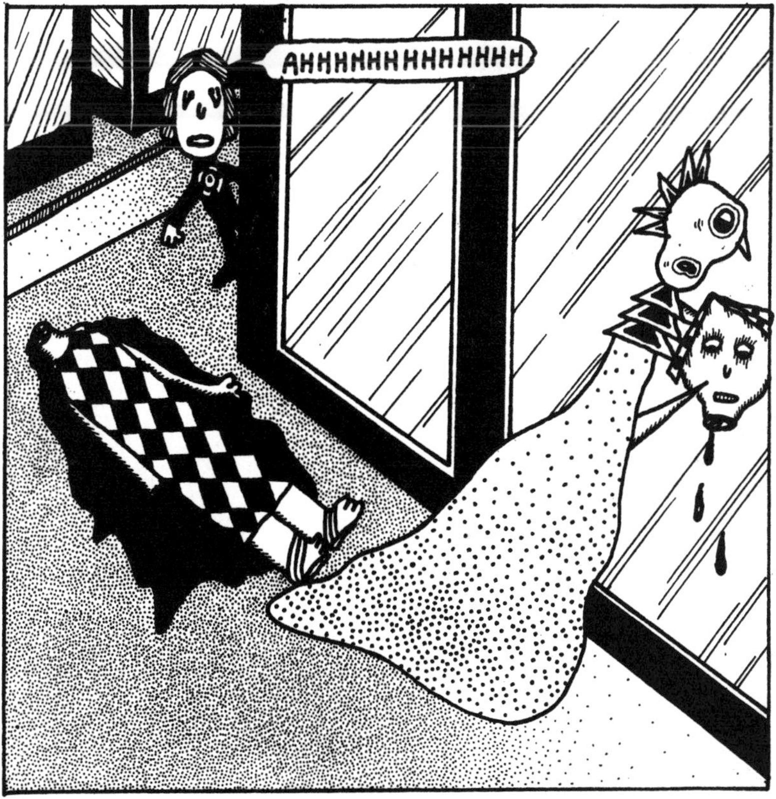
AHHHHHHHHHHHHH

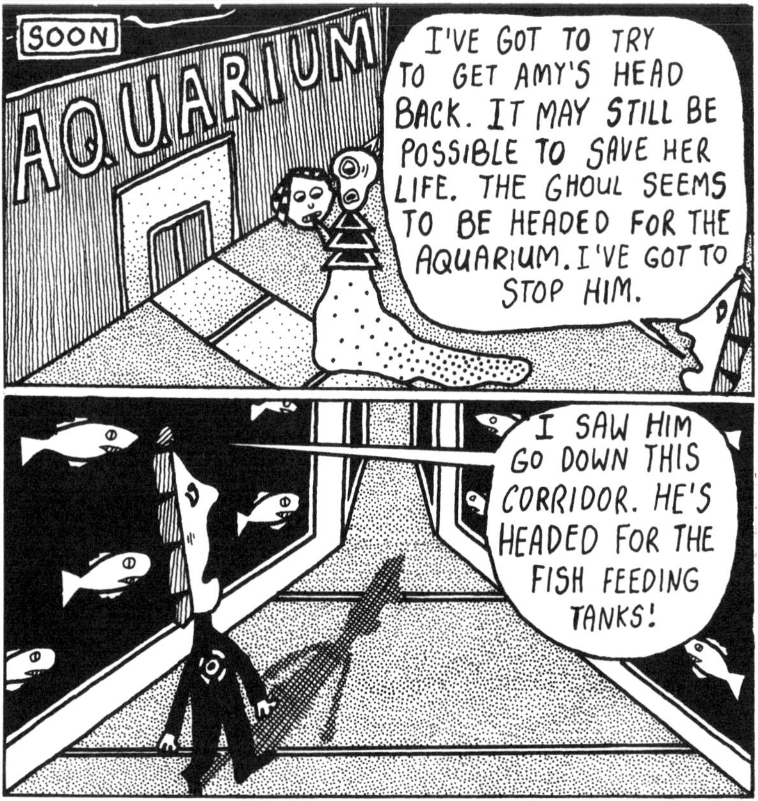
SOON
AQUARIUM
I'VE GOT TO TRY TO GET AMY'S HEAD BACK. IT MAY STILL BE POSSIBLE TO SAVE HER LIFE. THE GHOUL SEEMS TO BE HEADED FOR THE AQUARIUM. I'VE GOT TO STOP HIM.
I SAW HIM GO DOWN THIS CORRIDOR. HE'S HEADED FOR THE FISH FEEDING TANKS!

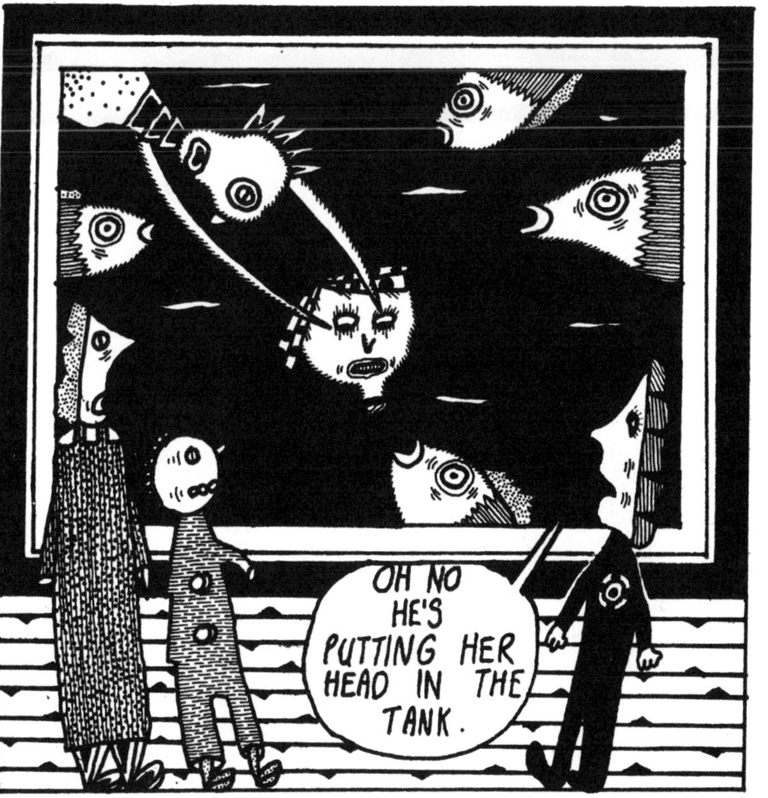
OH NO HE'S PUTTING HER HEAD IN THE TANK.

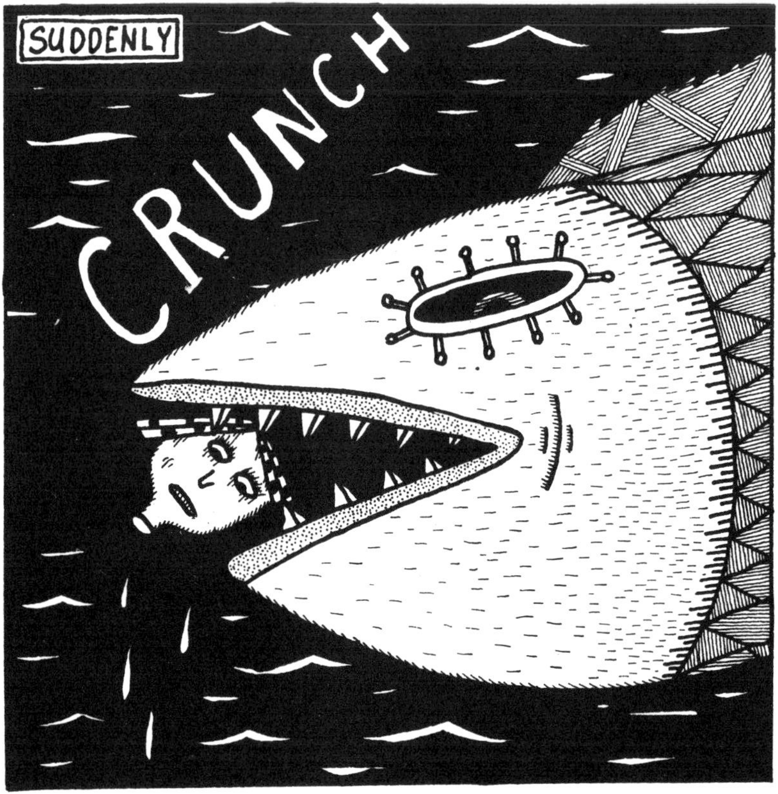
SUDDENLY
CRUNCH

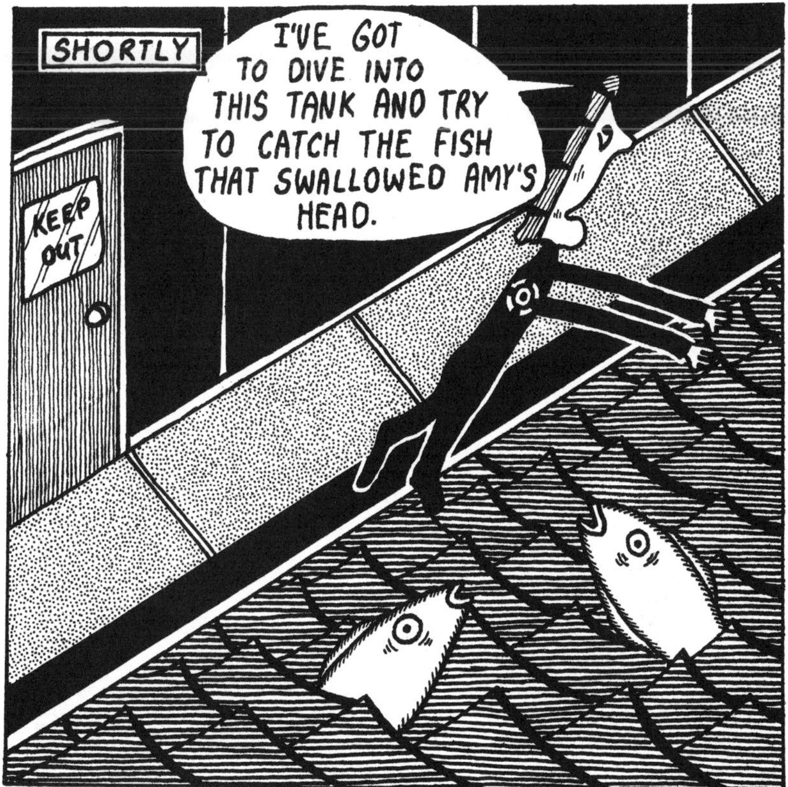
SHORTLY
I'VE GOT TO DIVE INTO THIS TANK AND TRY TO CATCH THE FISH THAT SWALLOWED AMY'S HEAD.
KEEP OUT

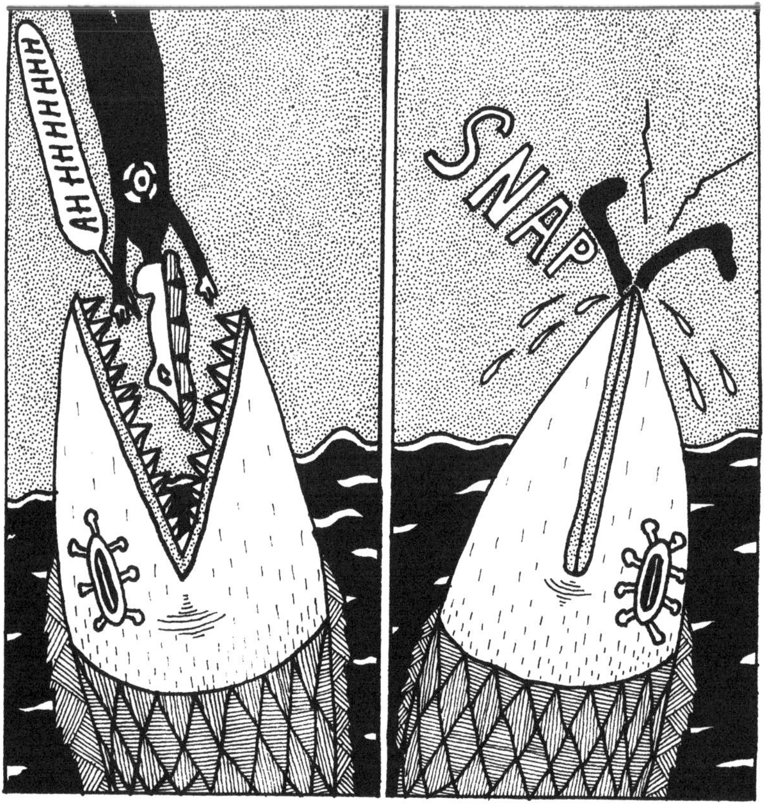
AHHHHHHHHHH
SNAP

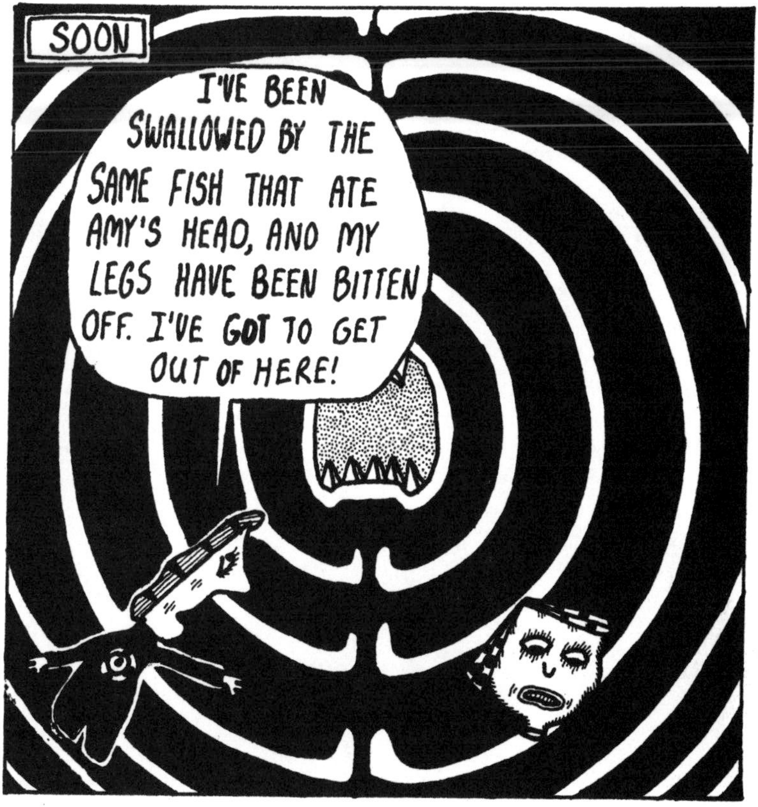
SOON
I'VE BEEN SWALLOWED BY THE SAME FISH THAT ATE AMY'S HEAD, AND MY LEGS HAVE BEEN BITTEN OFF. I'VE GOT TO GET OUT OF HERE!

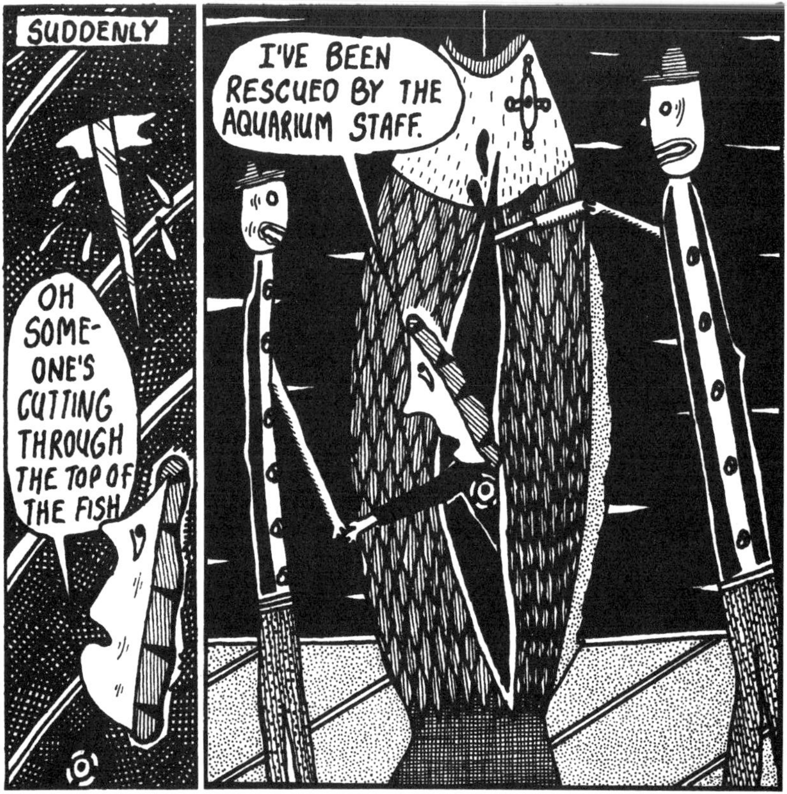
SUDDENLY
OH SOME-ONE'S CUTTING THROUGH THE TOP OF THE FISH
I'VE BEEN RESCUED BY THE AQUARIUM STAFF.

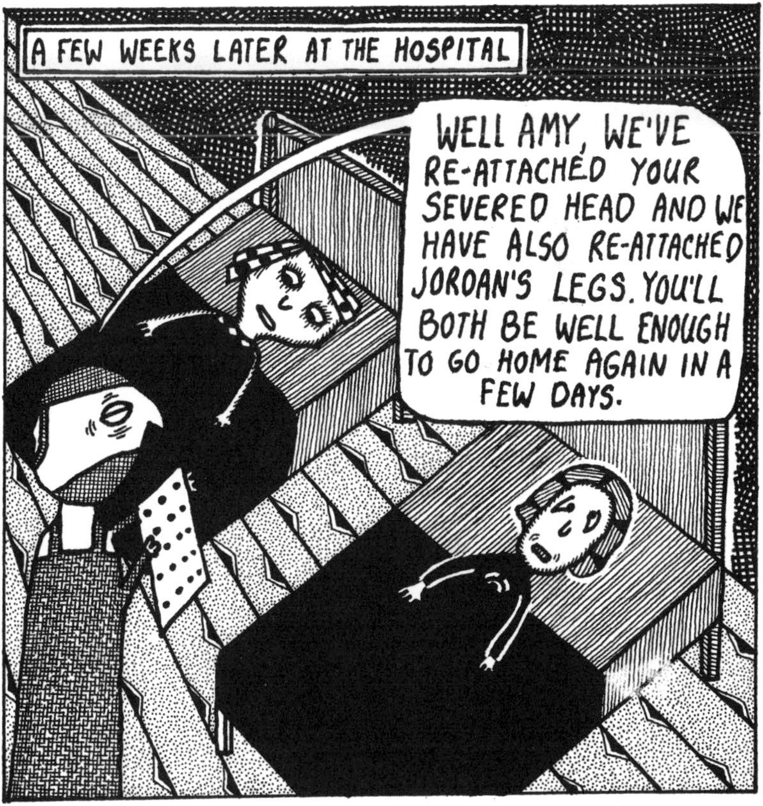
A FEW WEEKS LATER AT THE HOSPITAL
WELL AMY, WE'VE RE-ATTACHED YOUR SEVERED HEAD AND WE HAVE ALSO RE-ATTACHED JORDAN'S LEGS. YOU'LL BOTH BE WELL ENOUGH TO GO HOME AGAIN IN A FEW DAYS.

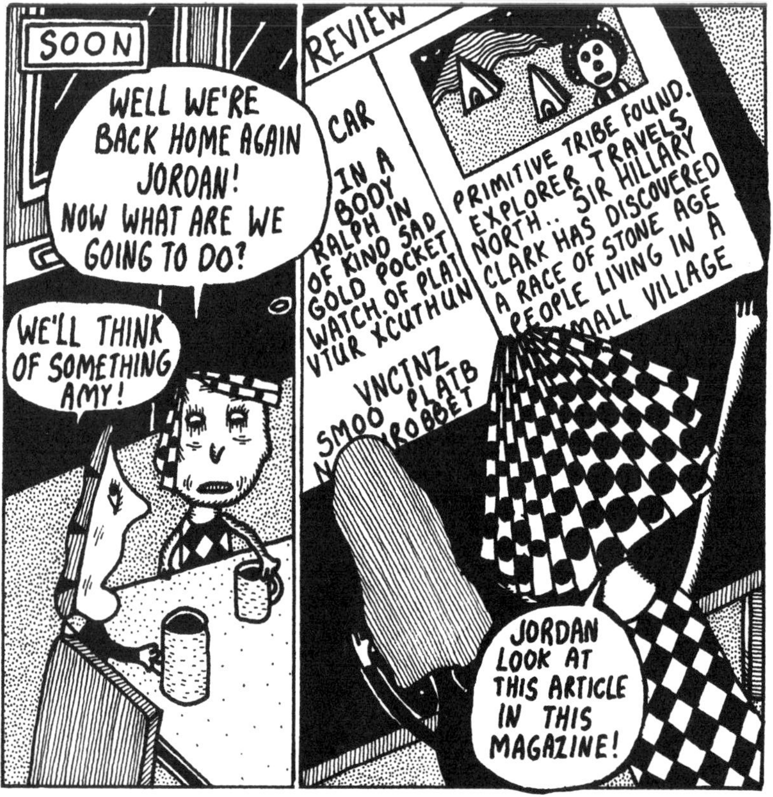
SOON
WELL WE'RE BACK HOME AGAIN JORDAN! NOW WHAT ARE WE GOING TO DO?
WE'LL THINK OF SOMETHING AMY!
REVIEW
CAR
IN A BODY RALPH IN OF KIND SAD GOLD POCKET WATCH.OF PLAT VTUR XCUTHUN
VNCTNZ SMOO PLATB ROBBET
PRIMITIVE TRIBE FOUND. EXPLORER TRAVELS NORTH.. SIR HILLARY CLARK HAS DISCOVERED A RACE OF STONE AGE PEOPLE LIVING IN A MALL VILLAGE
JORDAN LOOK AT THIS ARTICLE IN THIS MAGAZINE!

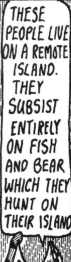

A RACE OF PRIMITIVE PEOPLE HAVE BEEN DISCOVERED UP NORTH. MAYBE WE COULD MOVE UP THERE AND LIVE WITH THEM.

THESE PEOPLE LIVE ON A REMOTE ISLAND. THEY SUBSIST ENTIRELY ON FISH AND BEAR WHICH THEY HUNT ON THEIR ISLAND

WE COULD LIVE UP THERE. THEN WE WOULDN'T HAVE TO WORRY ABOUT JOBS EVER AGAIN. WE'D LIVE OFF THE LAND.

AMY HAVE YOU TOTALLY LOST YOUR MIND? WE WOULD NEVER SURVIVE. AND EVEN IF WE DID, WE WOULD HATE IT!

YOU'VE GOT THE ATTENTION SPAN OF AN INSECT. AS SOON AS WE DECIDE TO DO ONE THING YOU WANT TO DO SOMETHING ELSE!

19

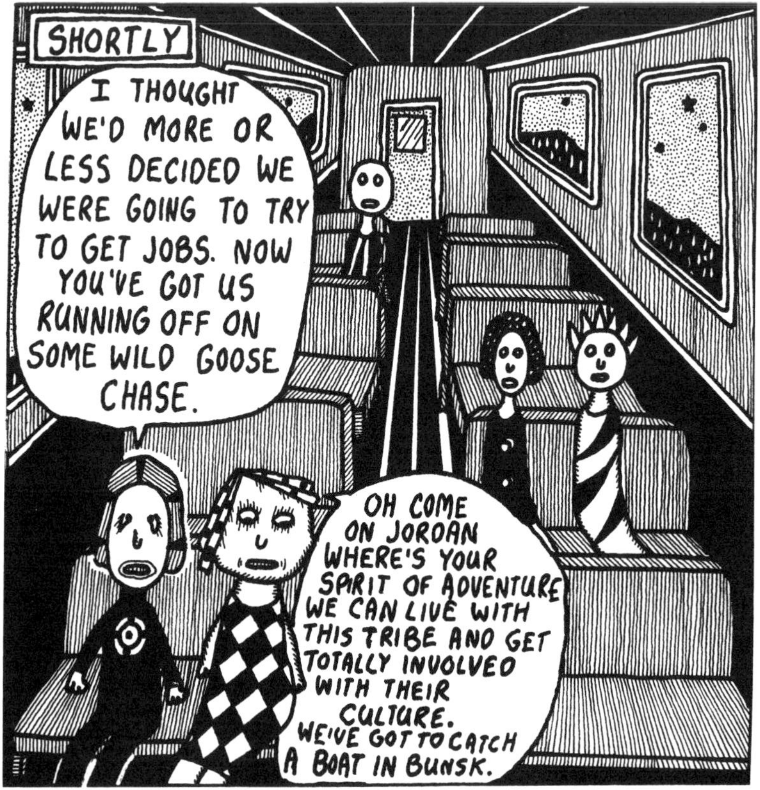
SHORTLY
I THOUGHT WE'D MORE OR LESS DECIDED WE WERE GOING TO TRY TO GET JOBS. NOW YOU'VE GOT US RUNNING OFF ON SOME WILD GOOSE CHASE.
OH COME ON JORDAN WHERE'S YOUR SPIRIT OF ADVENTURE WE CAN LIVE WITH THIS TRIBE AND GET TOTALLY INVOLVED WITH THEIR CULTURE. WE'VE GOT TO CATCH A BOAT IN BUNSK.

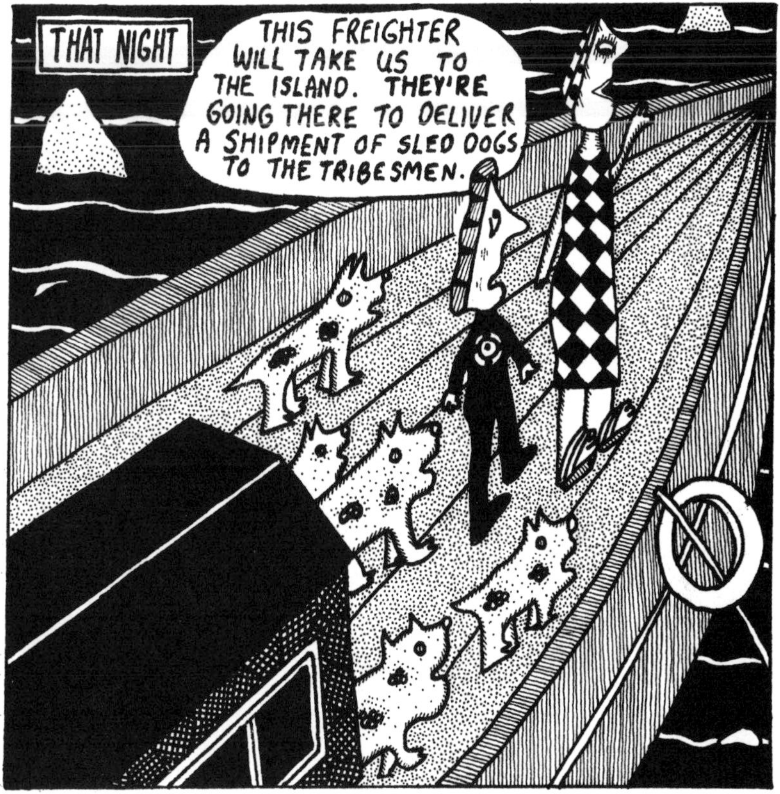
THAT NIGHT
THIS FREIGHTER WILL TAKE US TO THE ISLAND. THEY'RE GOING THERE TO DELIVER A SHIPMENT OF SLED DOGS TO THE TRIBESMEN.

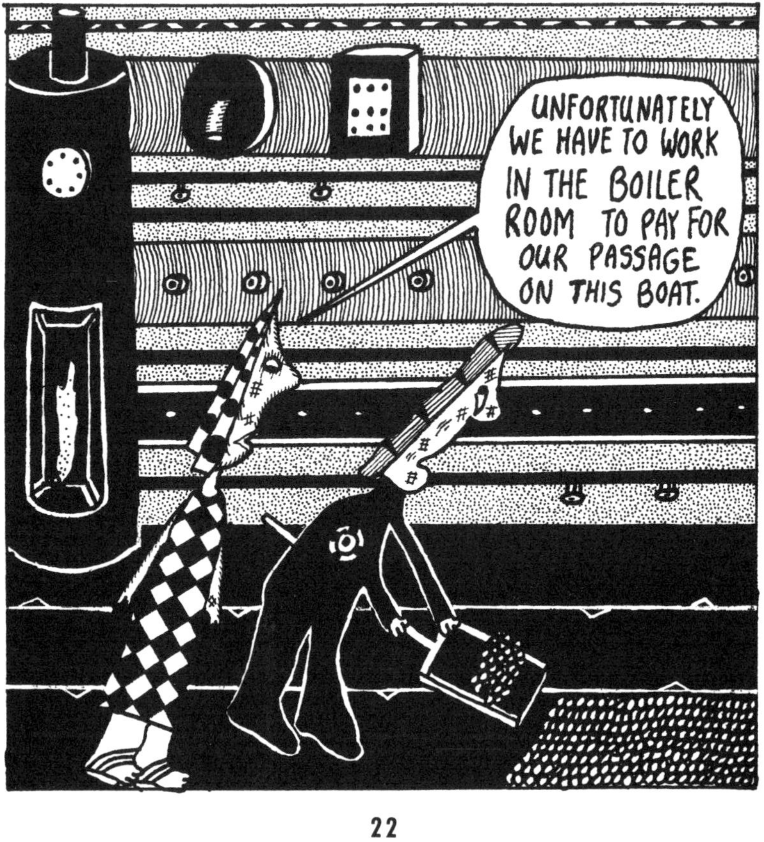
UNFORTUNATELY WE HAVE TO WORK IN THE BOILER ROOM TO PAY FOR OUR PASSAGE ON THIS BOAT.

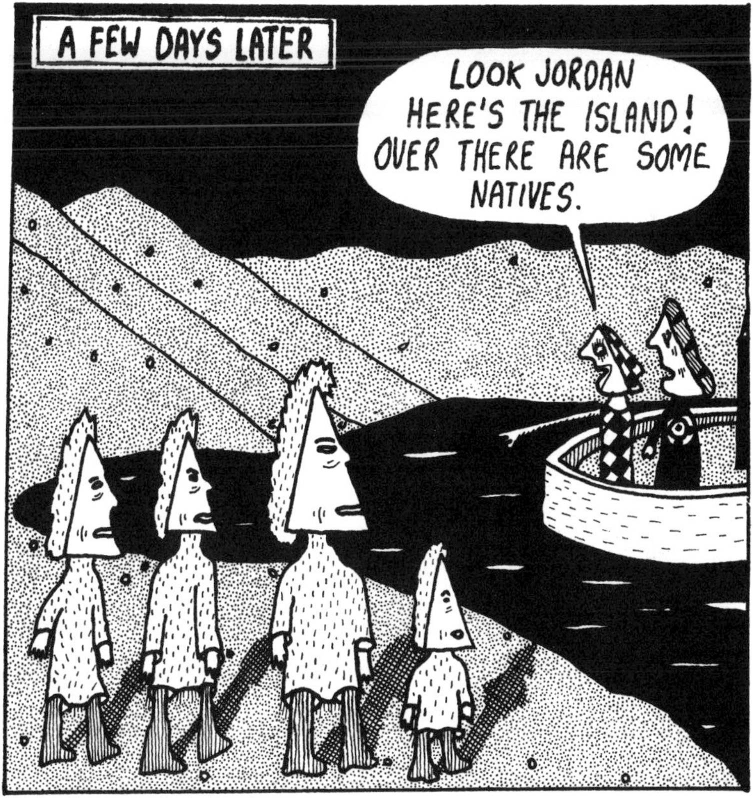
A FEW DAYS LATER
LOOK JORDAN HERE'S THE ISLAND! OVER THERE ARE SOME NATIVES.

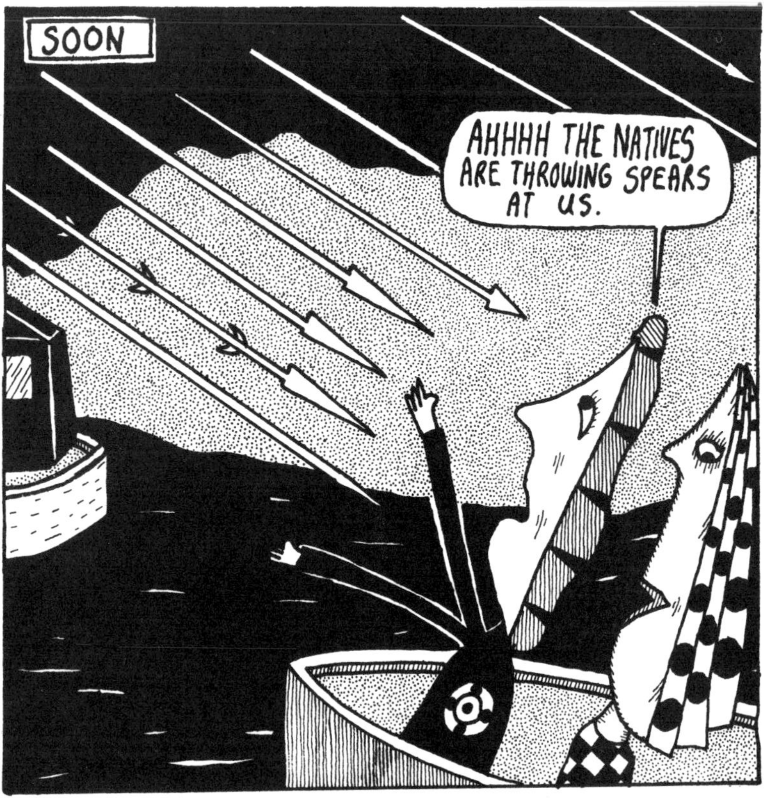
SOON
AHHHH THE NATIVES ARE THROWING SPEARS AT US.

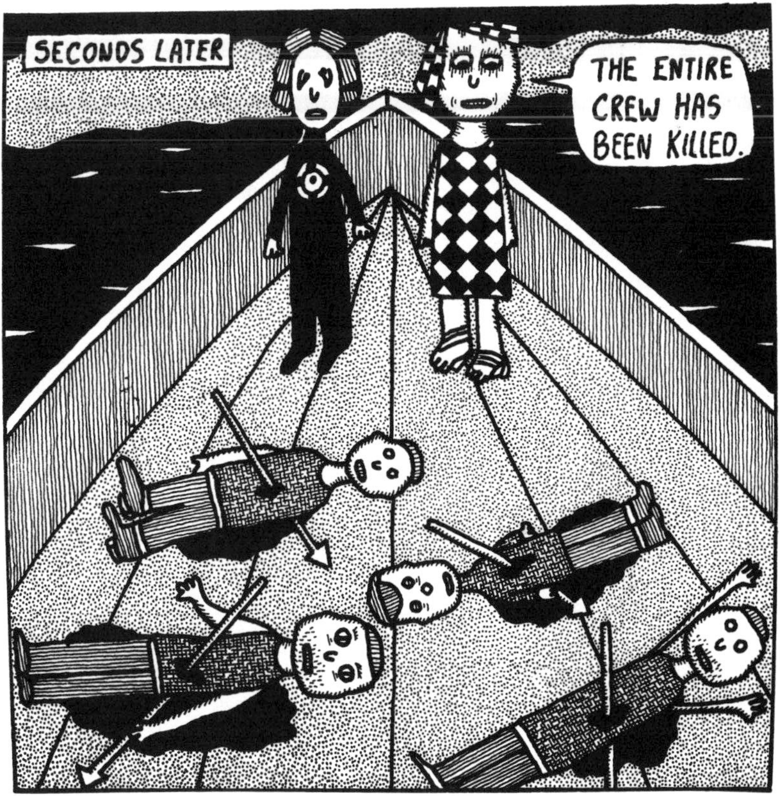
SECONDS LATER
THE ENTIRE CREW HAS BEEN KILLED.

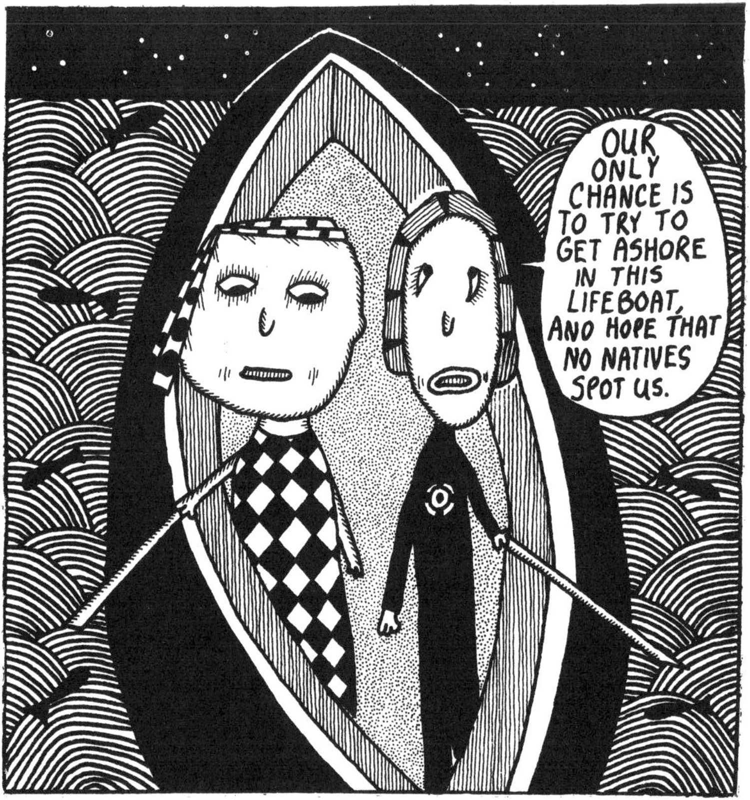
OUR ONLY CHANCE IS TO TRY TO GET ASHORE IN THIS LIFEBOAT, AND HOPE THAT NO NATIVES SPOT US.

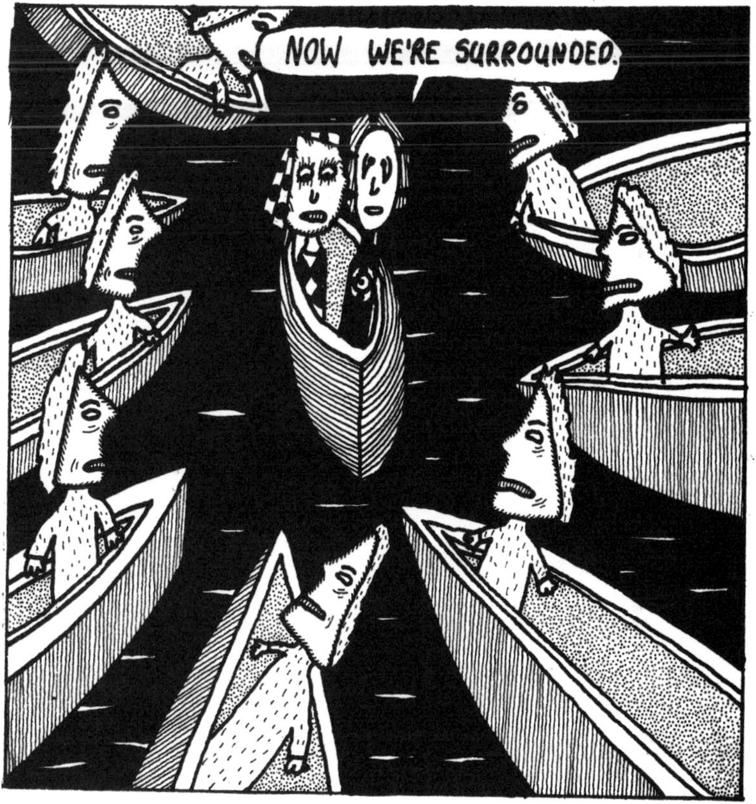
NOW WE'RE SURROUNDED.

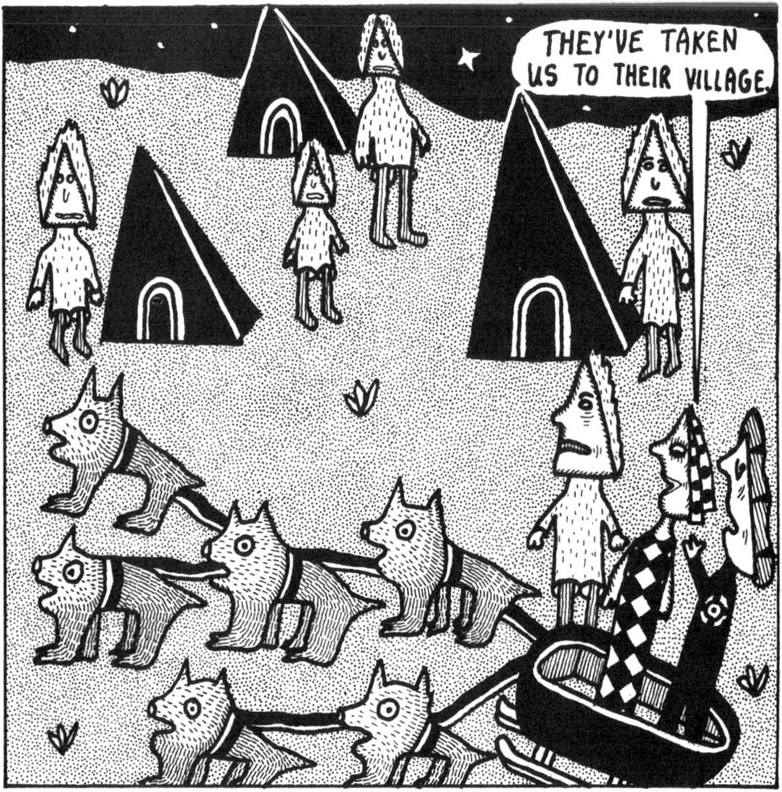
THEY'VE TAKEN US TO THEIR VILLAGE.

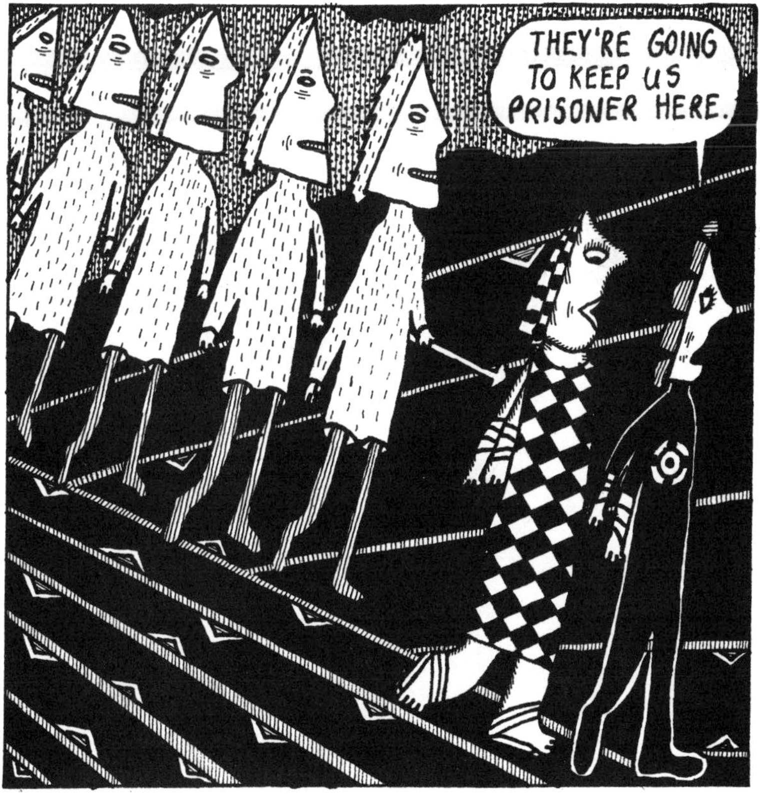
THEY'RE GOING TO KEEP US PRISONER HERE.

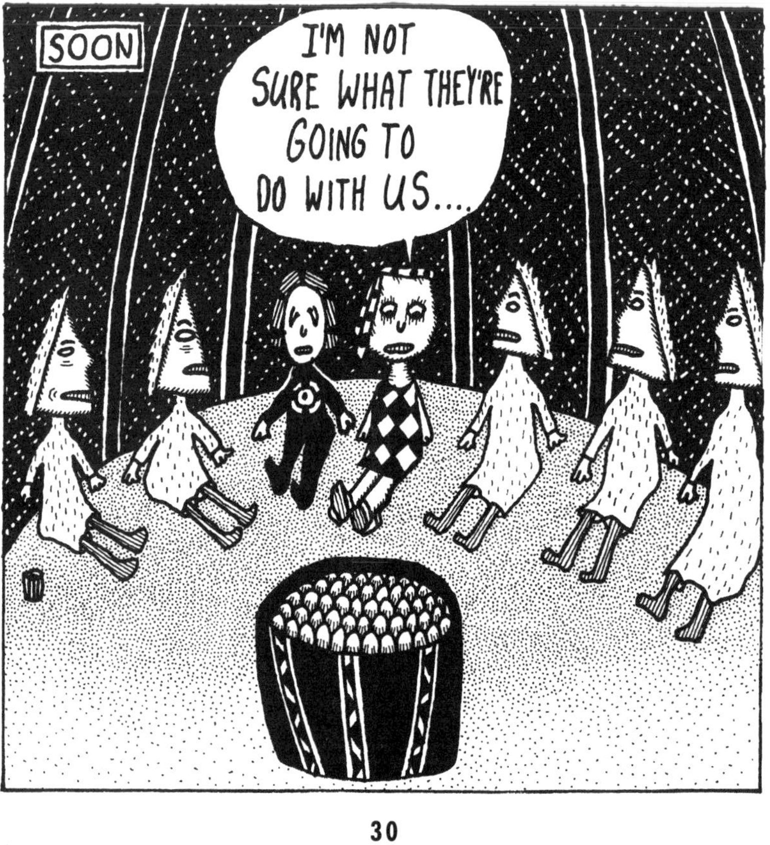
SOON
I'M NOT SURE WHAT THEY'RE GOING TO DO WITH US....

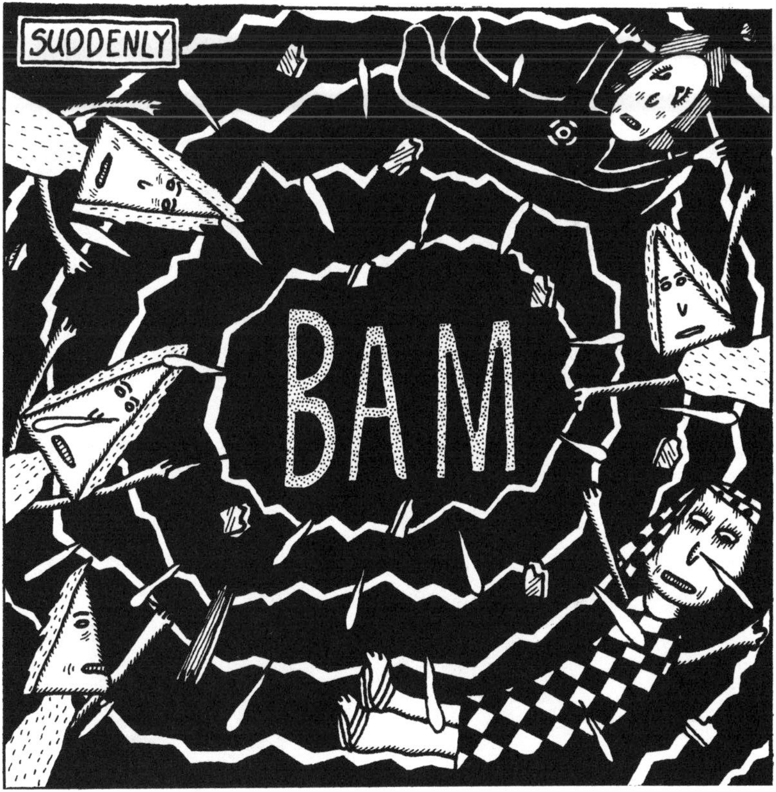
SUDDENLY
BAM

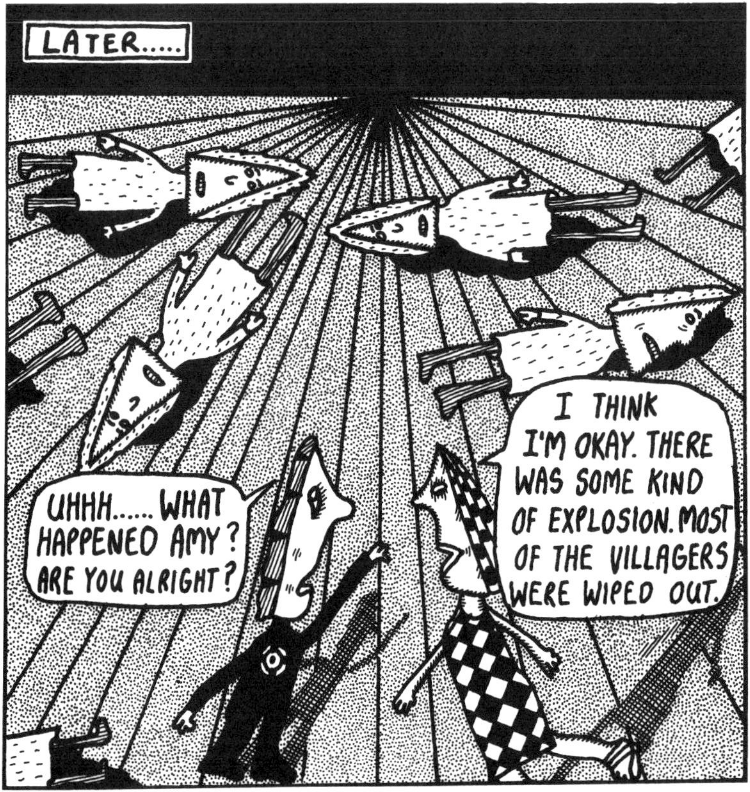
LATER.....
UHHH...... WHAT HAPPENED AMY? ARE YOU ALRIGHT?
I THINK I'M OKAY. THERE WAS SOME KIND OF EXPLOSION. MOST OF THE VILLAGERS WERE WIPED OUT.

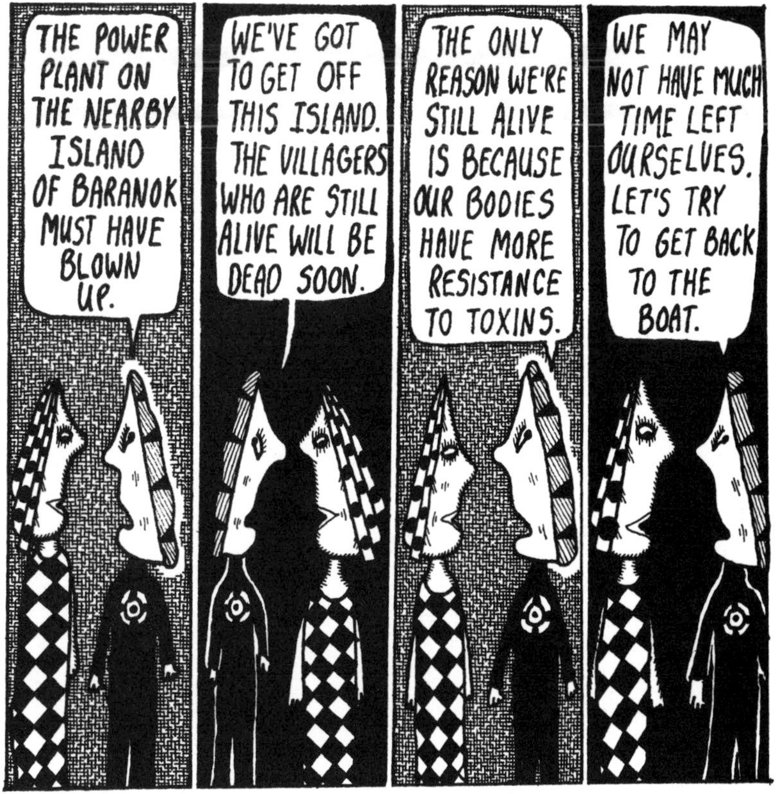
THE POWER PLANT ON THE NEARBY ISLAND OF BARANOK MUST HAVE BLOWN UP.
WE'VE GOT TO GET OFF THIS ISLAND. THE VILLAGERS WHO ARE STILL ALIVE WILL BE DEAD SOON.
THE ONLY REASON WE'RE STILL ALIVE IS BECAUSE OUR BODIES HAVE MORE RESISTANCE TO TOXINS.
WE MAY NOT HAVE MUCH TIME LEFT OURSELVES. LET'S TRY TO GET BACK TO THE BOAT.

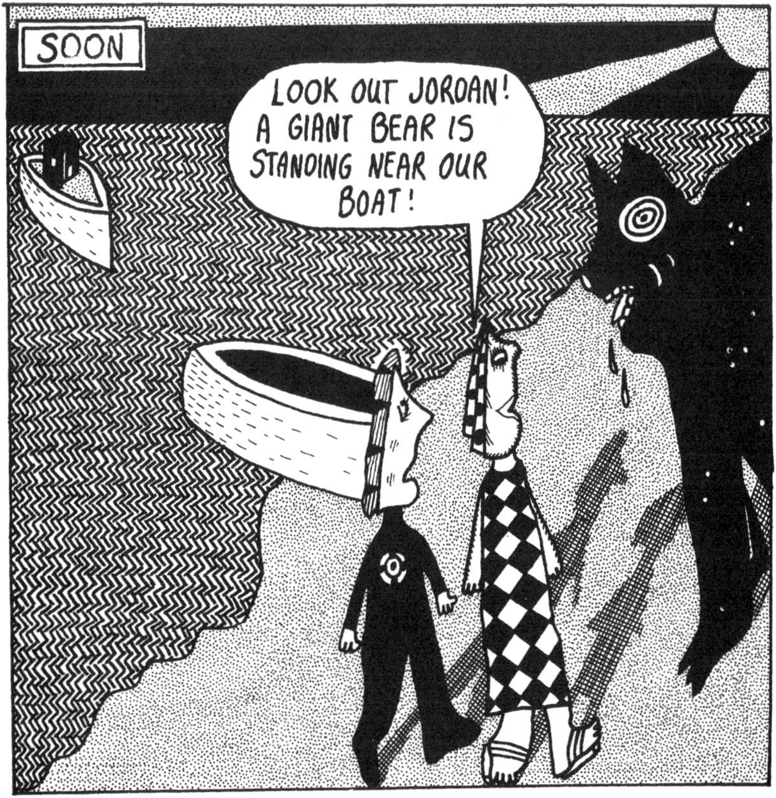
SOON
LOOK OUT JORDAN! A GIANT BEAR IS STANDING NEAR OUR BOAT!

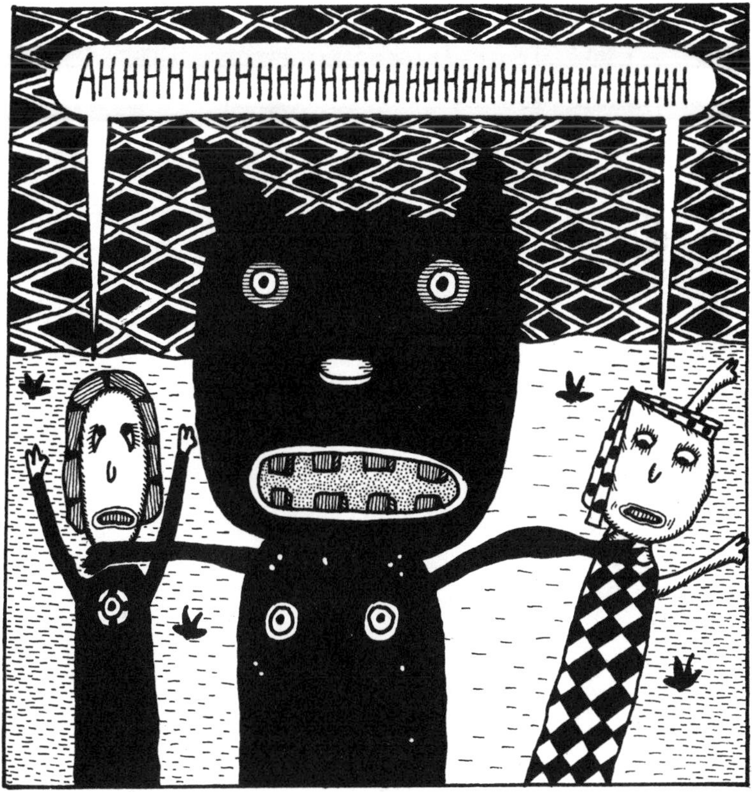
AHHHHHHHHHHHHHHHHHHHHHHHHHHHHH

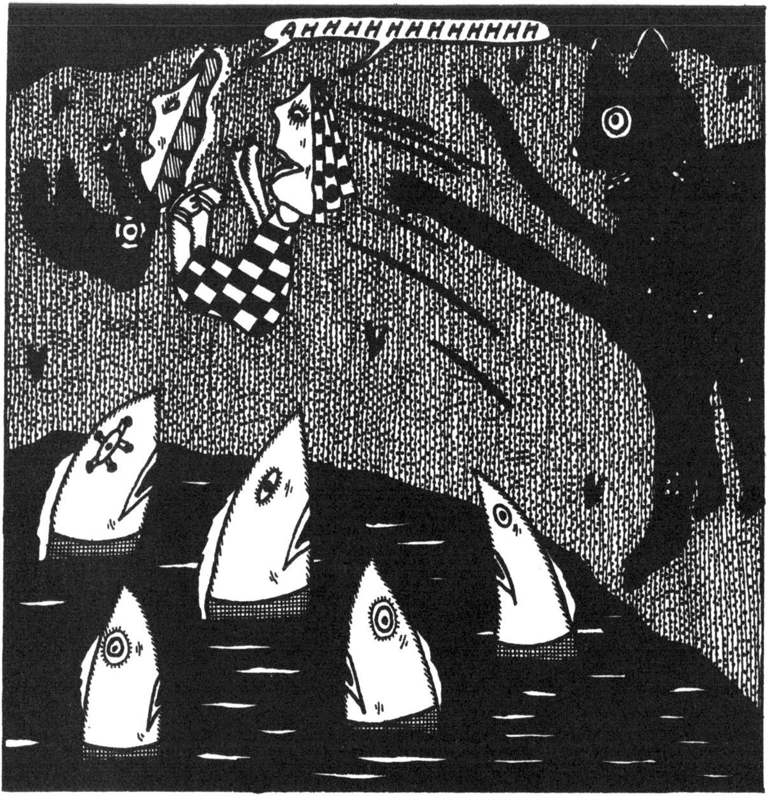
AHHHHHHHHHHHHH

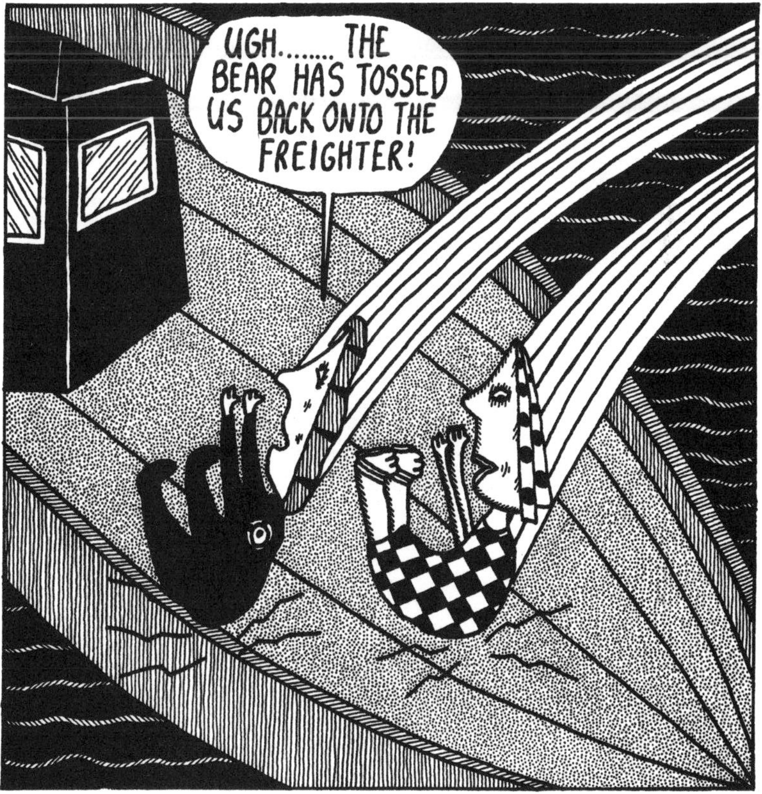
UGH........ THE BEAR HAS TOSSED US BACK ONTO THE FREIGHTER!

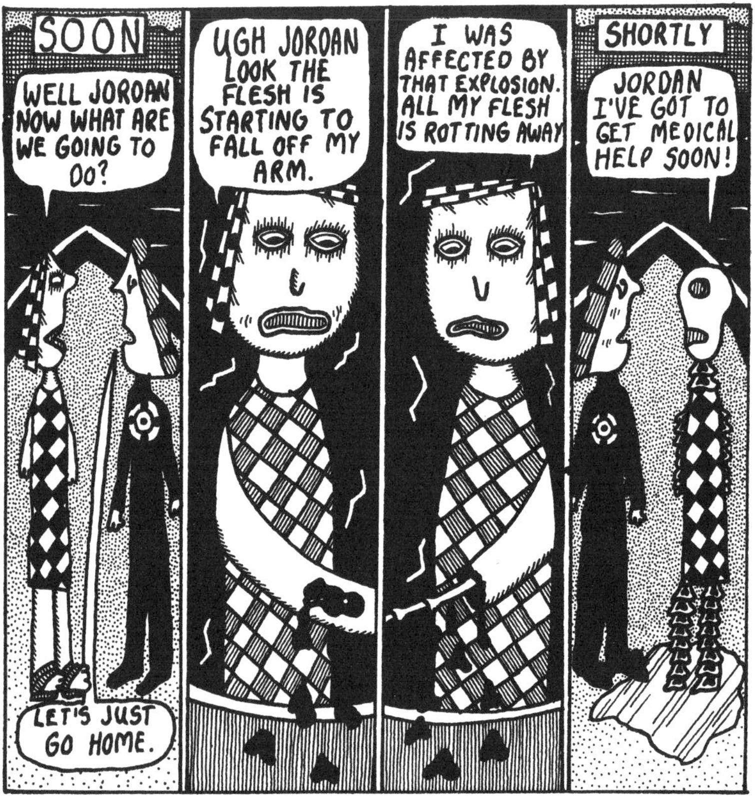
SOON
WELL JOROAN NOW WHAT ARE WE GOING TO DO?
LET'S JUST GO HOME.
UGH JOROAN LOOK THE FLESH IS STARTING TO FALL OFF MY ARM.
I WAS AFFECTED BY THAT EXPLOSION. ALL MY FLESH IS ROTTING AWAY
SHORTLY
JORDAN I'VE GOT TO GET MEDICAL HELP SOON!

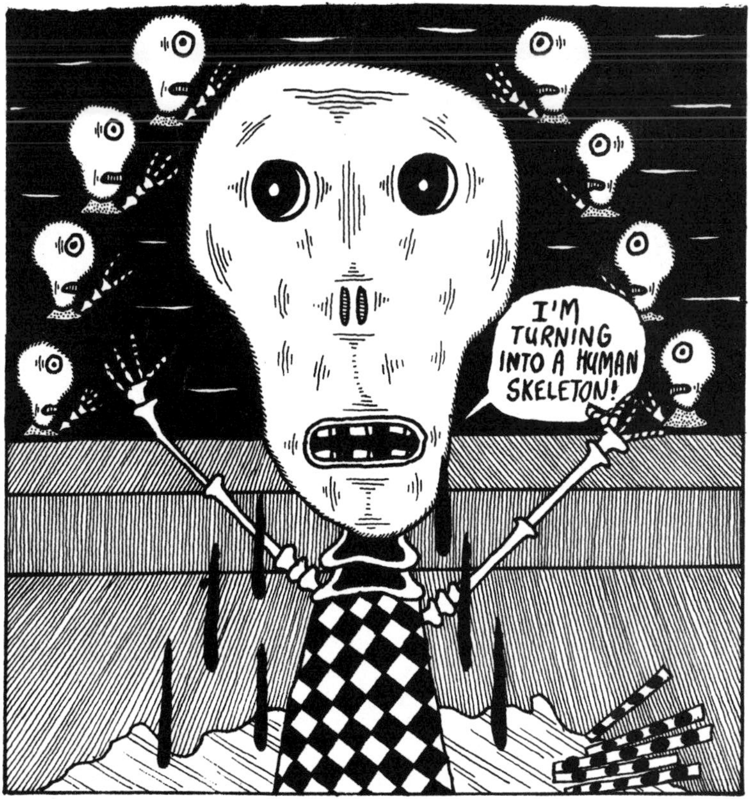
I'M TURNING INTO A HUMAN SKELETON!

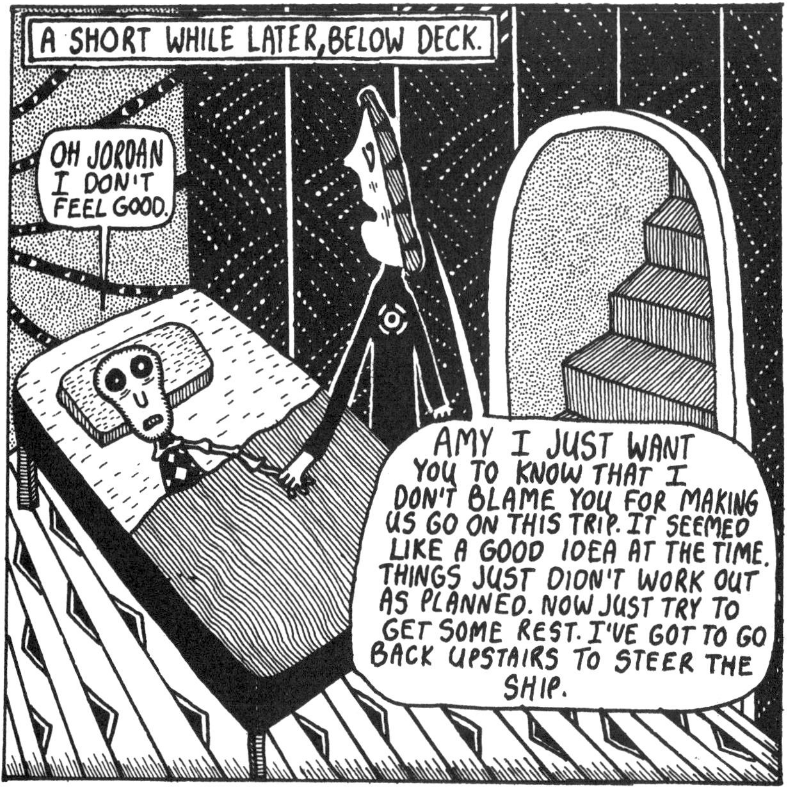
A SHORT WHILE LATER, BELOW DECK.
OH JORDAN I DON'T FEEL GOOD.
AMY I JUST WANT YOU TO KNOW THAT I DON'T BLAME YOU FOR MAKING US GO ON THIS TRIP. IT SEEMED LIKE A GOOD IDEA AT THE TIME. THINGS JUST DIDN'T WORK OUT AS PLANNED. NOW JUST TRY TO GET SOME REST. I'VE GOT TO GO BACK UPSTAIRS TO STEER THE SHIP.

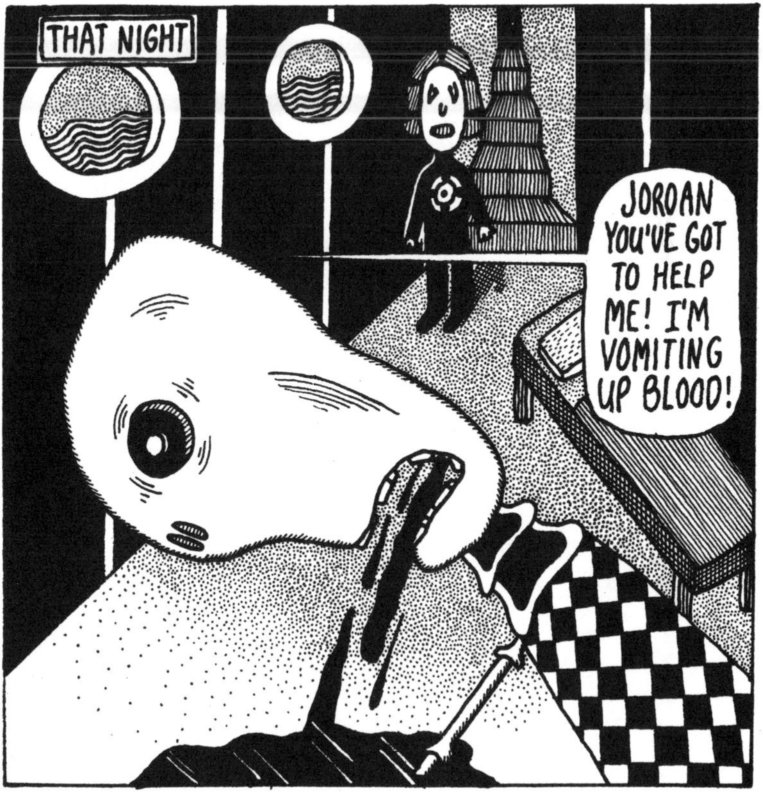
THAT NIGHT
JORDAN YOU'VE GOT TO HELP ME! I'M VOMITING UP BLOOD!

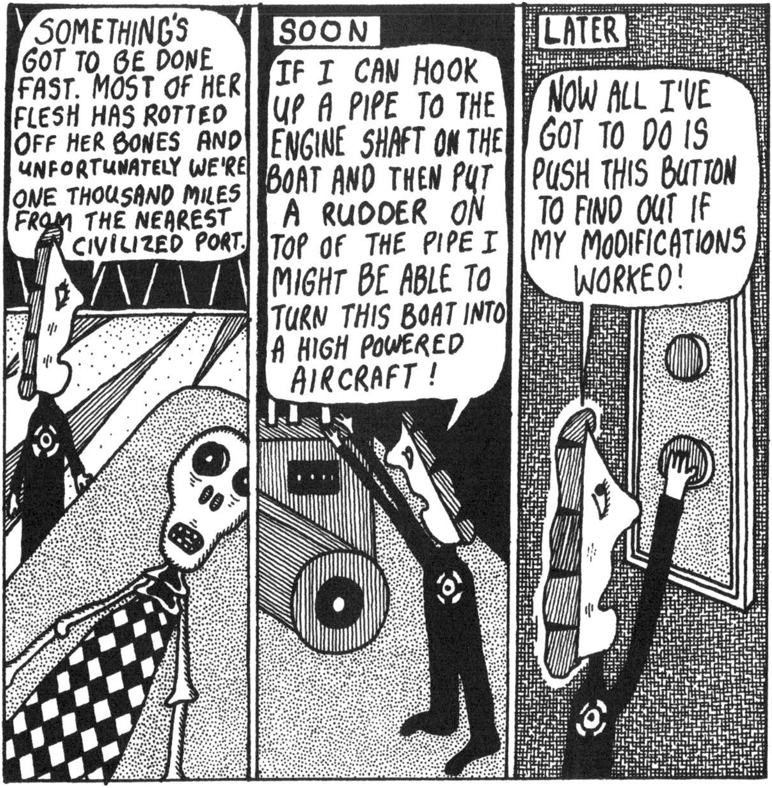
SOMETHING'S GOT TO BE DONE FAST. MOST OF HER FLESH HAS ROTTED OFF HER BONES AND UNFORTUNATELY WE'RE ONE THOUSAND MILES FROM THE NEAREST CIVILIZED PORT.
SOON
IF I CAN HOOK UP A PIPE TO THE ENGINE SHAFT ON THE BOAT AND THEN PUT A RUDDER ON TOP OF THE PIPE I MIGHT BE ABLE TO TURN THIS BOAT INTO A HIGH POWERED AIRCRAFT!
LATER
NOW ALL I'VE GOT TO DO IS PUSH THIS BUTTON TO FIND OUT IF MY MODIFICATIONS WORKED!

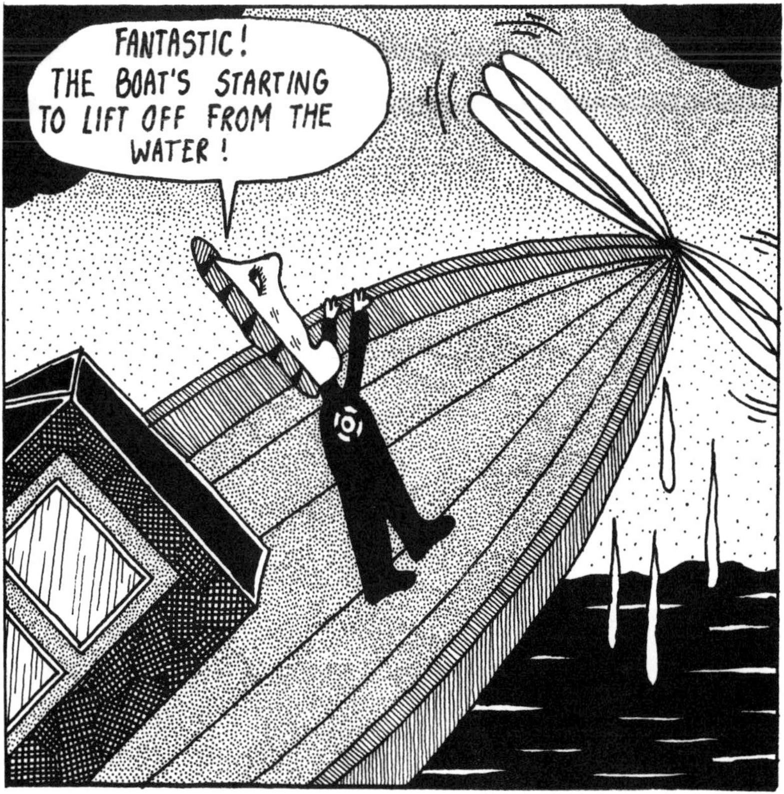
FANTASTIC! THE BOAT'S STARTING TO LIFT OFF FROM THE WATER!

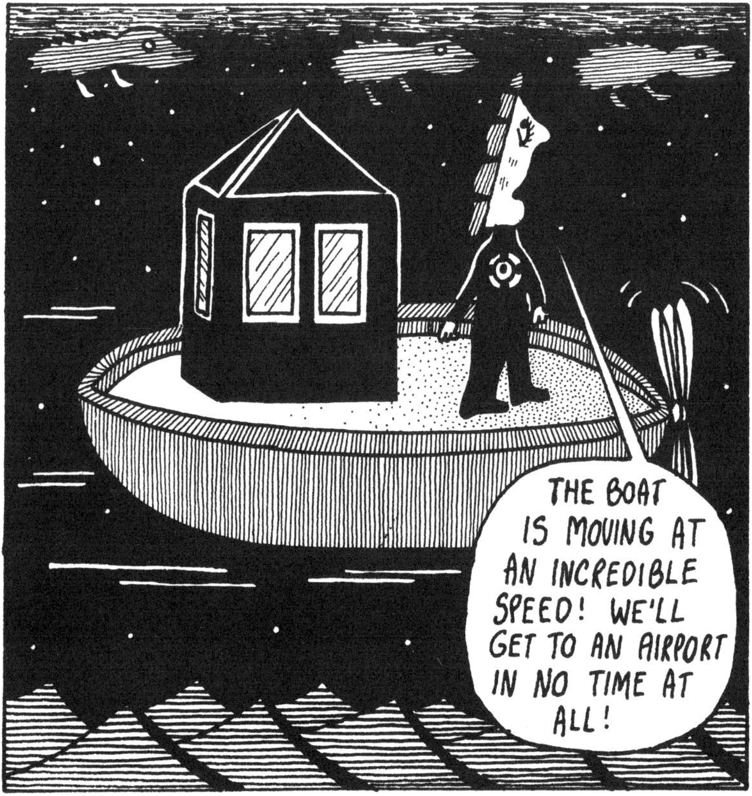
THE BOAT IS MOVING AT AN INCREDIBLE SPEED! WE'LL GET TO AN AIRPORT IN NO TIME AT ALL!

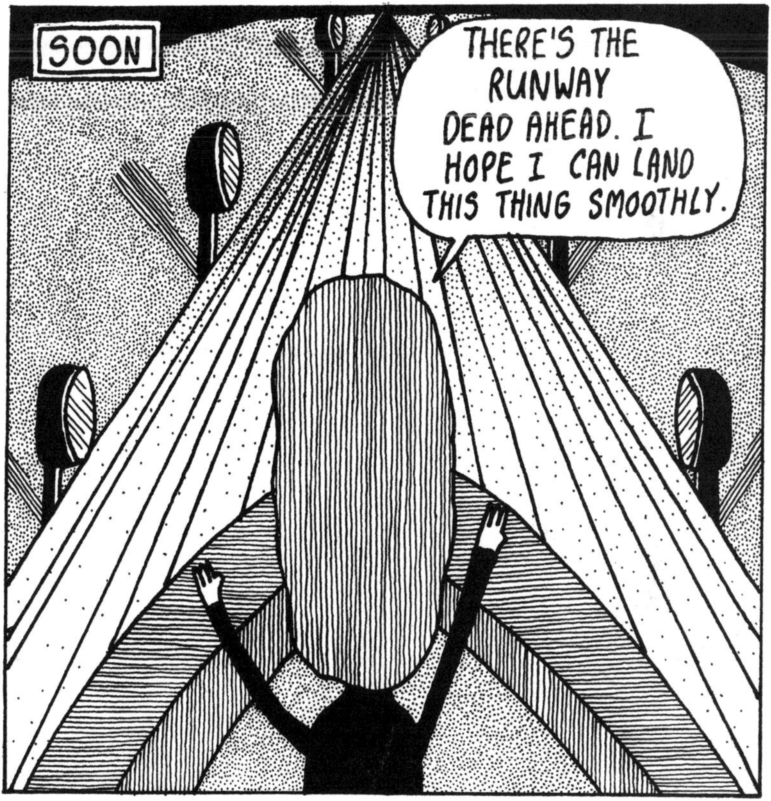
SOON
THERE'S THE RUNWAY DEAD AHEAD. I HOPE I CAN LAND THIS THING SMOOTHLY.

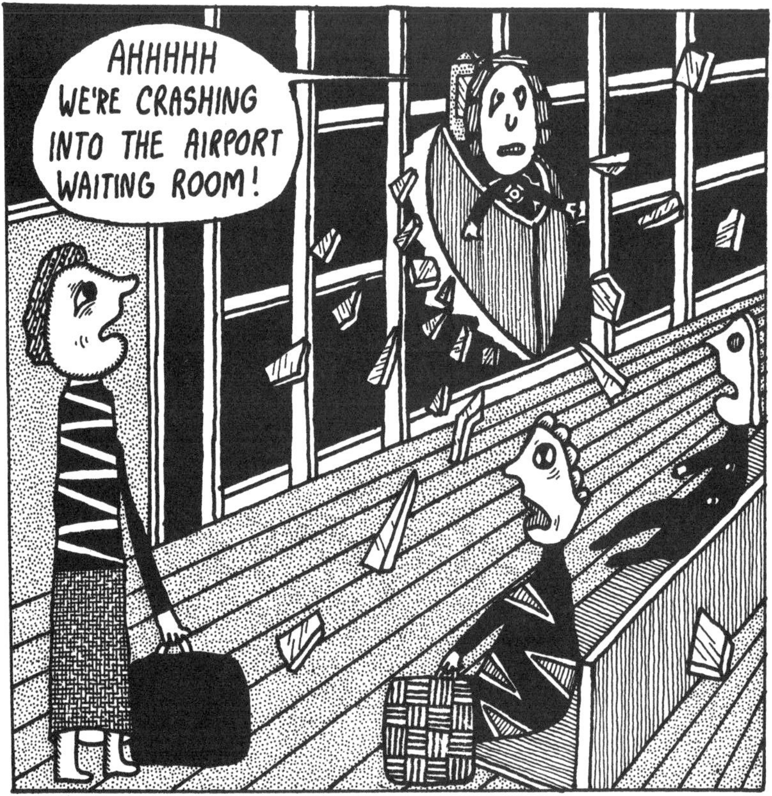
AHHHHH WE'RE CRASHING INTO THE AIRPORT WAITING ROOM!

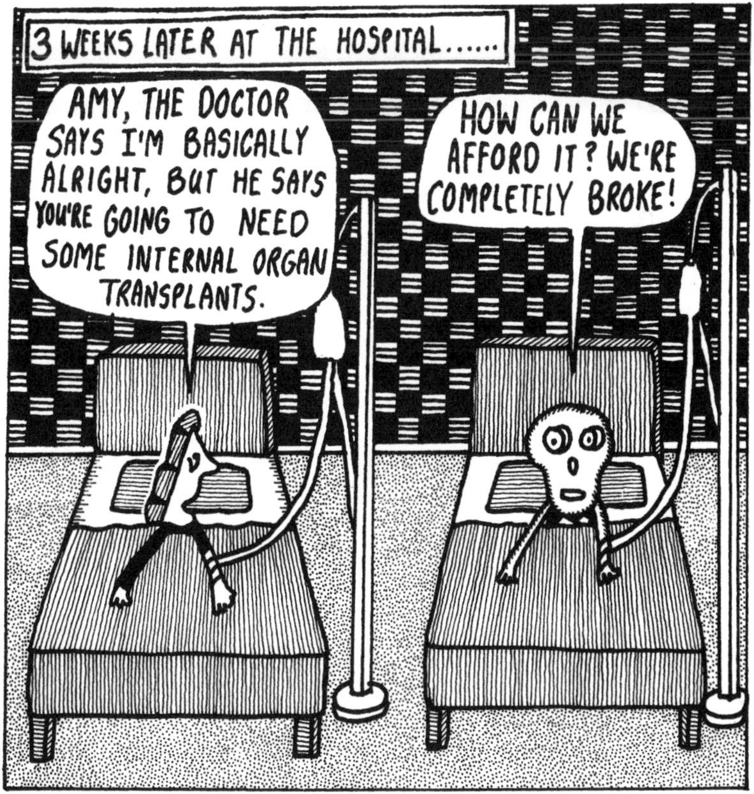
3 WEEKS LATER AT THE HOSPITAL......
AMY, THE DOCTOR SAYS I'M BASICALLY ALRIGHT, BUT HE SAYS YOU'RE GOING TO NEED SOME INTERNAL ORGAN TRANSPLANTS.
HOW CAN WE AFFORD IT? WE'RE COMPLETELY BROKE!

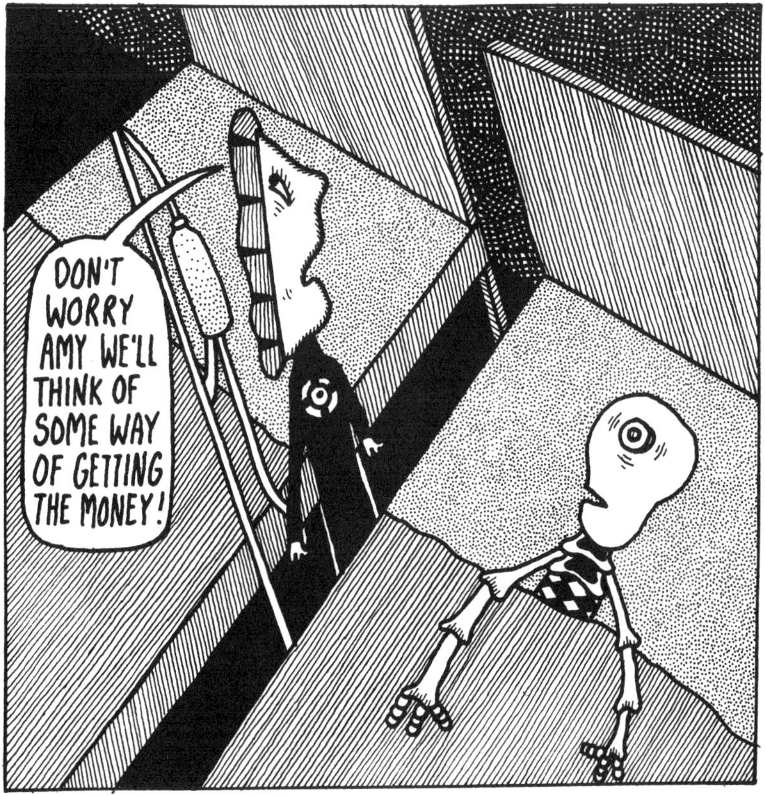
DON'T WORRY AMY WE'LL THINK OF SOME WAY OF GETTING THE MONEY!

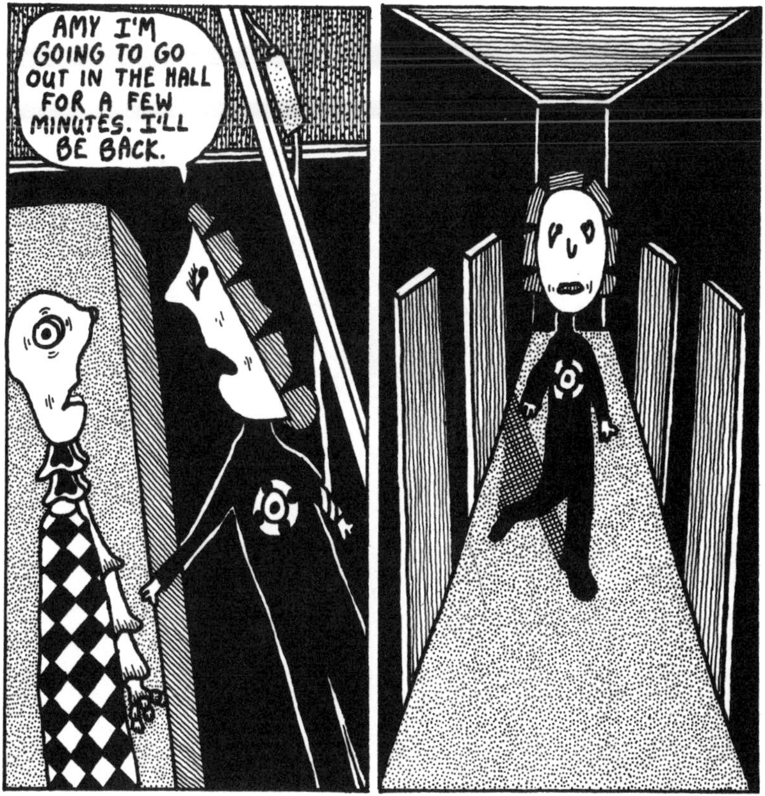
AMY I'M GOING TO GO OUT IN THE HALL FOR A FEW MINUTES. I'LL BE BACK.

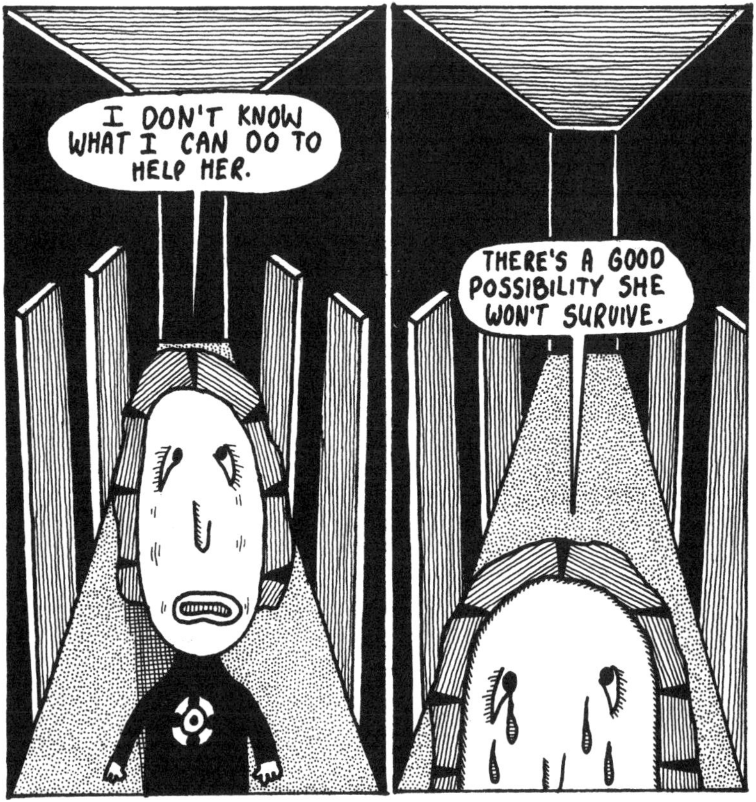
I DON'T KNOW WHAT I CAN DO TO HELP HER.
THERE'S A GOOD POSSIBILITY SHE WON'T SURVIVE.

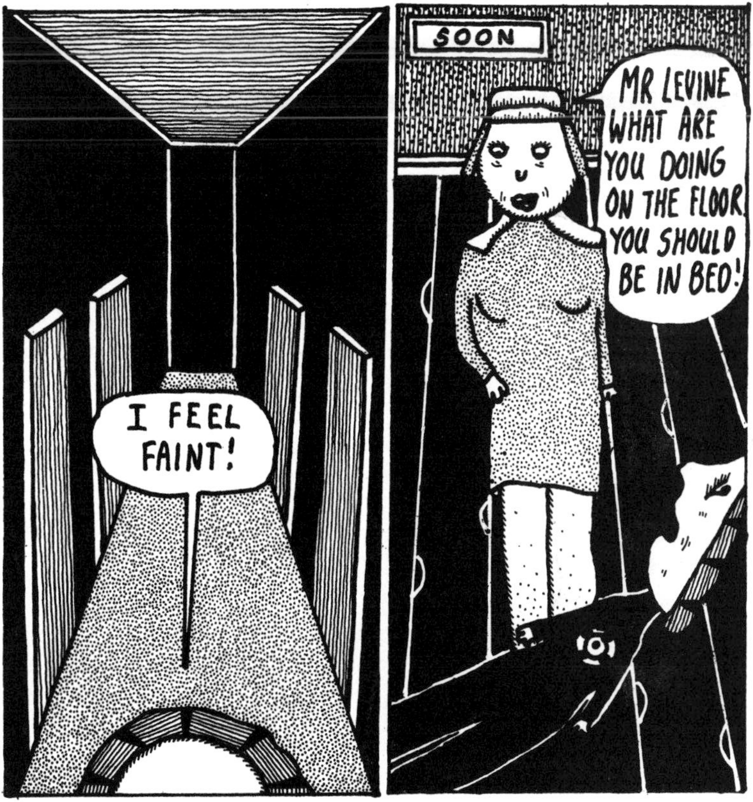
I FEEL FAINT!
SOON
MR LEVINE WHAT ARE YOU DOING ON THE FLOOR YOU SHOULD BE IN BED!

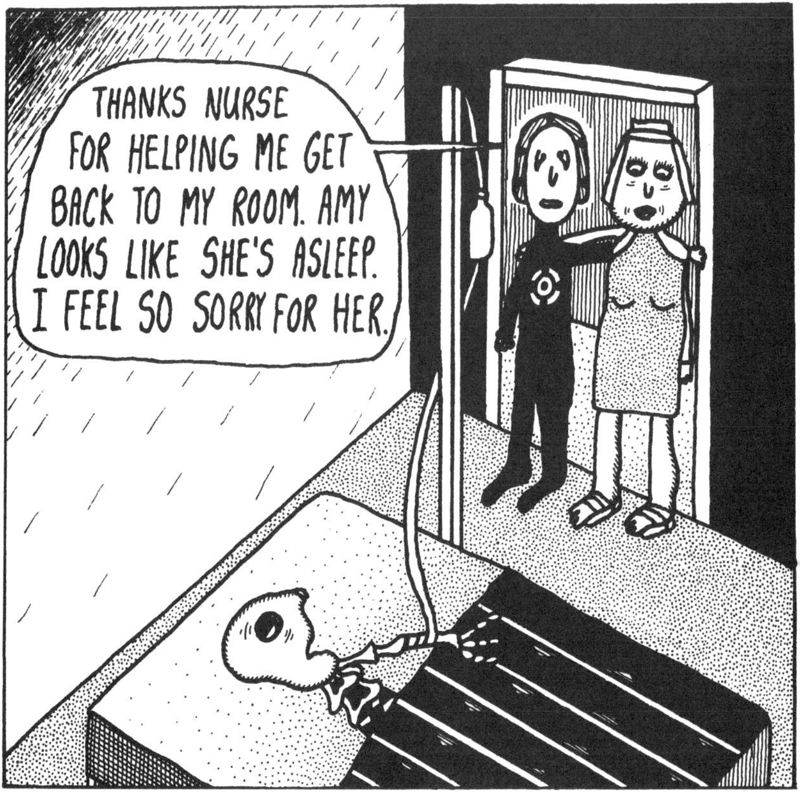
THANKS NURSE FOR HELPING ME GET BACK TO MY ROOM. AMY LOOKS LIKE SHE'S ASLEEP. I FEEL SO SORRY FOR HER.

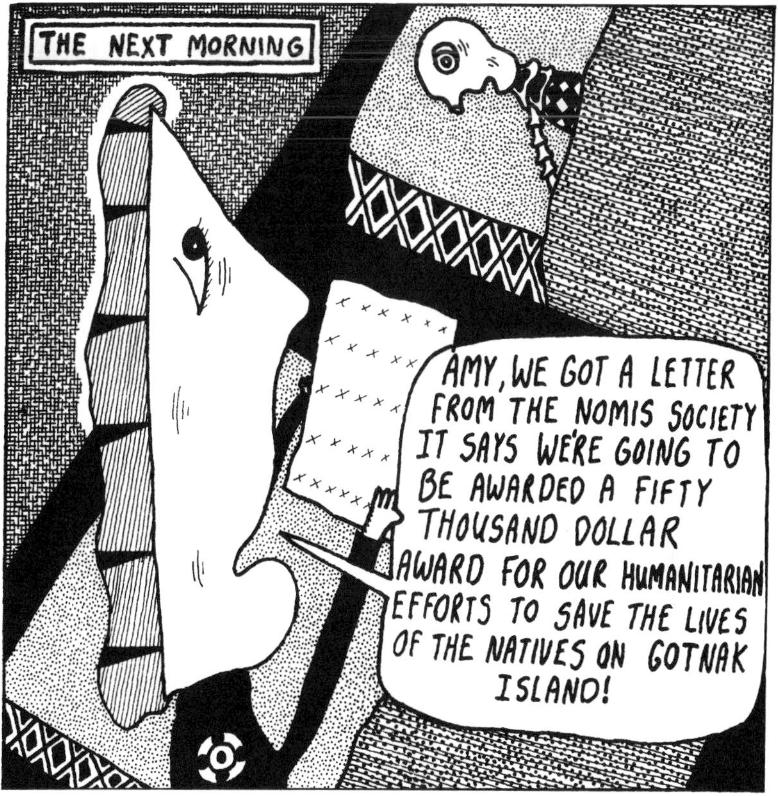
THE NEXT MORNING
AMY, WE GOT A LETTER FROM THE NOMIS SOCIETY IT SAYS WE'RE GOING TO BE AWARDED A FIFTY THOUSAND DOLLAR AWARD FOR OUR HUMANITARIAN EFFORTS TO SAVE THE LIVES OF THE NATIVES ON GOTNAK ISLAND!

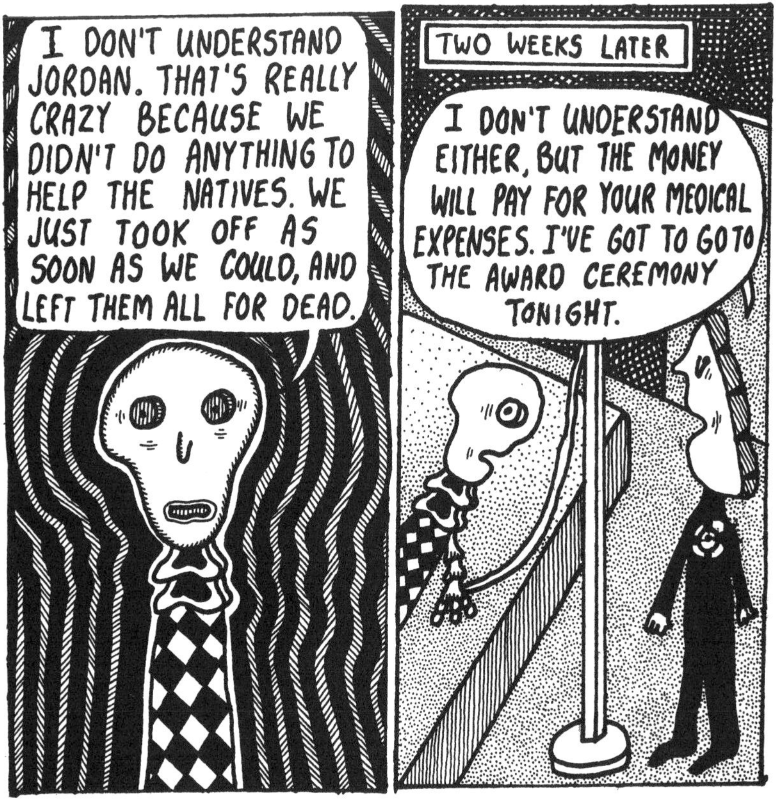
I DON'T UNDERSTAND JORDAN. THAT'S REALLY CRAZY BECAUSE WE DIDN'T DO ANYTHING TO HELP THE NATIVES. WE JUST TOOK OFF AS SOON AS WE COULD, AND LEFT THEM ALL FOR DEAD.
TWO WEEKS LATER
I DON'T UNDERSTAND EITHER, BUT THE MONEY WILL PAY FOR YOUR MEDICAL EXPENSES. I'VE GOT TO GO TO THE AWARD CEREMONY TONIGHT.

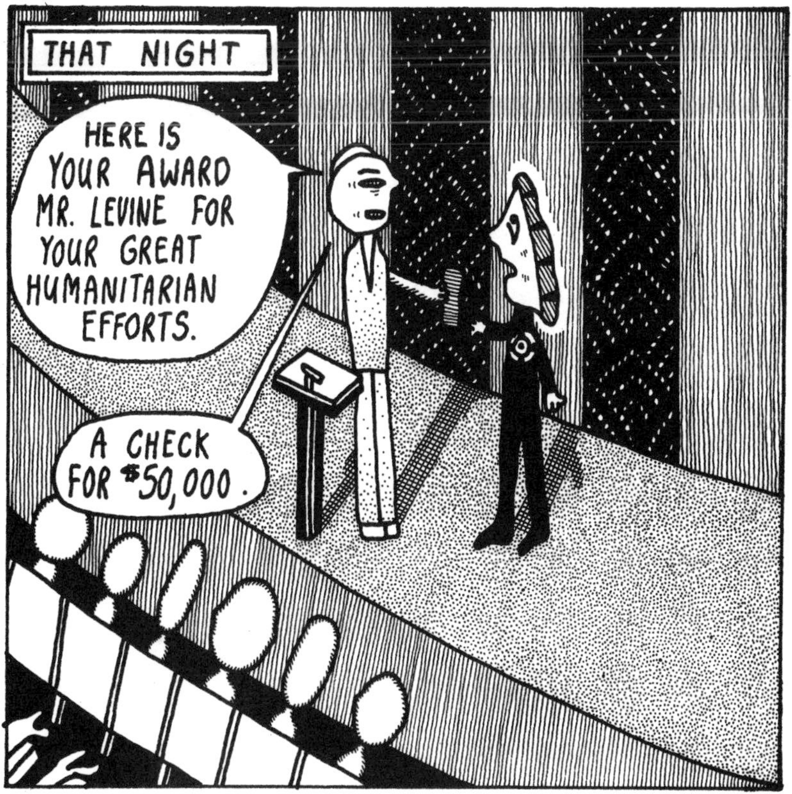
THAT NIGHT
HERE IS YOUR AWARD MR. LEVINE FOR YOUR GREAT HUMANITARIAN EFFORTS.
A CHECK FOR $50,000.

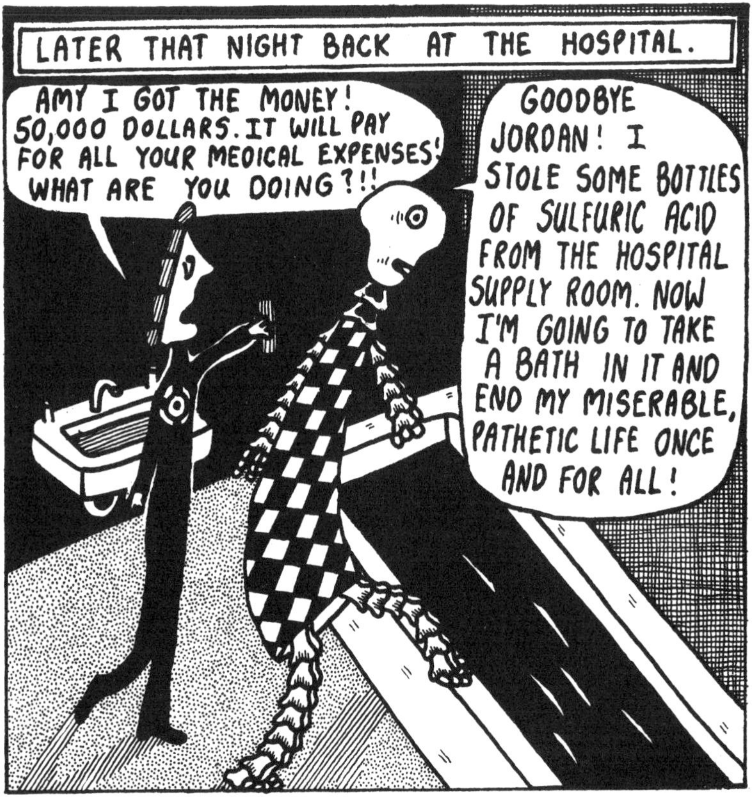
LATER THAT NIGHT BACK AT THE HOSPITAL.
AMY I GOT THE MONEY! 50,000 DOLLARS. IT WILL PAY FOR ALL YOUR MEDICAL EXPENSES! WHAT ARE YOU DOING?!!
GOODBYE JORDAN! I STOLE SOME BOTTLES OF SULFURIC ACID FROM THE HOSPITAL SUPPLY ROOM. NOW I'M GOING TO TAKE A BATH IN IT AND END MY MISERABLE, PATHETIC LIFE ONCE AND FOR ALL!

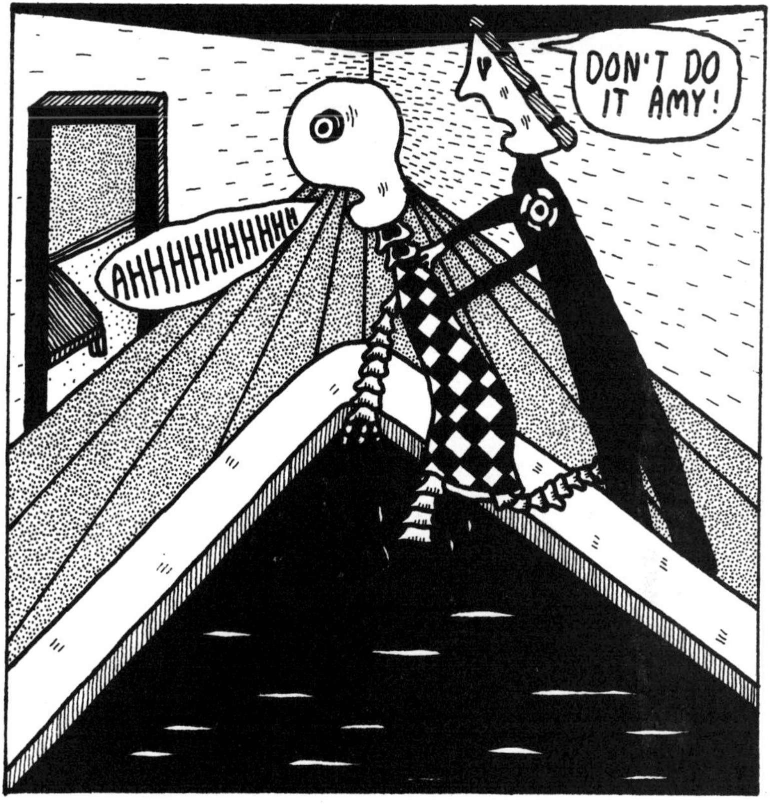
DON'T DO IT AMY!
AHHHHHHHHHH

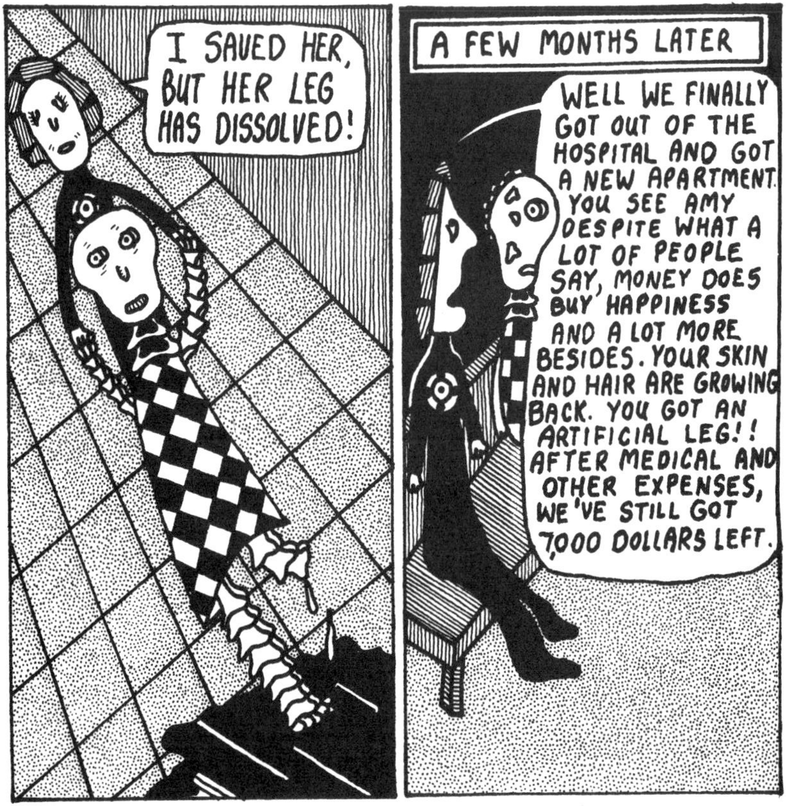
I SAVED HER, BUT HER LEG HAS DISSOLVED!
A FEW MONTHS LATER
WELL WE FINALLY GOT OUT OF THE HOSPITAL AND GOT A NEW APARTMENT. YOU SEE AMY DESPITE WHAT A LOT OF PEOPLE SAY, MONEY DOES BUY HAPPINESS AND A LOT MORE BESIDES. YOUR SKIN AND HAIR ARE GROWING BACK. YOU GOT AN ARTIFICIAL LEG!! AFTER MEDICAL AND OTHER EXPENSES, WE'VE STILL GOT 7,000 DOLLARS LEFT.

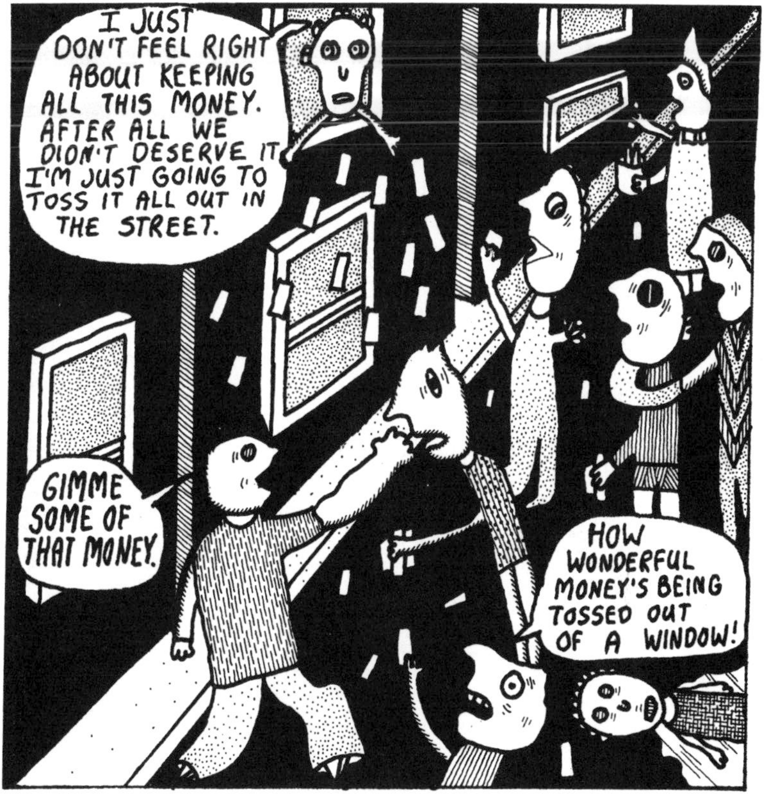
I JUST DON'T FEEL RIGHT ABOUT KEEPING ALL THIS MONEY. AFTER ALL WE DIDN'T DESERVE IT. I'M JUST GOING TO TOSS IT ALL OUT IN THE STREET.
GIMME SOME OF THAT MONEY.
HOW WONDERFUL MONEY'S BEING TOSSED OUT OF A WINDOW!

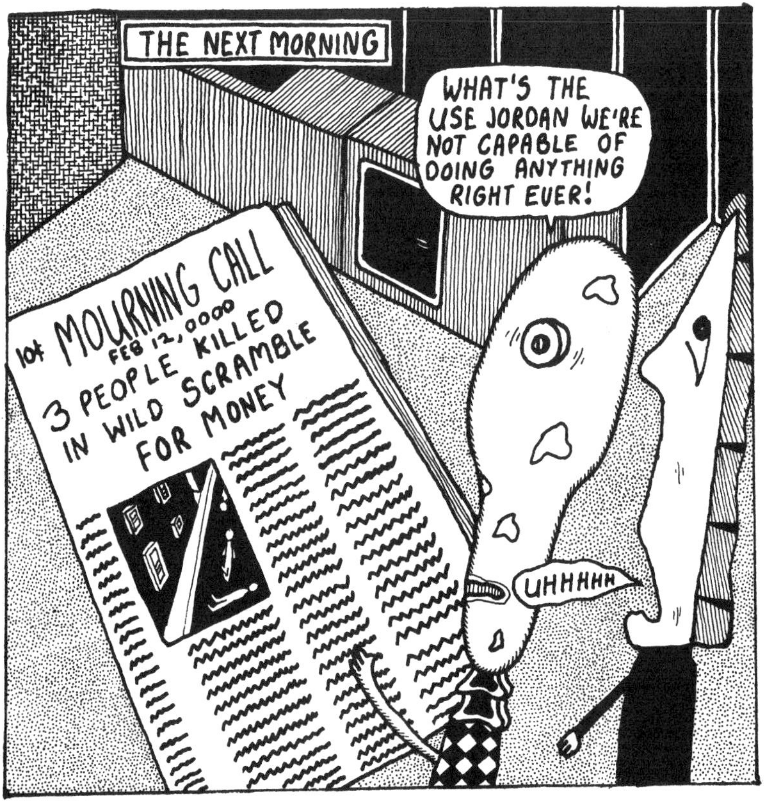
THE NEXT MORNING
WHAT'S THE USE JORDAN WE'RE NOT CAPABLE OF DOING ANYTHING RIGHT EVER!
10¢ MOURNING CALL
FEB 12, 0000
3 PEOPLE KILLED IN WILD SCRAMBLE FOR MONEY
UHHHHH

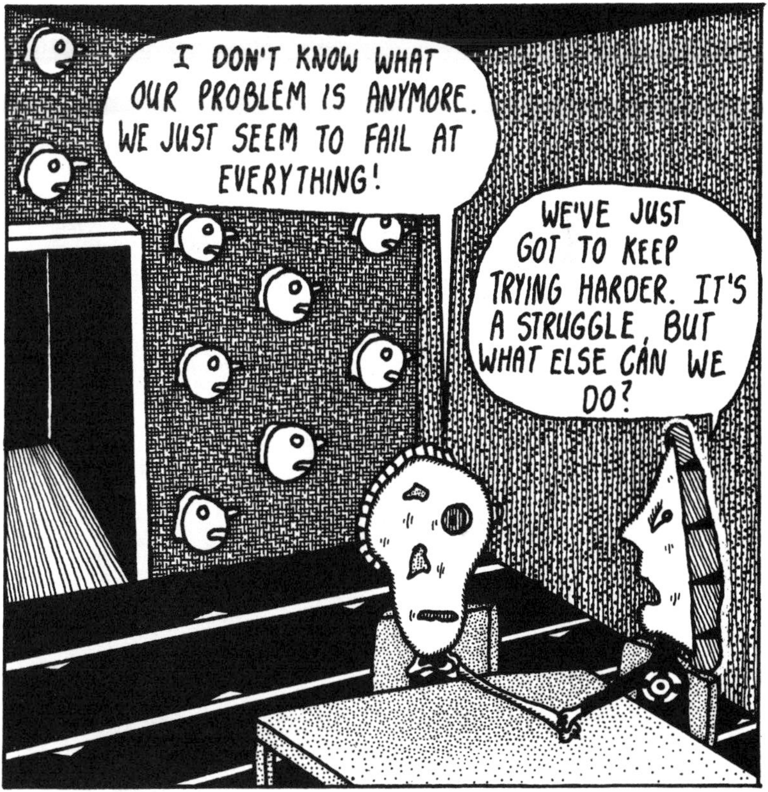
I DON'T KNOW WHAT OUR PROBLEM IS ANYMORE. WE JUST SEEM TO FAIL AT EVERYTHING!
WE'VE JUST GOT TO KEEP TRYING HARDER. IT'S A STRUGGLE, BUT WHAT ELSE CAN WE DO?

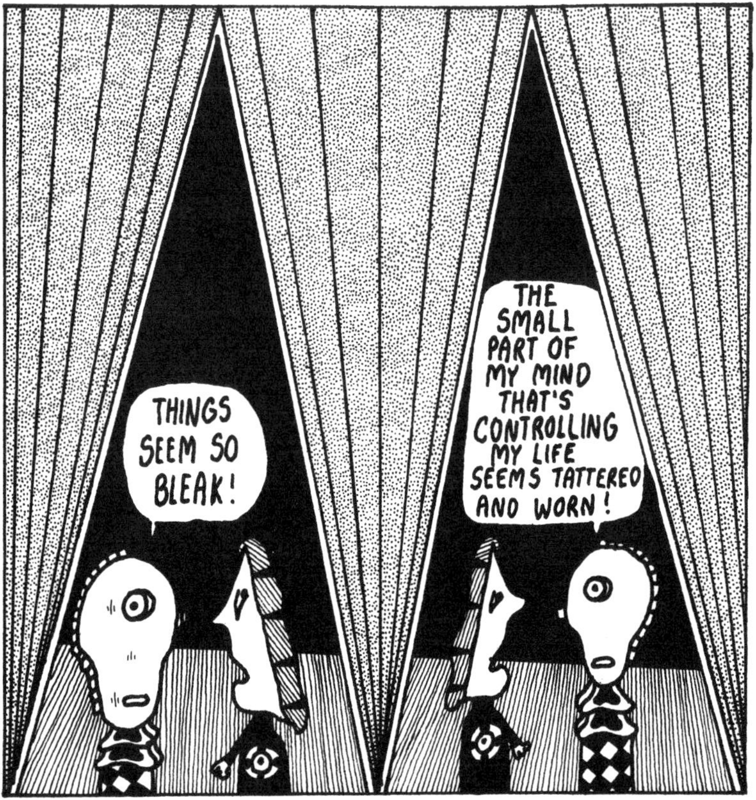
THINGS SEEM SO BLEAK!
THE SMALL PART OF MY MIND THAT'S CONTROLLING MY LIFE SEEMS TATTERED AND WORN!

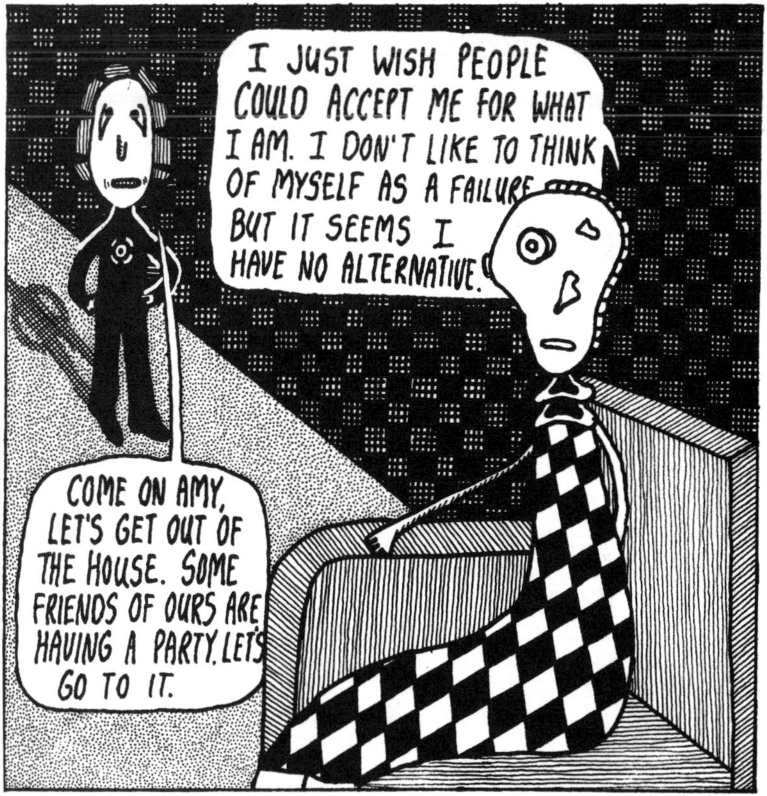
I JUST WISH PEOPLE COULD ACCEPT ME FOR WHAT I AM. I DON'T LIKE TO THINK OF MYSELF AS A FAILURE BUT IT SEEMS I HAVE NO ALTERNATIVE.
COME ON AMY, LET'S GET OUT OF THE HOUSE. SOME FRIENDS OF OURS ARE HAVING A PARTY. LET'S GO TO IT.

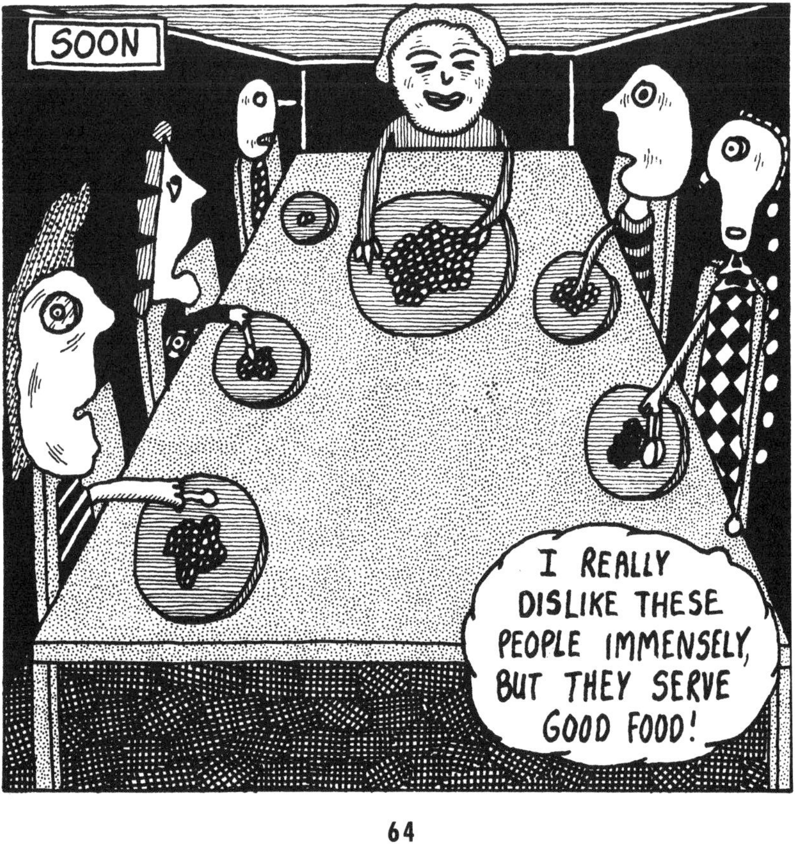
SOON
I REALLY DISLIKE THESE PEOPLE IMMENSELY, BUT THEY SERVE GOOD FOOD!

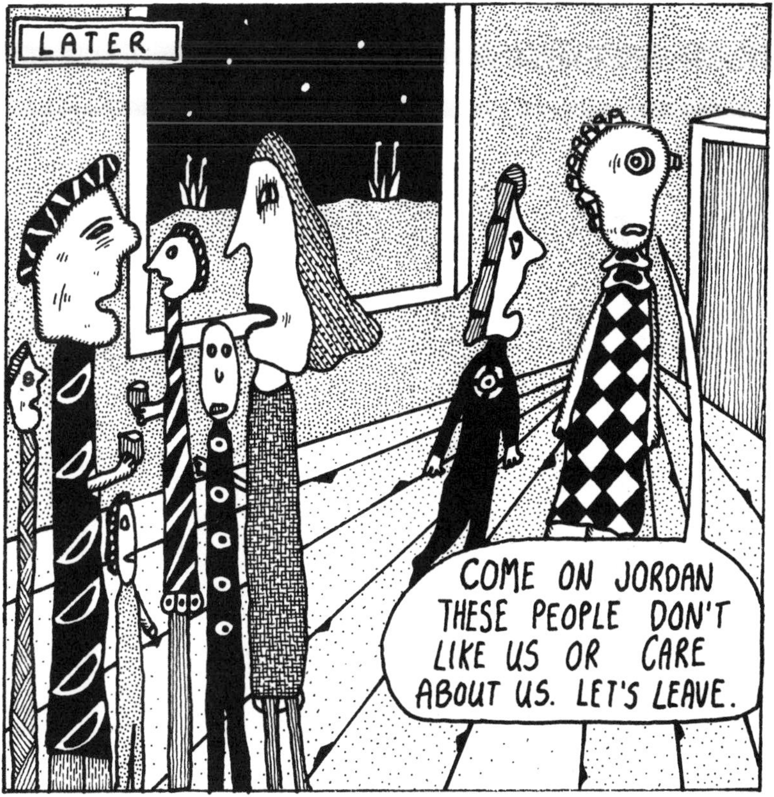
LATER
COME ON JORDAN THESE PEOPLE DON'T LIKE US OR CARE ABOUT US. LET'S LEAVE.

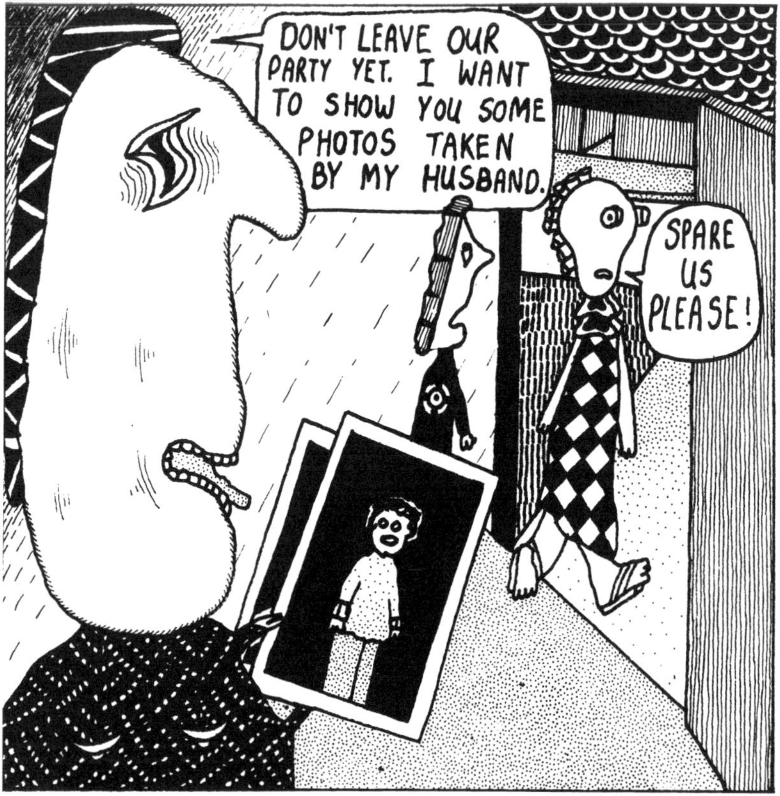
DON'T LEAVE OUR PARTY YET. I WANT TO SHOW YOU SOME PHOTOS TAKEN BY MY HUSBAND.
SPARE US PLEASE!

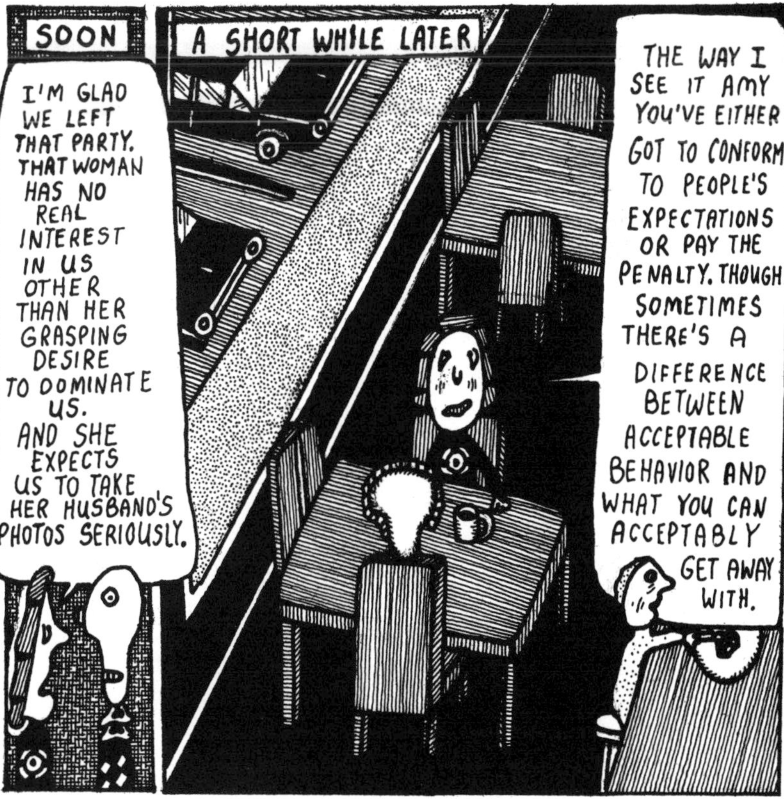
SOON
I'M GLAD WE LEFT THAT PARTY. THAT WOMAN HAS NO REAL INTEREST IN US OTHER THAN HER GRASPING DESIRE TO DOMINATE US. AND SHE EXPECTS US TO TAKE HER HUSBAND'S PHOTOS SERIOUSLY.
A SHORT WHILE LATER
THE WAY I SEE IT AMY YOU'VE EITHER GOT TO CONFORM TO PEOPLE'S EXPECTATIONS OR PAY THE PENALTY. THOUGH SOMETIMES THERE'S A DIFFERENCE BETWEEN ACCEPTABLE BEHAVIOR AND WHAT YOU CAN ACCEPTABLY GET AWAY WITH.

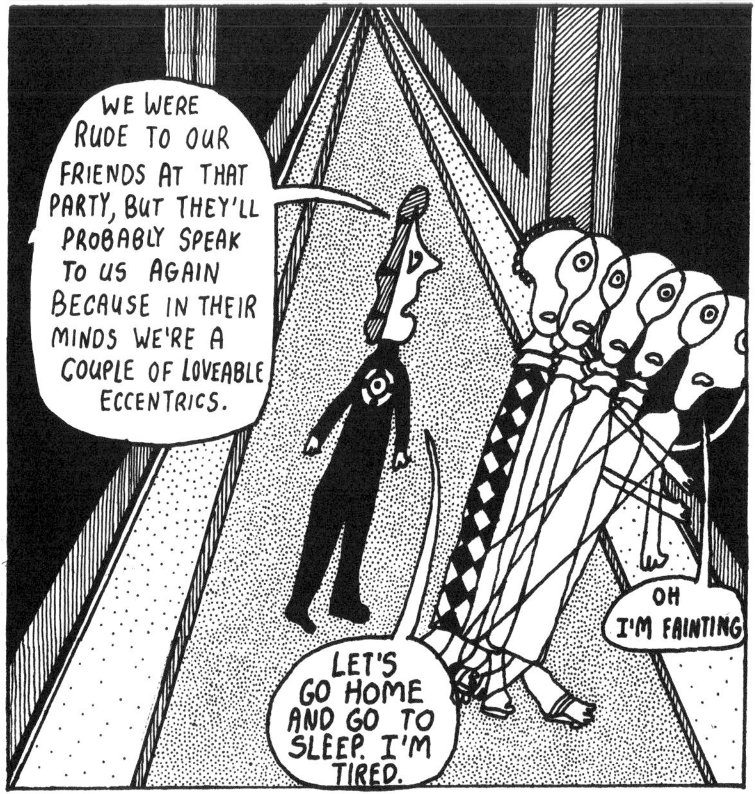
WE WERE RUDE TO OUR FRIENDS AT THAT PARTY, BUT THEY'LL PROBABLY SPEAK TO US AGAIN BECAUSE IN THEIR MINDS WE'RE A COUPLE OF LOVEABLE ECCENTRICS.
OH I'M FAINTING
LET'S GO HOME AND GO TO SLEEP. I'M TIRED.

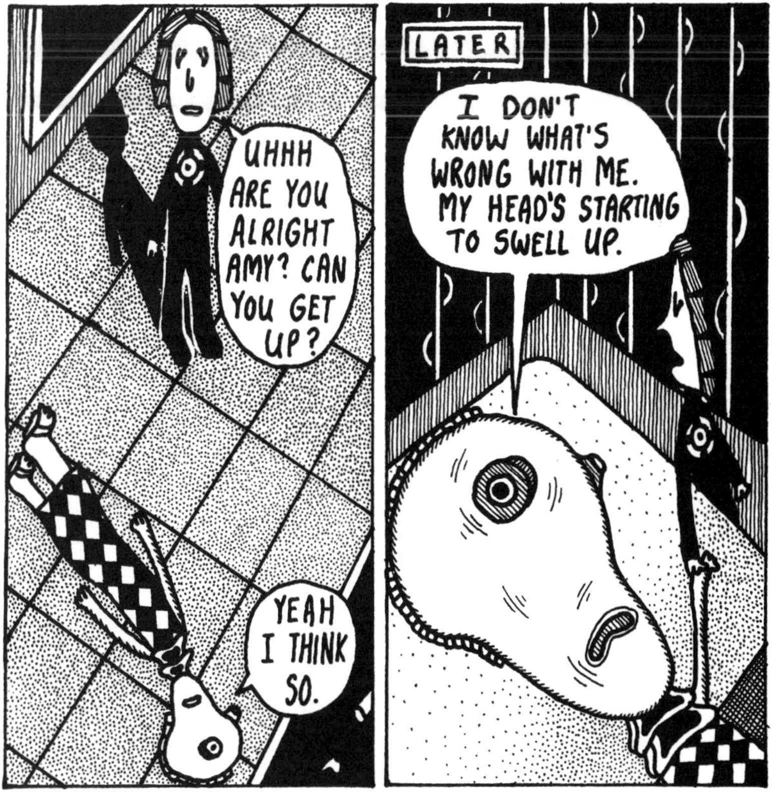
UHHH ARE YOU ALRIGHT AMY? CAN YOU GET UP?
YEAH I THINK SO.
LATER
I DON'T KNOW WHAT'S WRONG WITH ME. MY HEAD'S STARTING TO SWELL UP.

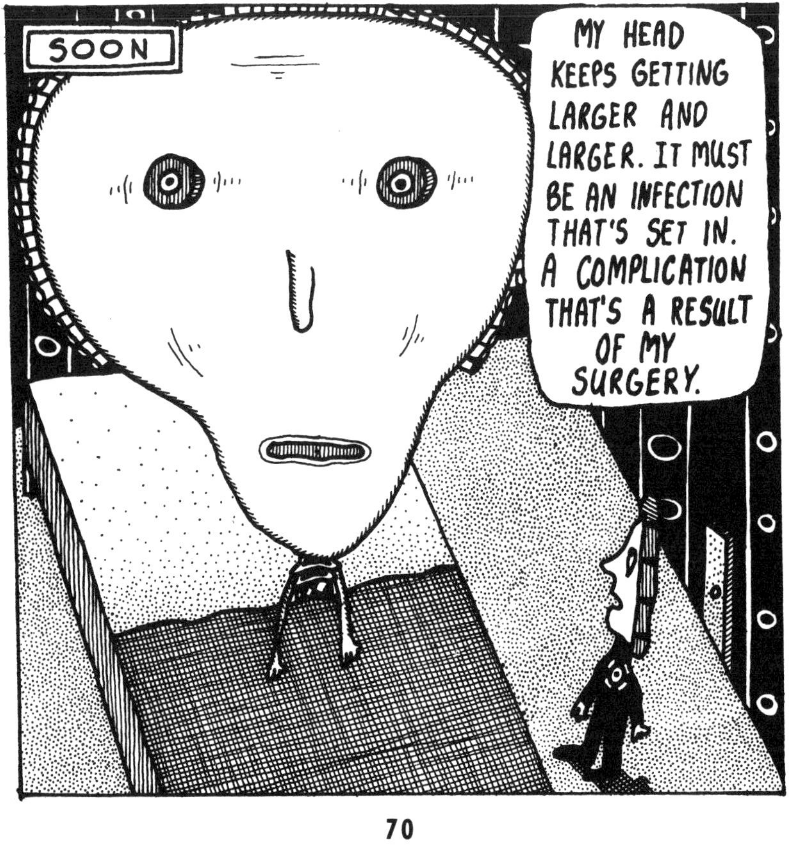
SOON
MY HEAD KEEPS GETTING LARGER AND LARGER. IT MUST BE AN INFECTION THAT'S SET IN. A COMPLICATION THAT'S A RESULT OF MY SURGERY.

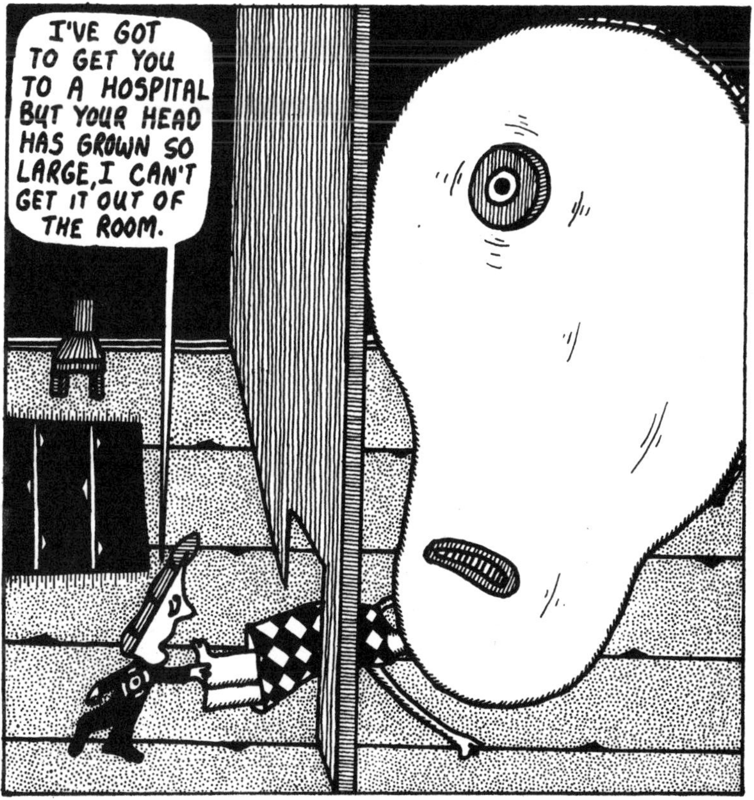
I'VE GOT TO GET YOU TO A HOSPITAL BUT YOUR HEAD HAS GROWN SO LARGE, I CAN'T GET IT OUT OF THE ROOM.

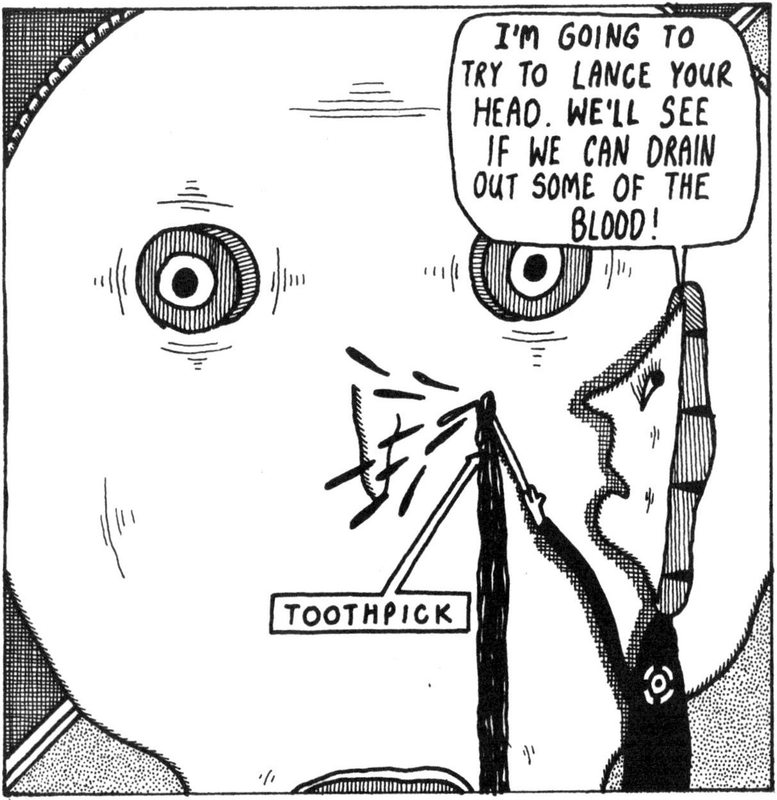
I'M GOING TO TRY TO LANCE YOUR HEAD. WE'LL SEE IF WE CAN DRAIN OUT SOME OF THE BLOOD!
TOOTHPICK

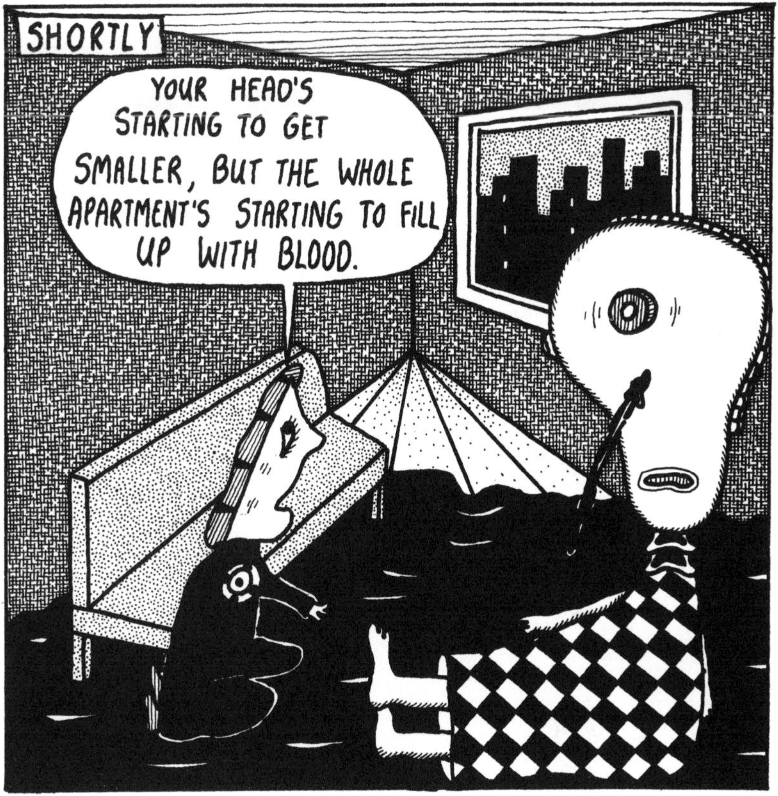
SHORTLY
YOUR HEAD'S STARTING TO GET SMALLER, BUT THE WHOLE APARTMENT'S STARTING TO FILL UP WITH BLOOD.

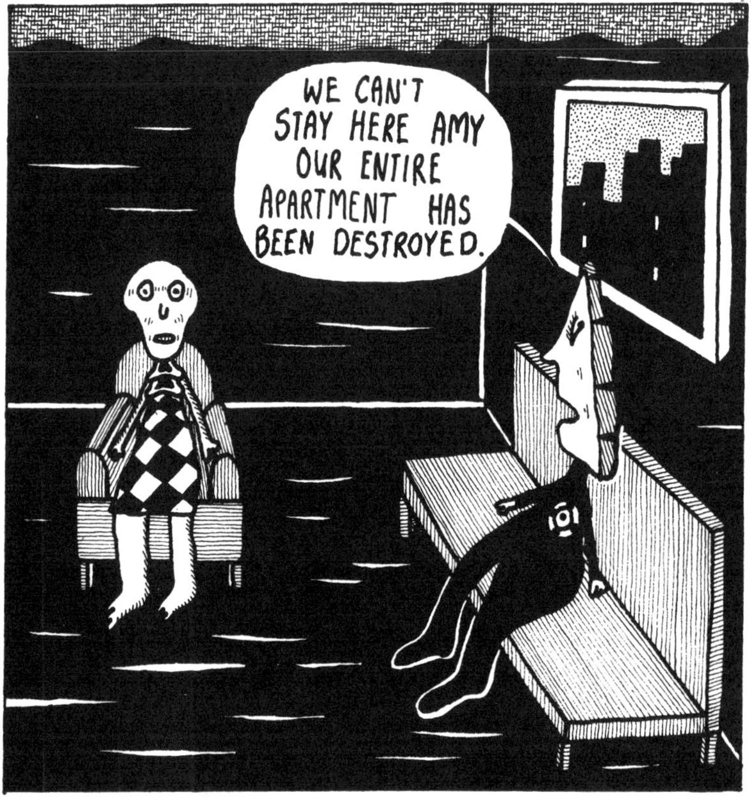
WE CAN'T STAY HERE AMY OUR ENTIRE APARTMENT HAS BEEN DESTROYED.

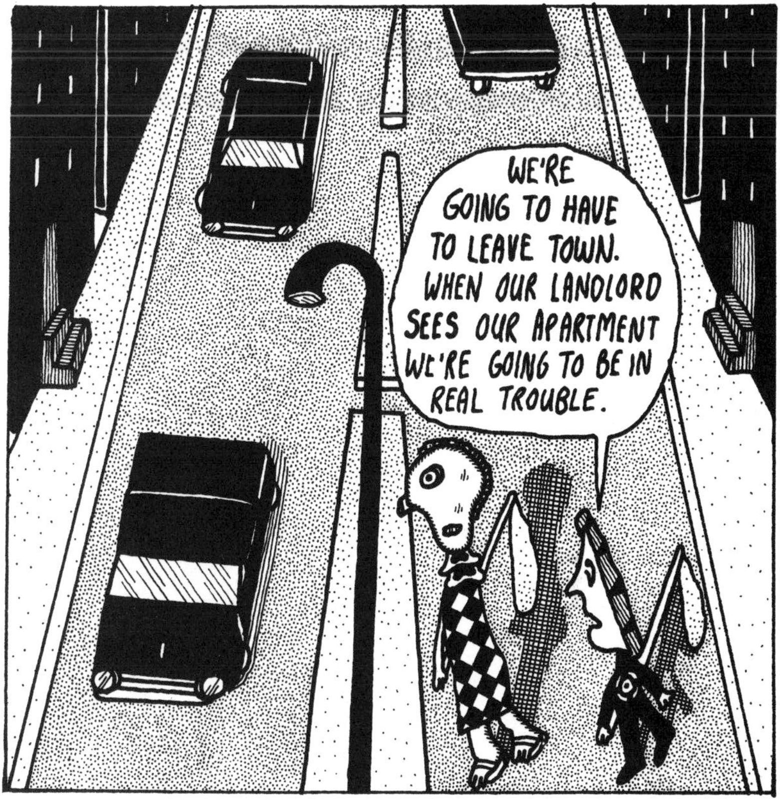
WE'RE GOING TO HAVE TO LEAVE TOWN. WHEN OUR LANDLORD SEES OUR APARTMENT WE'RE GOING TO BE IN REAL TROUBLE.

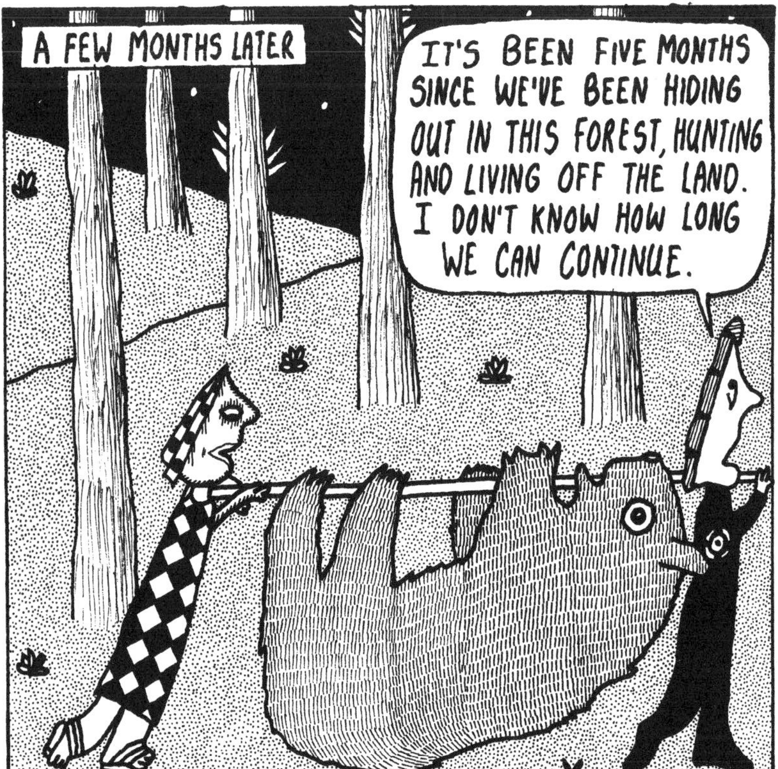
A FEW MONTHS LATER
IT'S BEEN FIVE MONTHS SINCE WE'VE BEEN HIDING OUT IN THIS FOREST, HUNTING AND LIVING OFF THE LAND. I DON'T KNOW HOW LONG WE CAN CONTINUE.

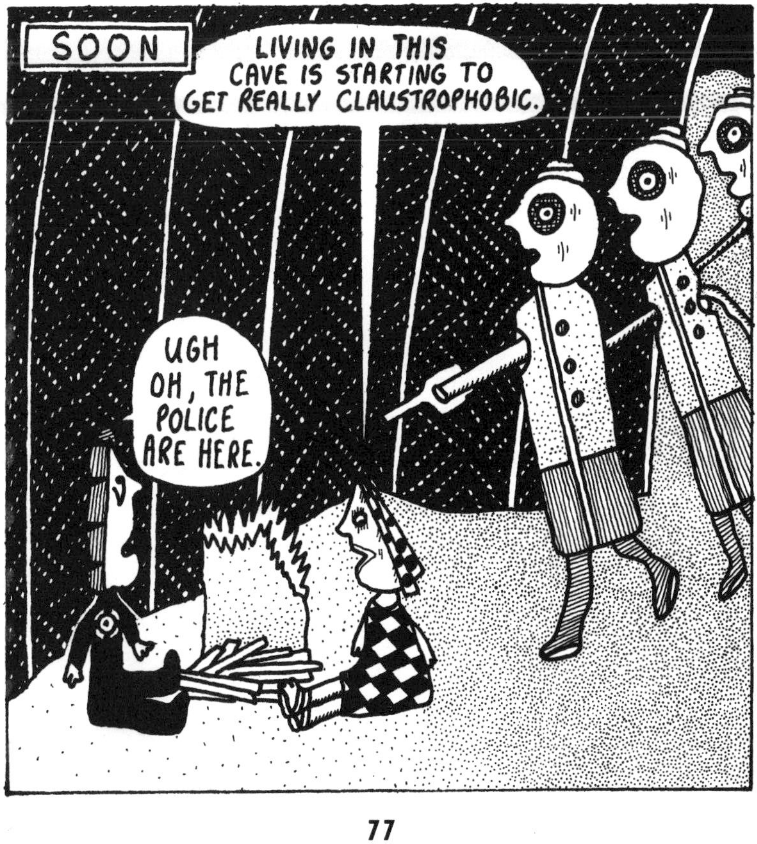
SOON
LIVING IN THIS CAVE IS STARTING TO GET REALLY CLAUSTROPHOBIC.
UGH OH, THE POLICE ARE HERE.

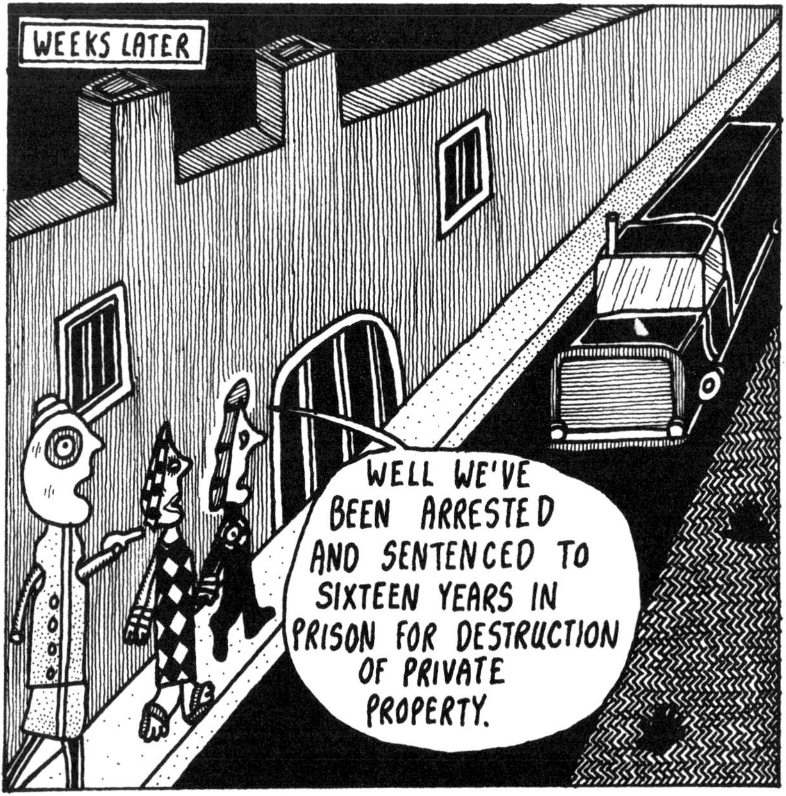
WEEKS LATER
WELL WE'VE BEEN ARRESTED AND SENTENCED TO SIXTEEN YEARS IN PRISON FOR DESTRUCTION OF PRIVATE PROPERTY.

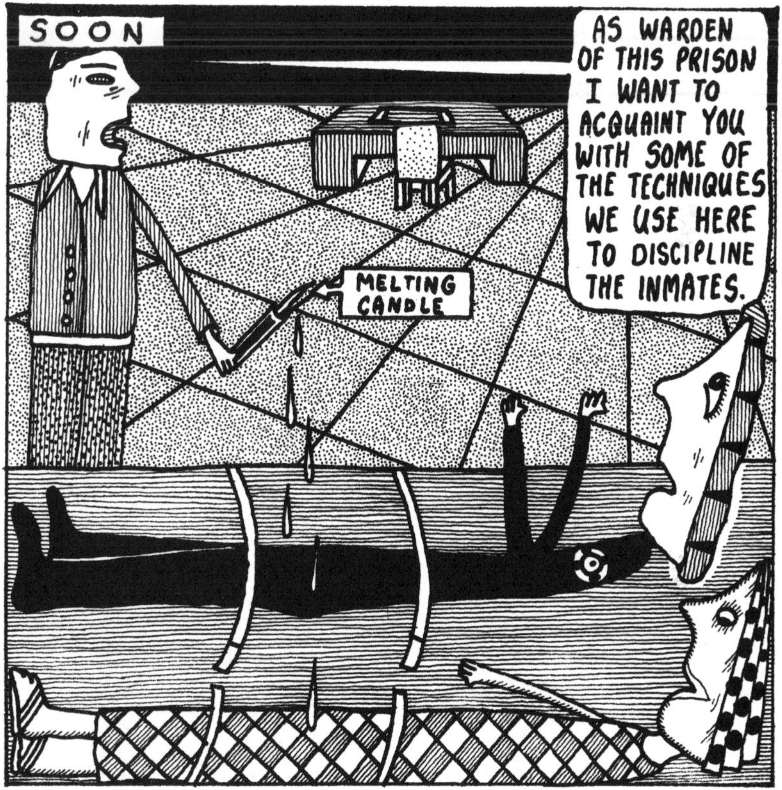
SOON
AS WARDEN OF THIS PRISON I WANT TO ACQUAINT YOU WITH SOME OF THE TECHNIQUES WE USE HERE TO DISCIPLINE THE INMATES.
MELTING CANDLE

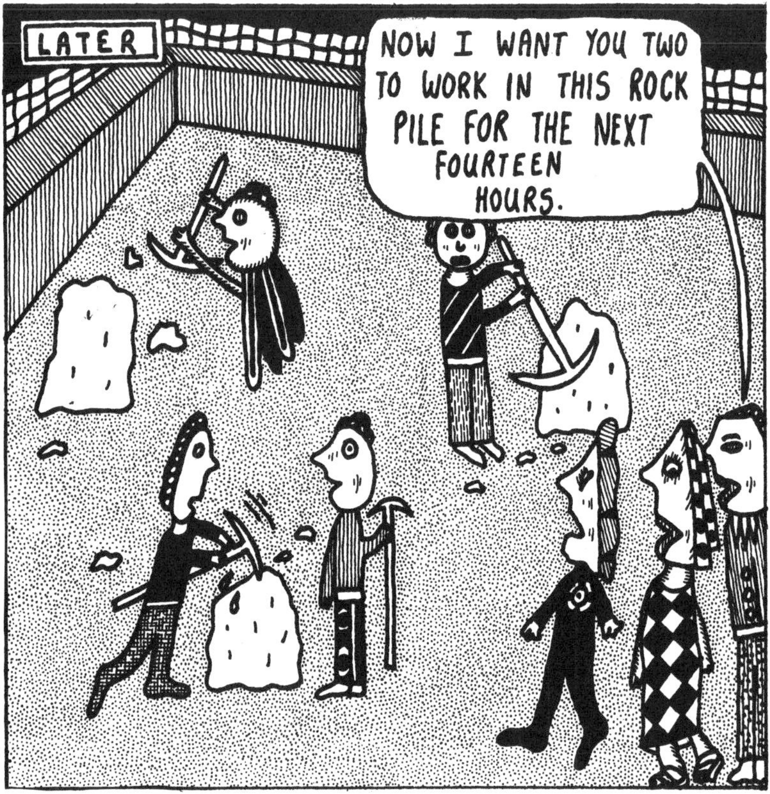
LATER
NOW I WANT YOU TWO TO WORK IN THIS ROCK PILE FOR THE NEXT FOURTEEN HOURS.

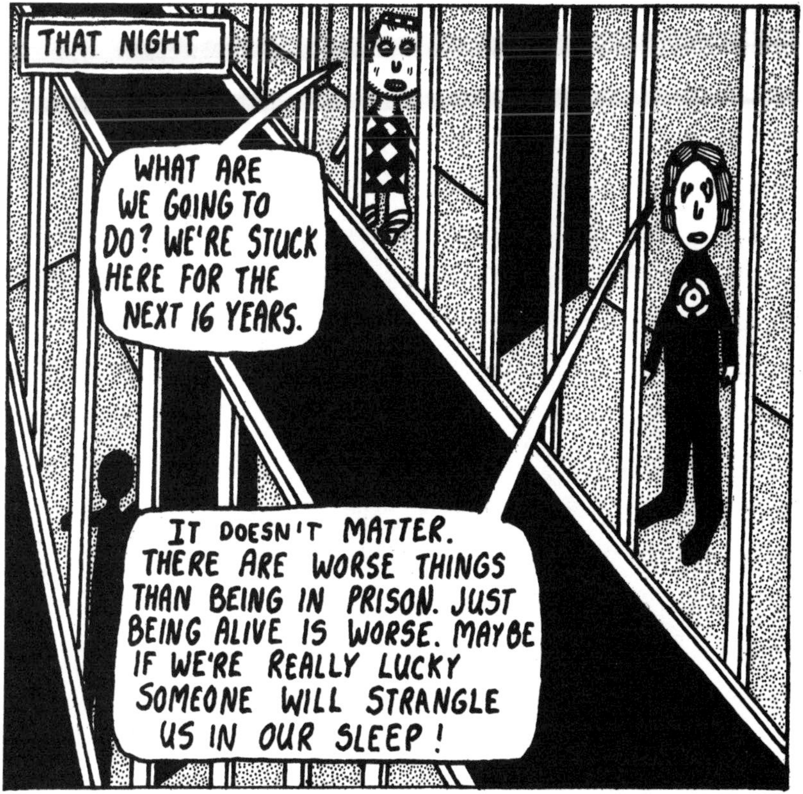
THAT NIGHT
WHAT ARE WE GOING TO DO? WE'RE STUCK HERE FOR THE NEXT 16 YEARS.
IT DOESN'T MATTER. THERE ARE WORSE THINGS THAN BEING IN PRISON. JUST BEING ALIVE IS WORSE. MAYBE IF WE'RE REALLY LUCKY SOMEONE WILL STRANGLE US IN OUR SLEEP!

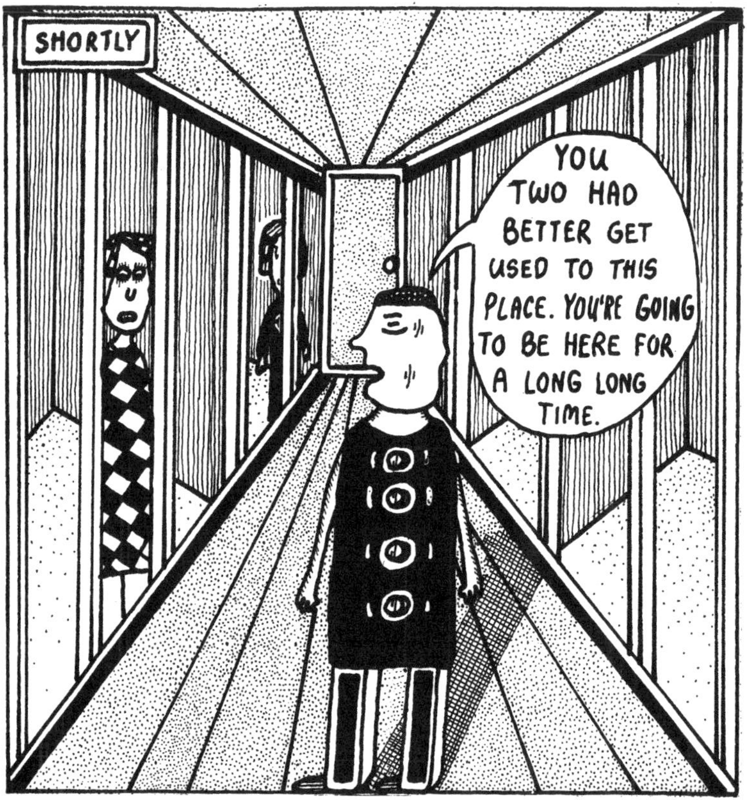
SHORTLY
YOU TWO HAD BETTER GET USED TO THIS PLACE. YOU'RE GOING TO BE HERE FOR A LONG LONG TIME.

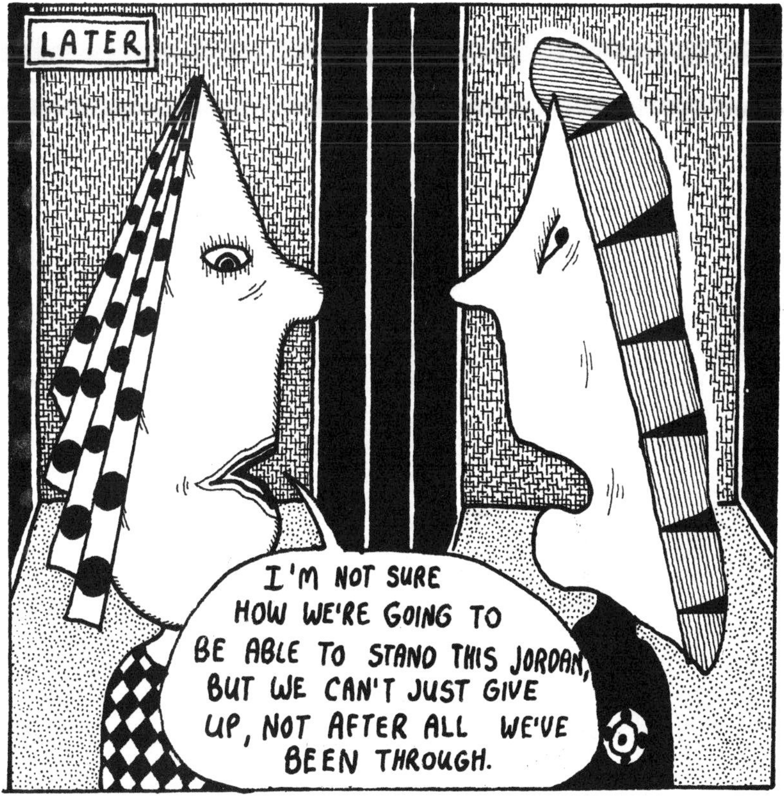
LATER
I'M NOT SURE HOW WE'RE GOING TO BE ABLE TO STAND THIS JORDAN, BUT WE CAN'T JUST GIVE UP, NOT AFTER ALL WE'VE BEEN THROUGH.

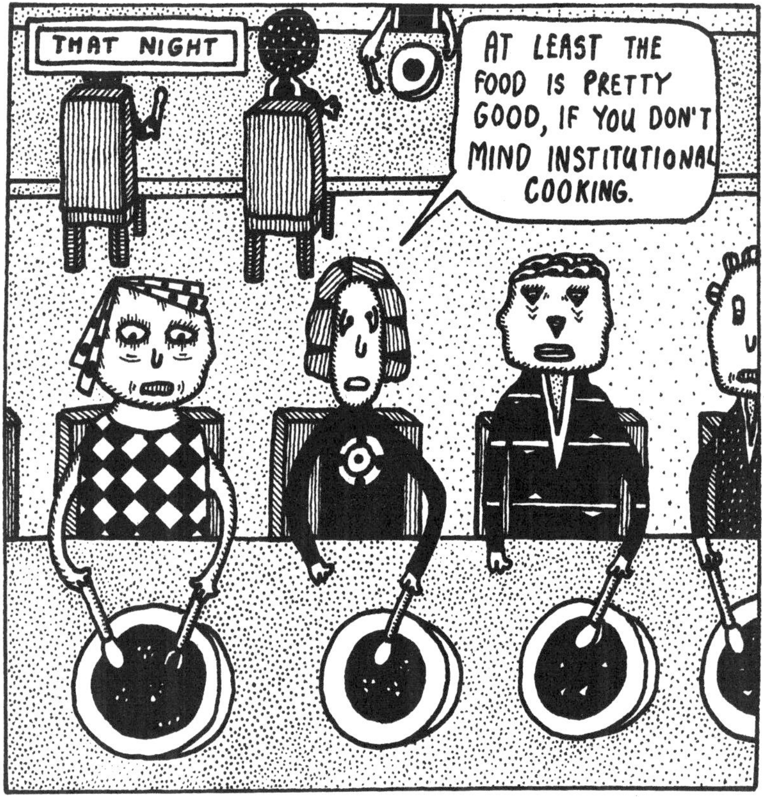
THAT NIGHT
AT LEAST THE FOOD IS PRETTY GOOD, IF YOU DON'T MIND INSTITUTIONAL COOKING.

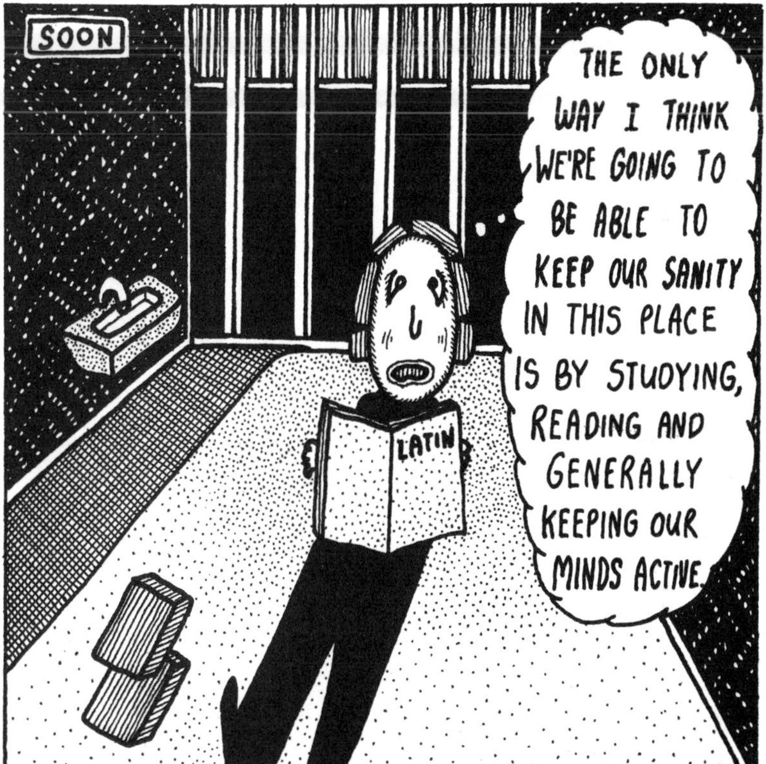
SOON
THE ONLY WAY I THINK WE'RE GOING TO BE ABLE TO KEEP OUR SANITY IN THIS PLACE IS BY STUDYING, READING AND GENERALLY KEEPING OUR MINDS ACTIVE.
LATIN

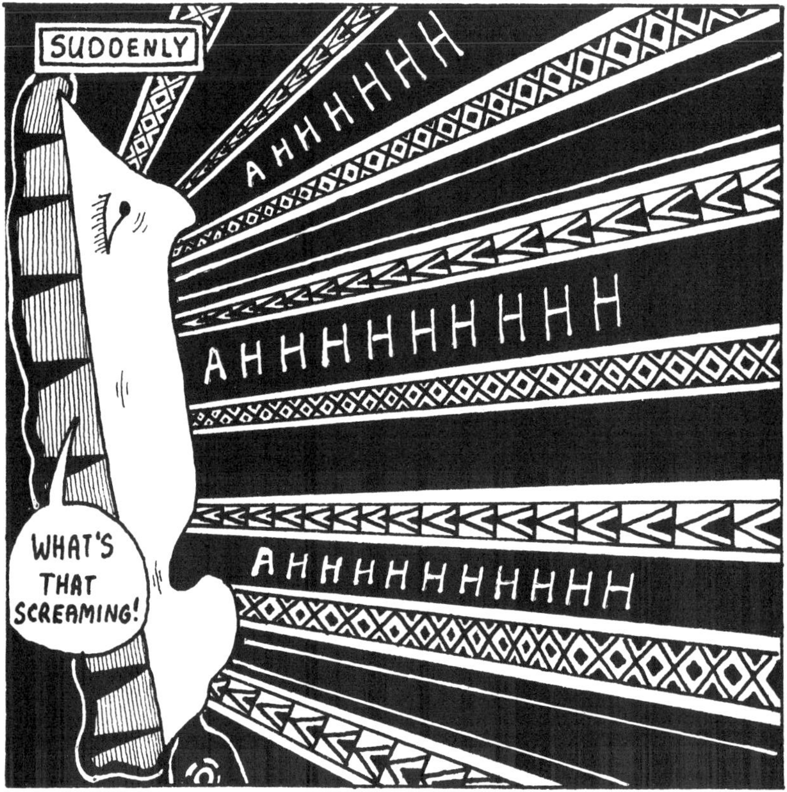
SUDDENLY
AHHHHHHH
AHHHHHHHHHH
AHHHHHHHHHHH
WHAT'S THAT SCREAMING!

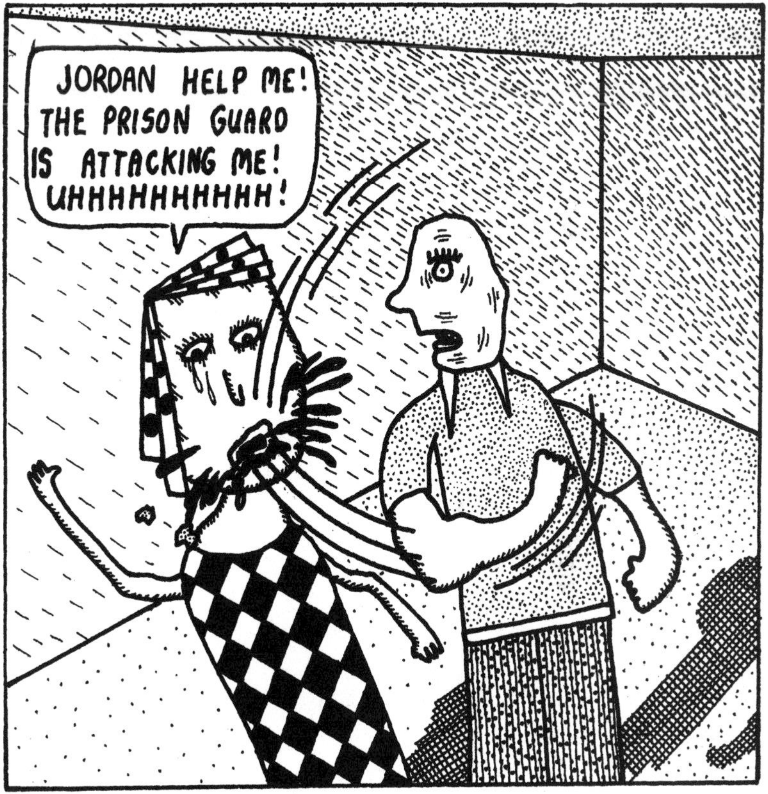
JORDAN HELP ME! THE PRISON GUARD IS ATTACKING ME! UHHHHHHHHHH!

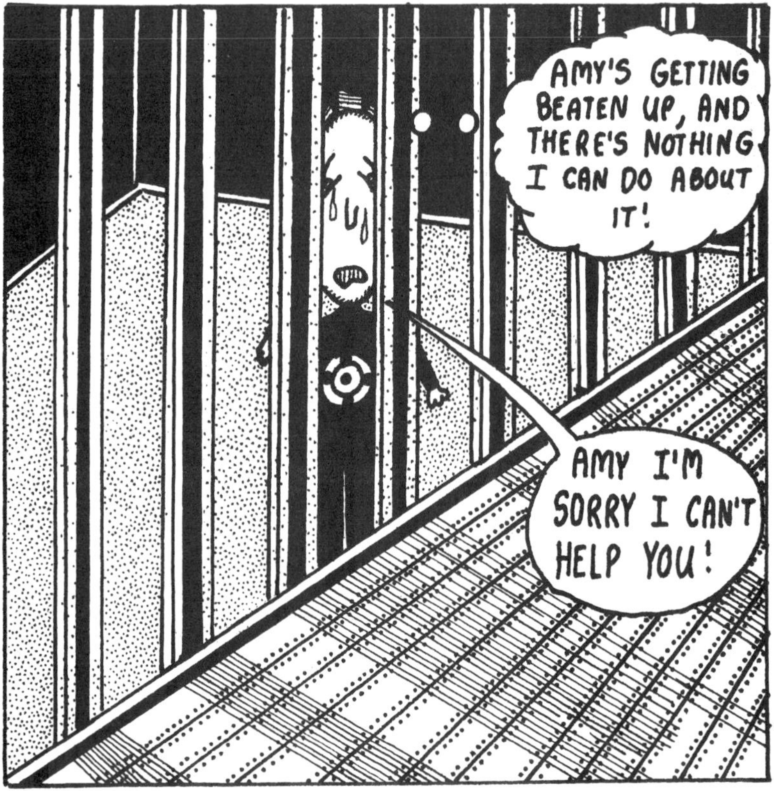
AMY'S GETTING BEATEN UP, AND THERE'S NOTHING I CAN DO ABOUT IT!
AMY I'M SORRY I CAN'T HELP YOU!

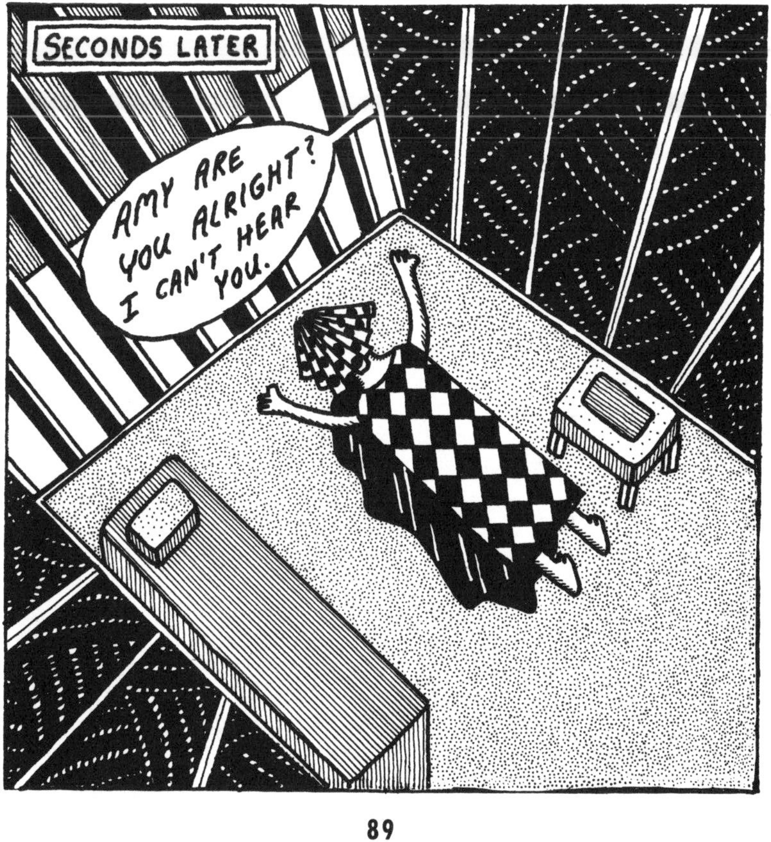
SECONDS LATER
AMY ARE YOU ALRIGHT? I CAN'T HEAR YOU.

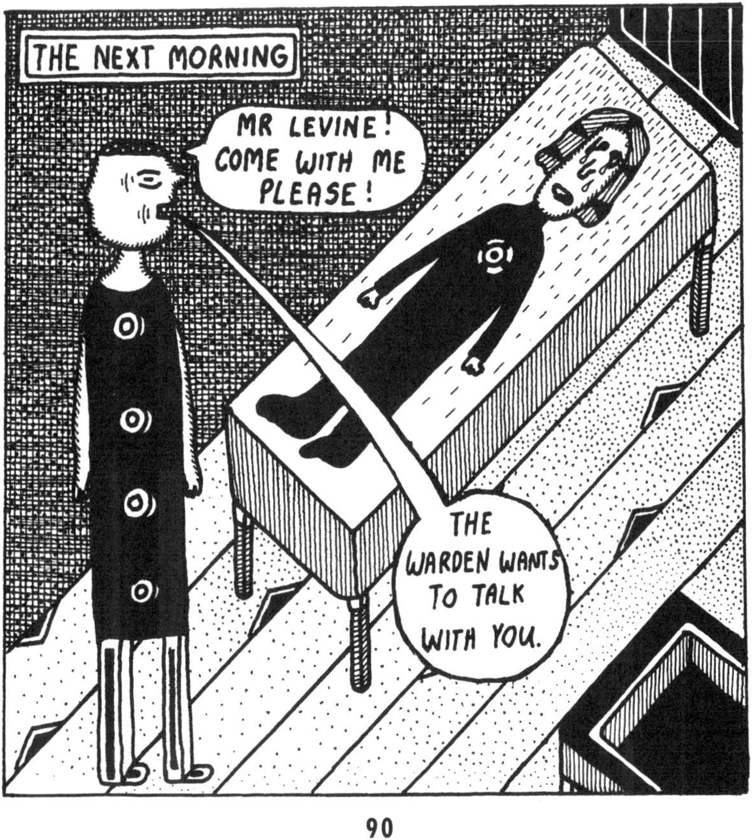
THE NEXT MORNING
MR LEVINE! COME WITH ME PLEASE!
THE WARDEN WANTS TO TALK WITH YOU.

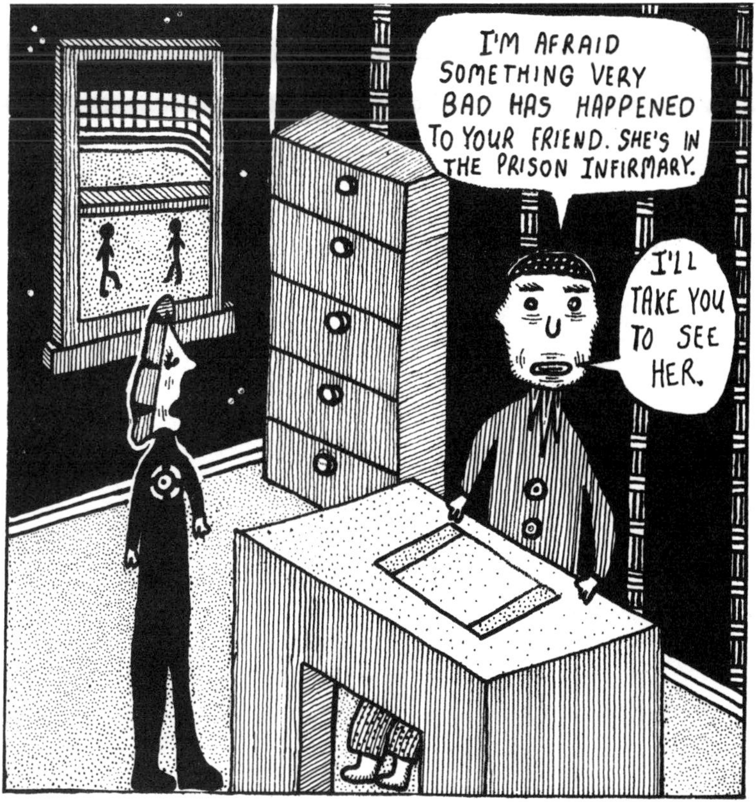
I'M AFRAID SOMETHING VERY BAD HAS HAPPENED TO YOUR FRIEND. SHE'S IN THE PRISON INFIRMARY.
I'LL TAKE YOU TO SEE HER.

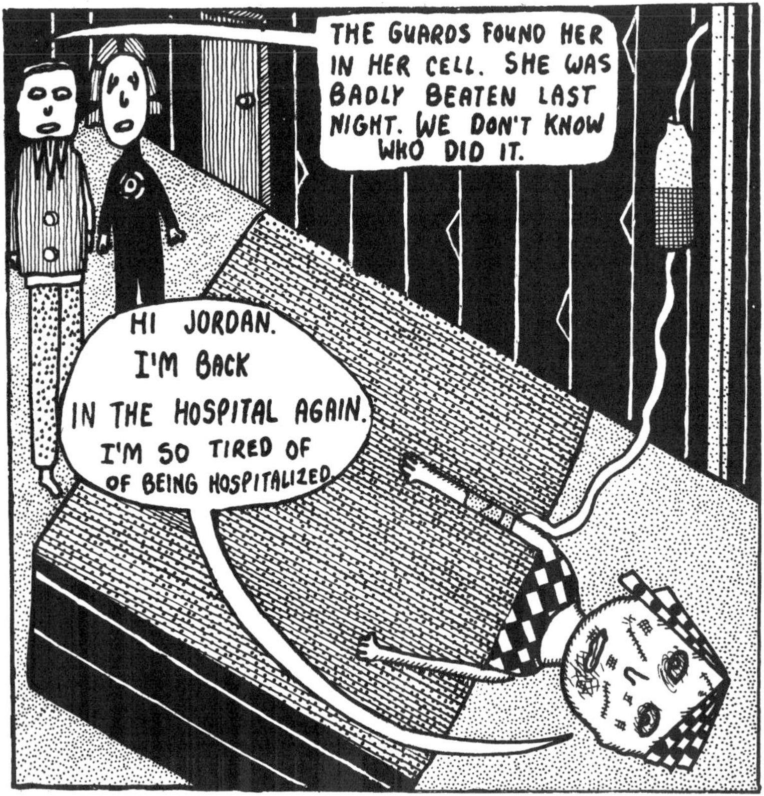
THE GUARDS FOUND HER IN HER CELL. SHE WAS BADLY BEATEN LAST NIGHT. WE DON'T KNOW WHO DID IT.
HI JORDAN. I'M BACK IN THE HOSPITAL AGAIN. I'M SO TIRED OF OF BEING HOSPITALIZED.

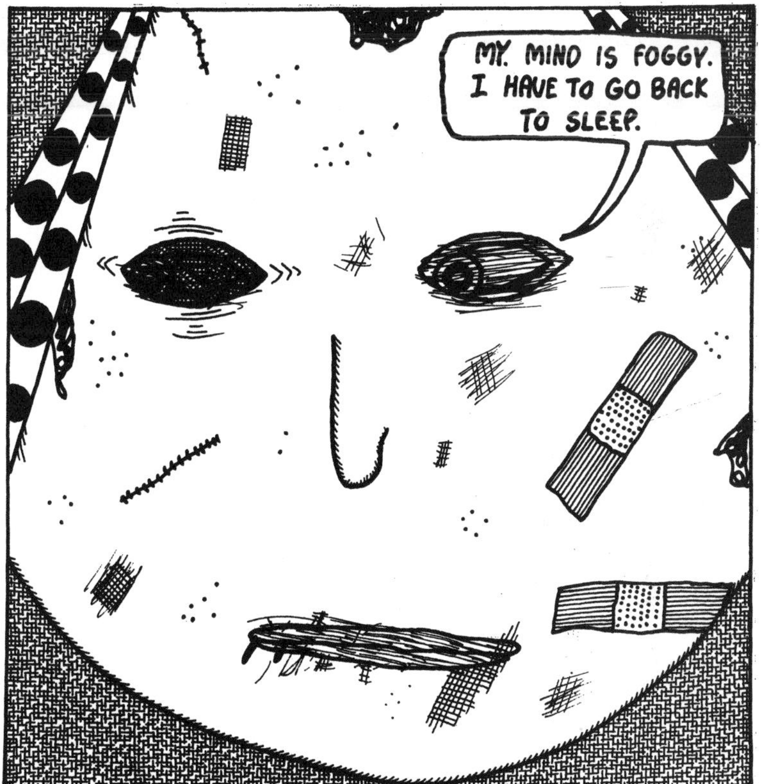
MY. MIND IS FOGGY. I HAVE TO GO BACK TO SLEEP.

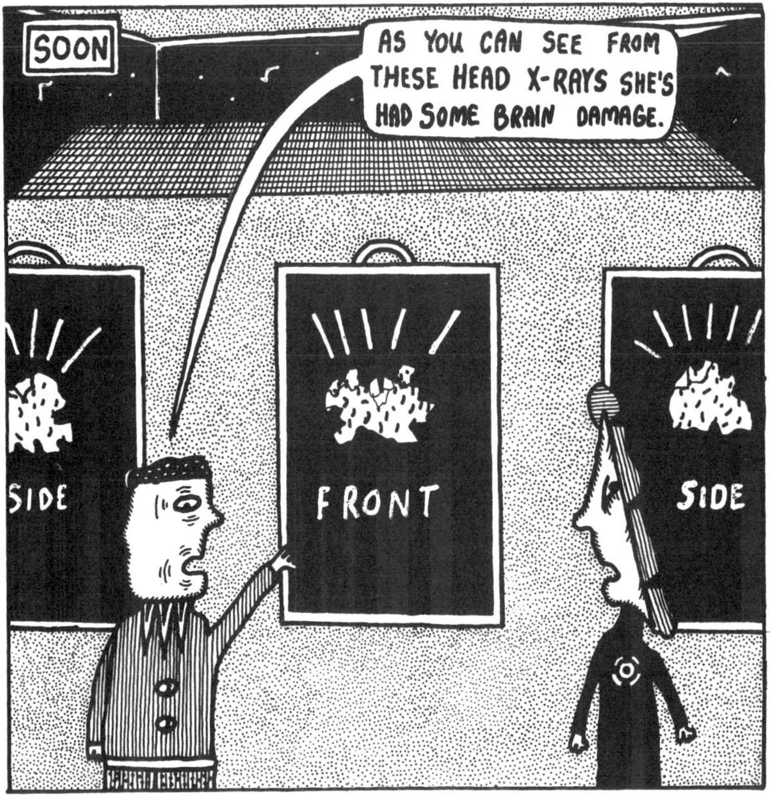
SOON
AS YOU CAN SEE FROM THESE HEAD X-RAYS SHE'S HAD SOME BRAIN DAMAGE.
SIDE
FRONT
SIDE

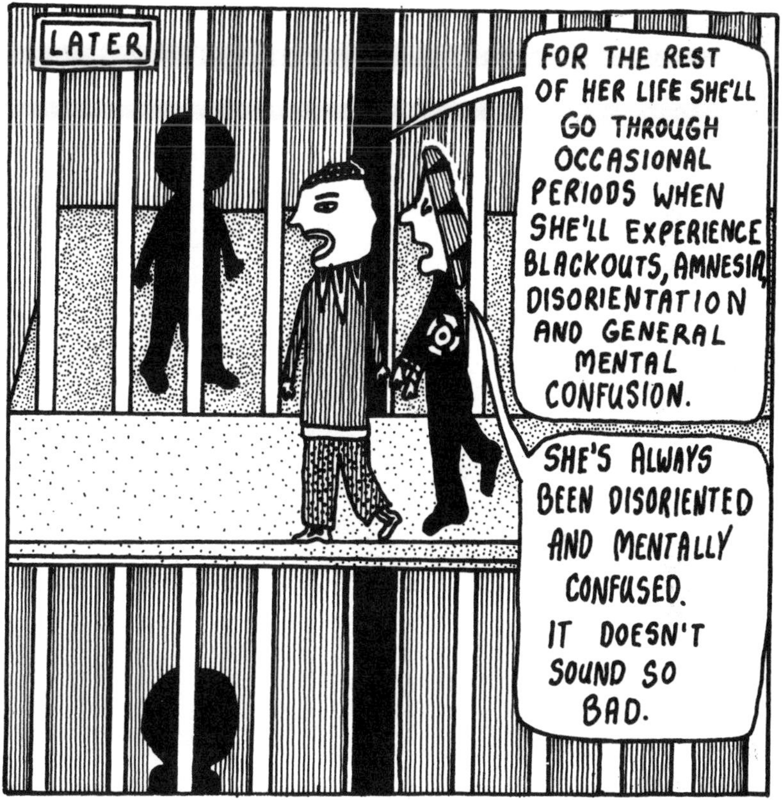
LATER
FOR THE REST OF HER LIFE SHE'LL GO THROUGH OCCASIONAL PERIODS WHEN SHE'LL EXPERIENCE BLACKOUTS, AMNESIA, DISORIENTATION AND GENERAL MENTAL CONFUSION.
SHE'S ALWAYS BEEN DISORIENTED AND MENTALLY CONFUSED. IT DOESN'T SOUND SO BAD.

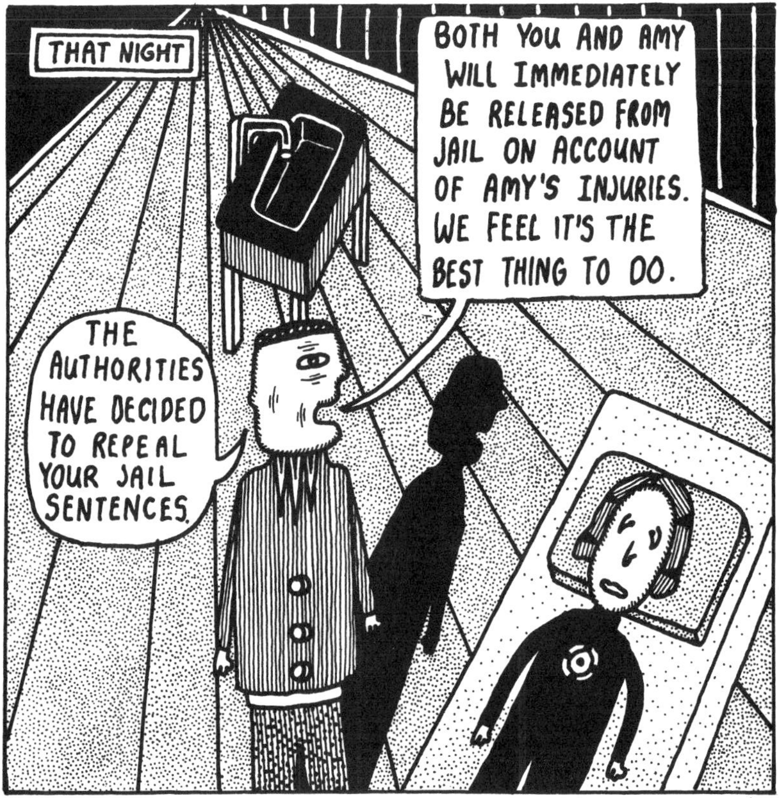
THAT NIGHT
THE AUTHORITIES HAVE DECIDED TO REPEAL YOUR JAIL SENTENCES.
BOTH YOU AND AMY WILL IMMEDIATELY BE RELEASED FROM JAIL ON ACCOUNT OF AMY'S INJURIES. WE FEEL IT'S THE BEST THING TO DO.

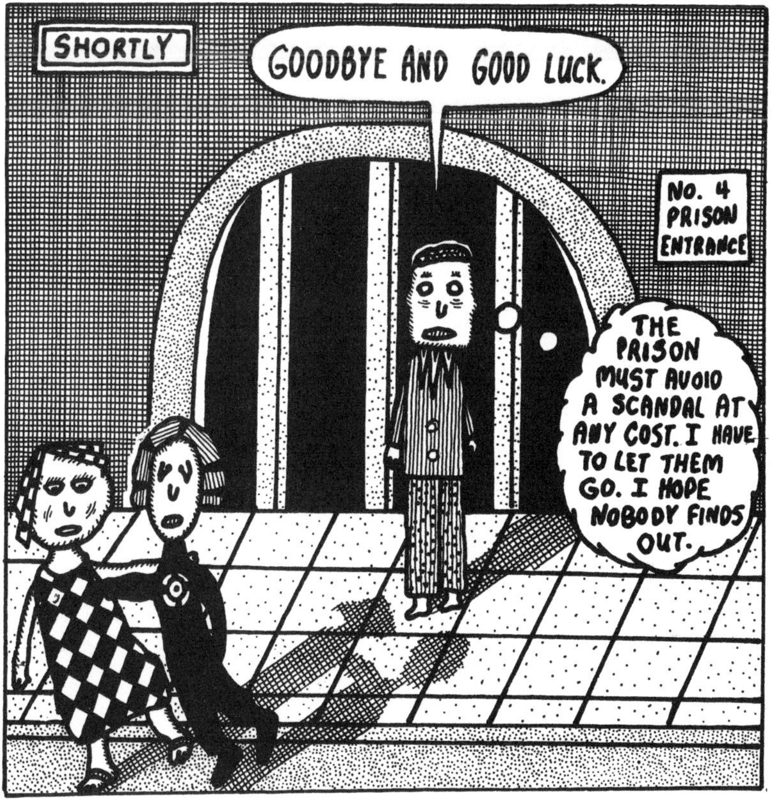
SHORTLY
GOODBYE AND GOOD LUCK.
NO. 4 PRISON ENTRANCE
THE PRISON MUST AVOID A SCANDAL AT ANY COST. I HAVE TO LET THEM GO. I HOPE NOBODY FINDS OUT.

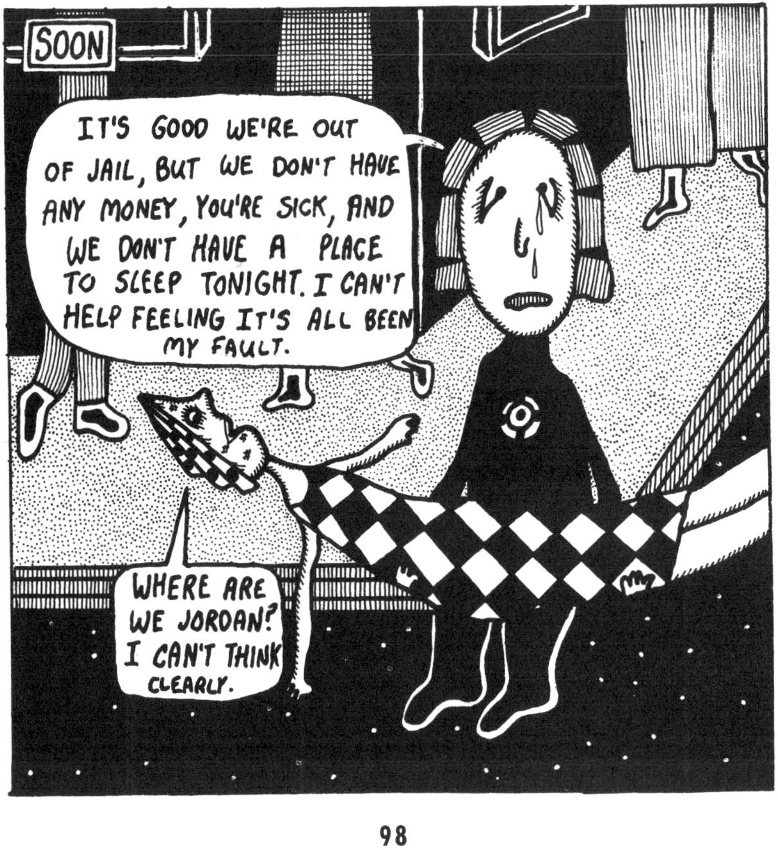
SOON
IT'S GOOD WE'RE OUT OF JAIL, BUT WE DON'T HAVE ANY MONEY, YOU'RE SICK, AND WE DON'T HAVE A PLACE TO SLEEP TONIGHT. I CAN'T HELP FEELING IT'S ALL BEEN MY FAULT.
WHERE ARE WE JORDAN? I CAN'T THINK CLEARLY.

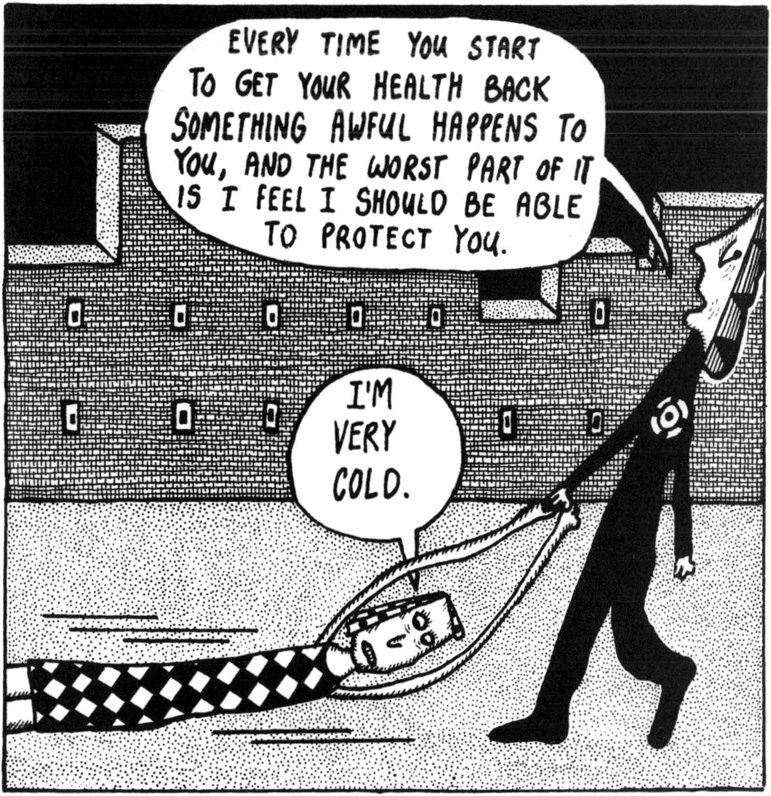
EVERY TIME YOU START TO GET YOUR HEALTH BACK SOMETHING AWFUL HAPPENS TO YOU, AND THE WORST PART OF IT IS I FEEL I SHOULD BE ABLE TO PROTECT YOU.
I'M VERY COLD.

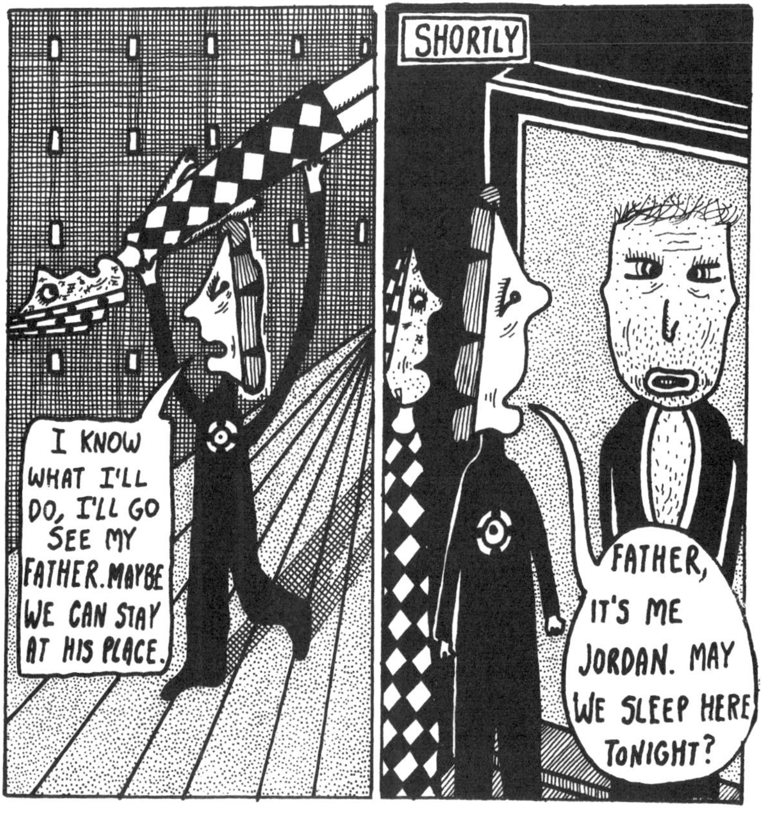
I KNOW WHAT I'LL DO, I'LL GO SEE MY FATHER. MAYBE WE CAN STAY AT HIS PLACE.
SHORTLY
FATHER, IT'S ME JORDAN. MAY WE SLEEP HERE TONIGHT?

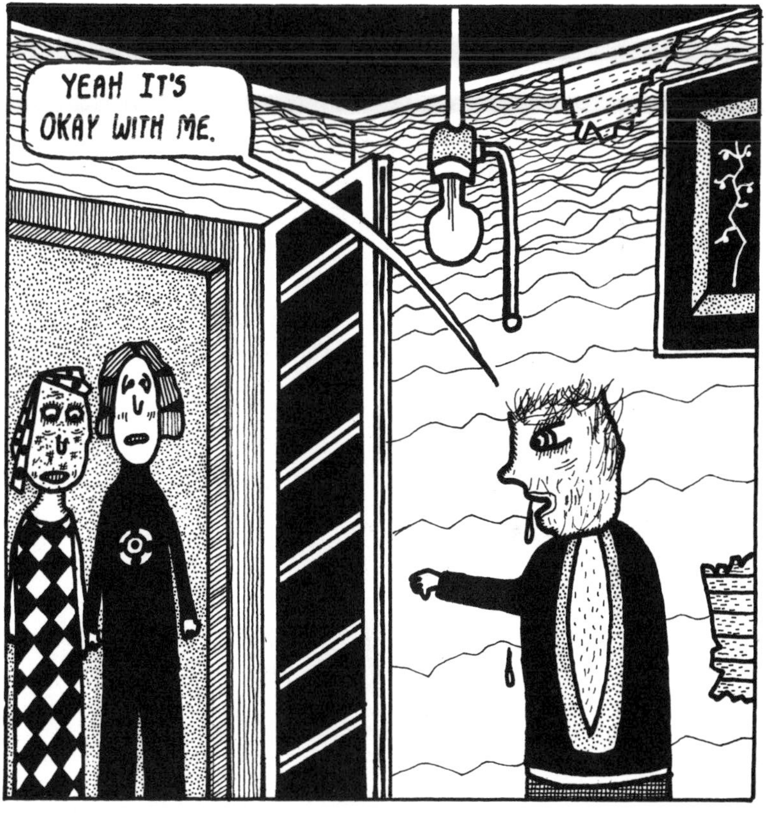
YEAH IT'S OKAY WITH ME.

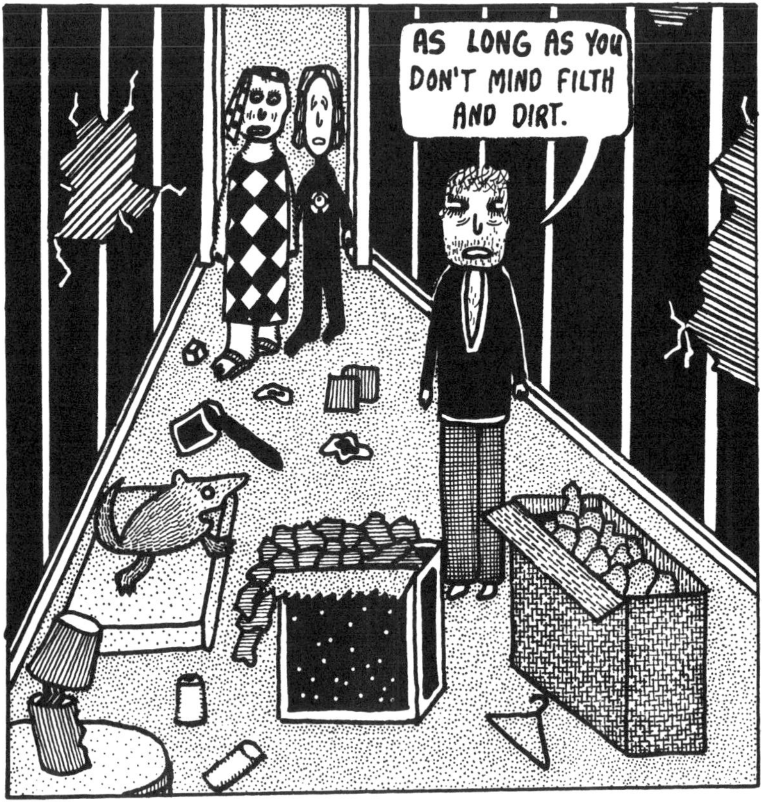
AS LONG AS YOU DON'T MIND FILTH AND DIRT.

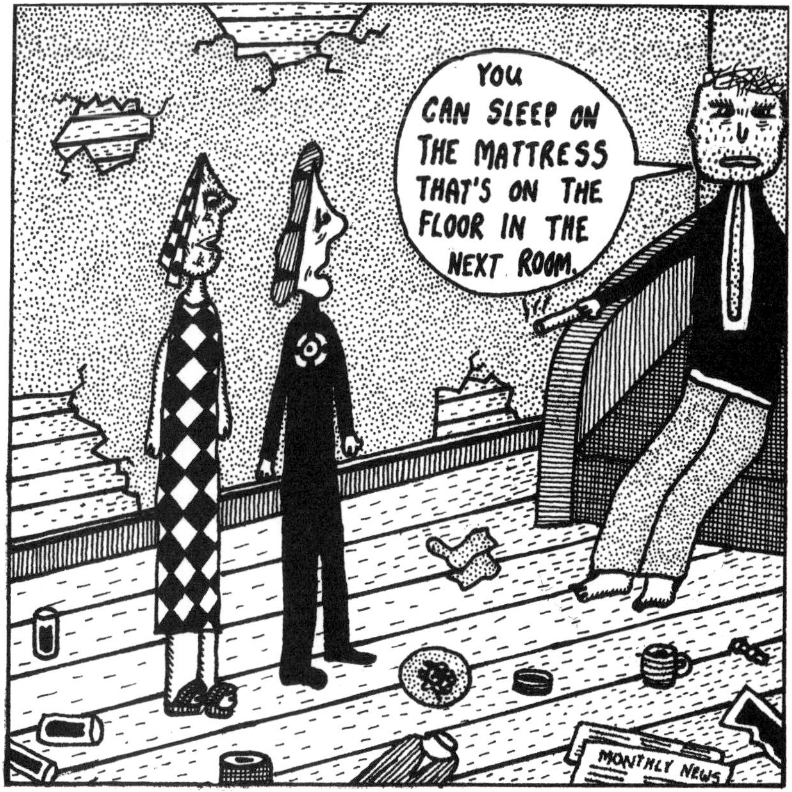
YOU CAN SLEEP ON THE MATTRESS THAT'S ON THE FLOOR IN THE NEXT ROOM.
MONTHLY NEWS

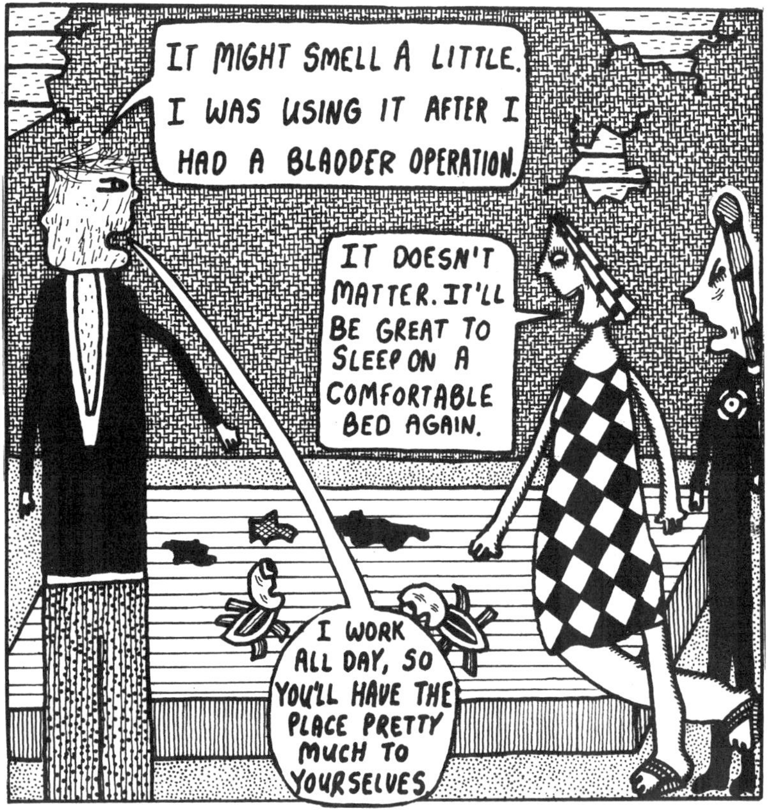
IT MIGHT SMELL A LITTLE. I WAS USING IT AFTER I HAD A BLADDER OPERATION.
IT DOESN'T MATTER. IT'LL BE GREAT TO SLEEP ON A COMFORTABLE BED AGAIN.
I WORK ALL DAY, SO YOU'LL HAVE THE PLACE PRETTY MUCH TO YOURSELVES

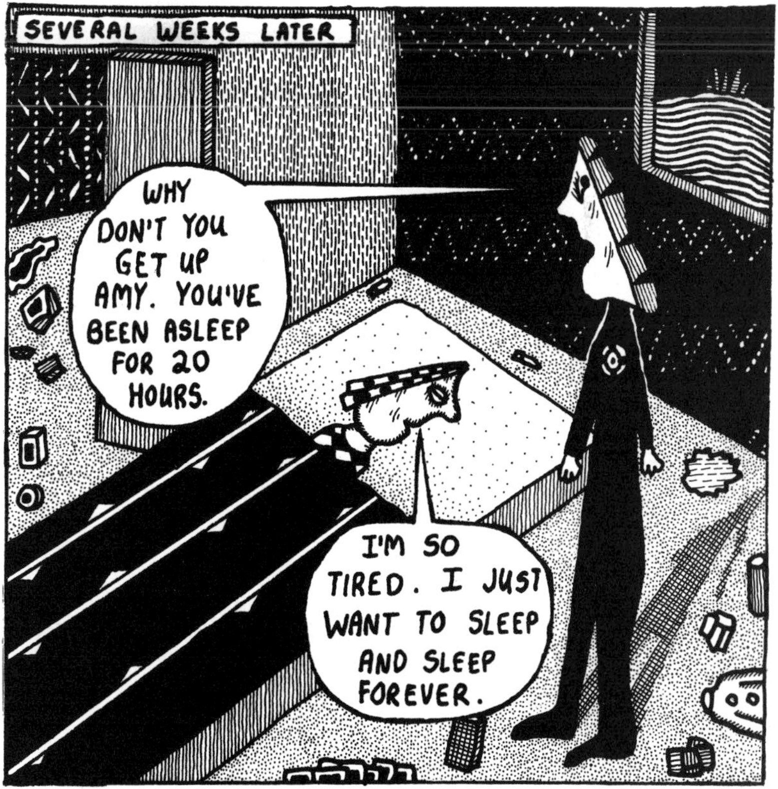
SEVERAL WEEKS LATER
WHY DON'T YOU GET UP AMY. YOU'VE BEEN ASLEEP FOR 20 HOURS.
I'M SO TIRED. I JUST WANT TO SLEEP AND SLEEP AND SLEEP FOREVER.

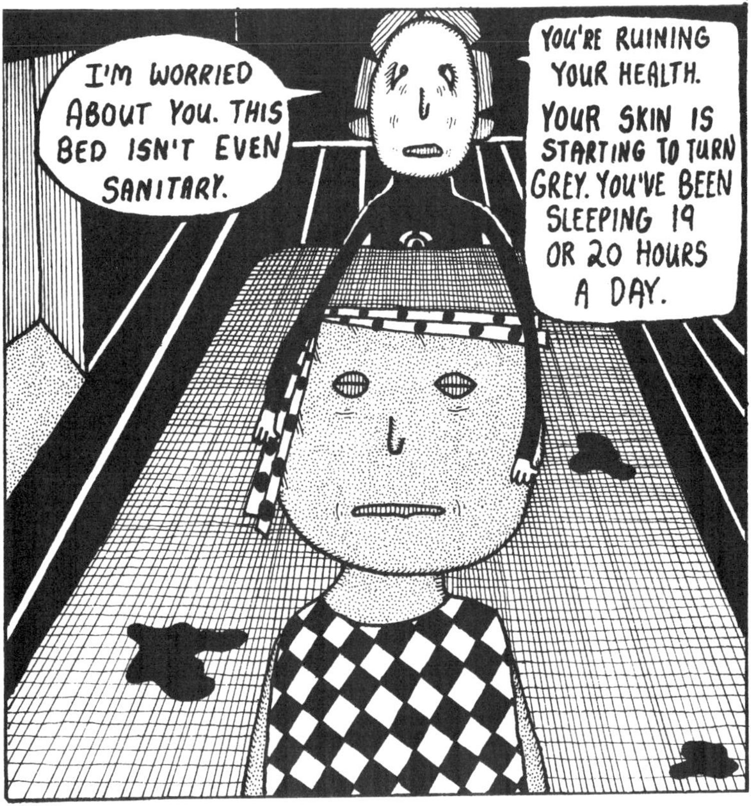
I'M WORRIED ABOUT YOU. THIS BED ISN'T EVEN SANITARY.
YOU'RE RUINING YOUR HEALTH.
YOUR SKIN IS STARTING TO TURN GREY. YOU'VE BEEN SLEEPING 19 OR 20 HOURS A DAY.

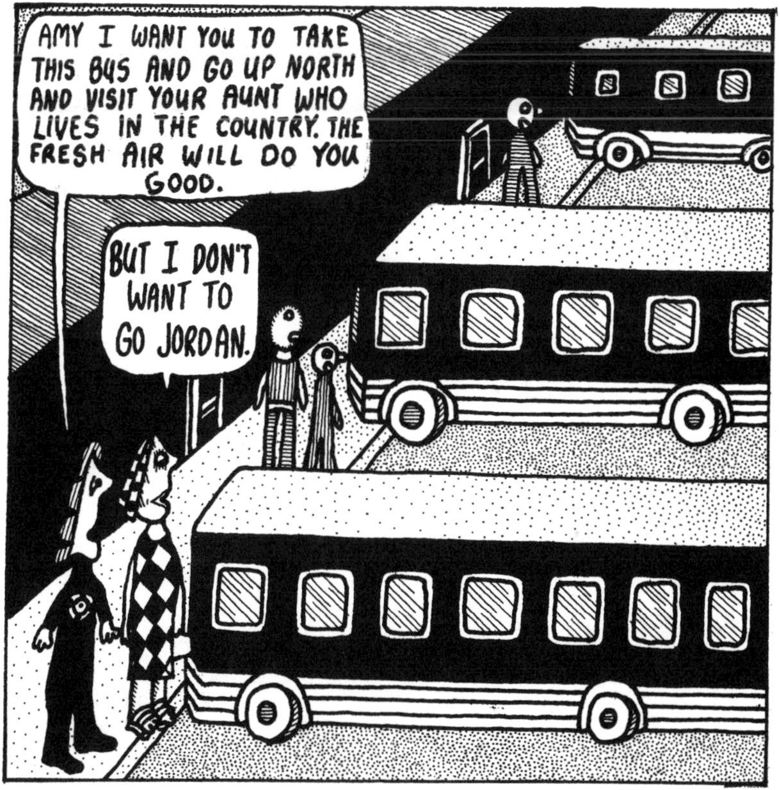
AMY I WANT YOU TO TAKE THIS BUS AND GO UP NORTH AND VISIT YOUR AUNT WHO LIVES IN THE COUNTRY. THE FRESH AIR WILL DO YOU GOOD.
BUT I DON'T WANT TO GO JORDAN.

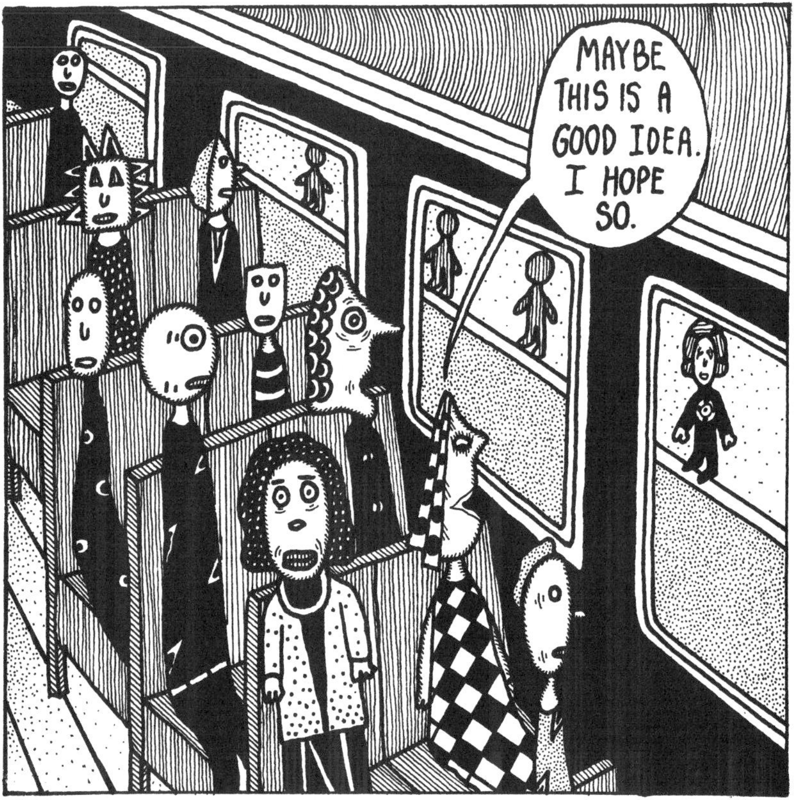
MAYBE THIS IS A GOOD IDEA. I HOPE SO.

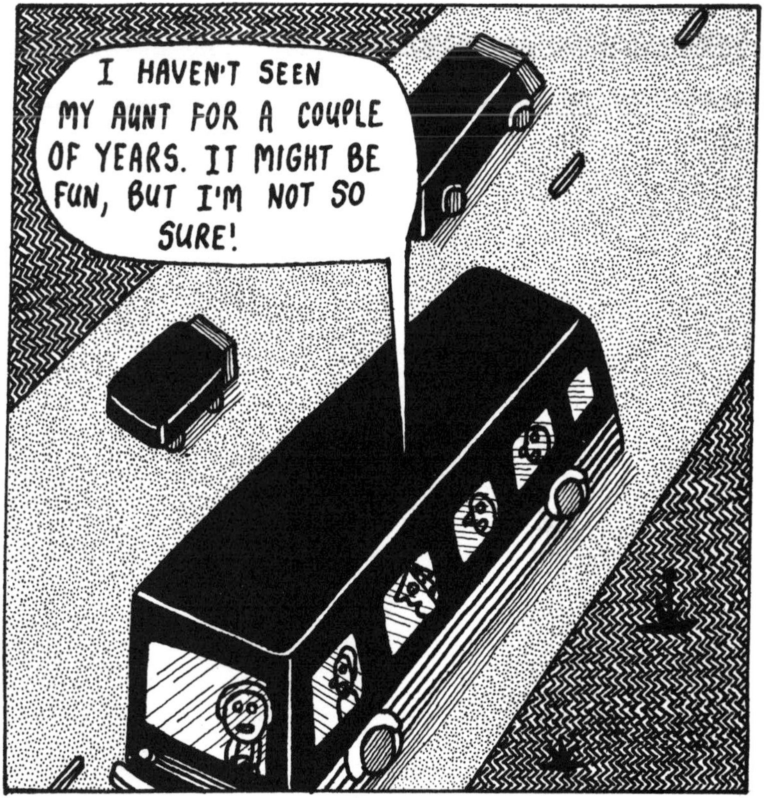
I HAVEN'T SEEN MY AUNT FOR A COUPLE OF YEARS. IT MIGHT BE FUN, BUT I'M NOT SO SURE!

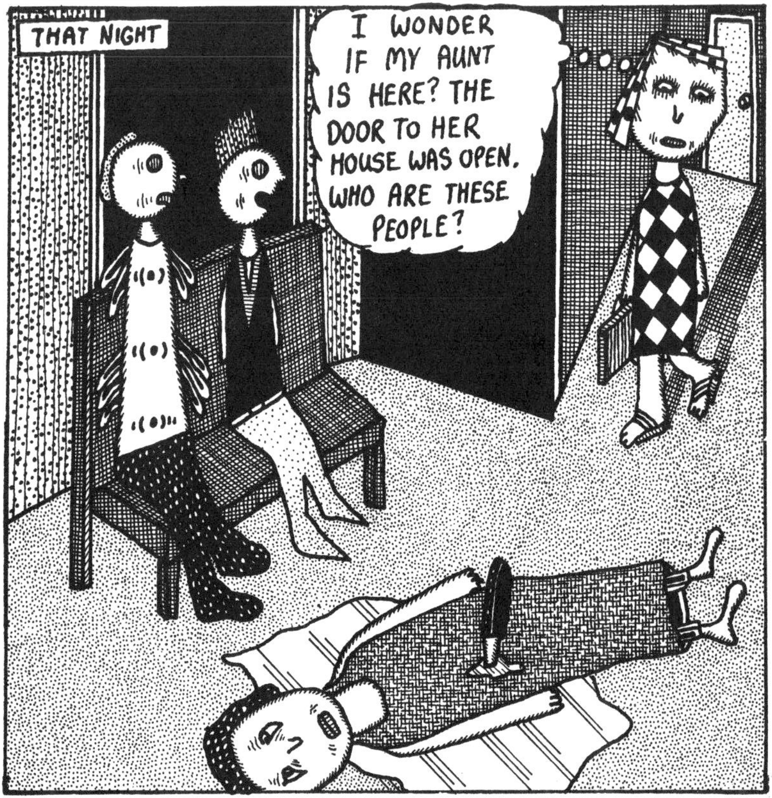
THAT NIGHT
I WONDER IF MY AUNT IS HERE? THE DOOR TO HER HOUSE WAS OPEN. WHO ARE THESE PEOPLE?

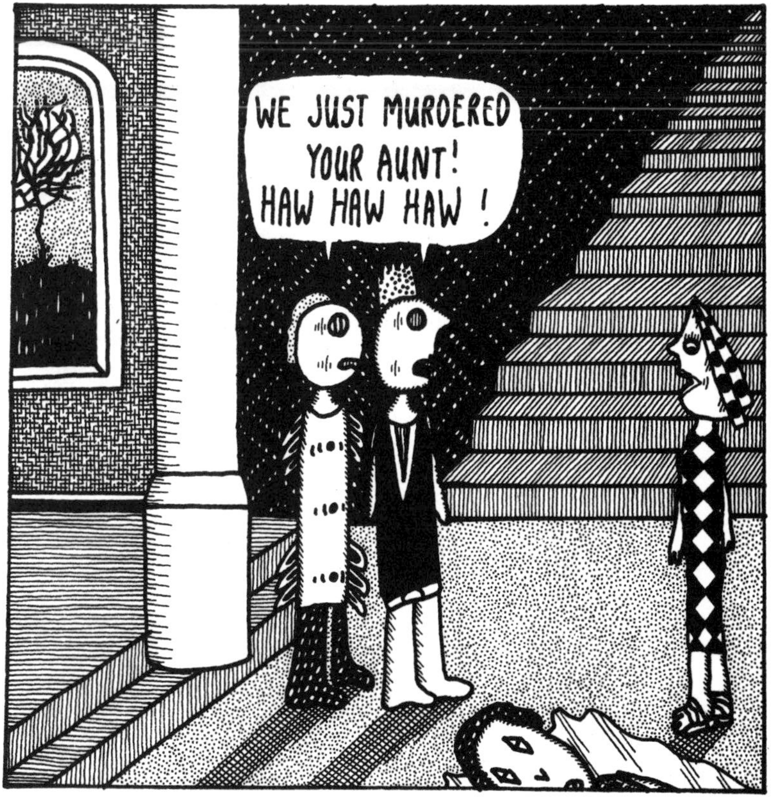
WE JUST MURDERED YOUR AUNT! HAW HAW HAW !

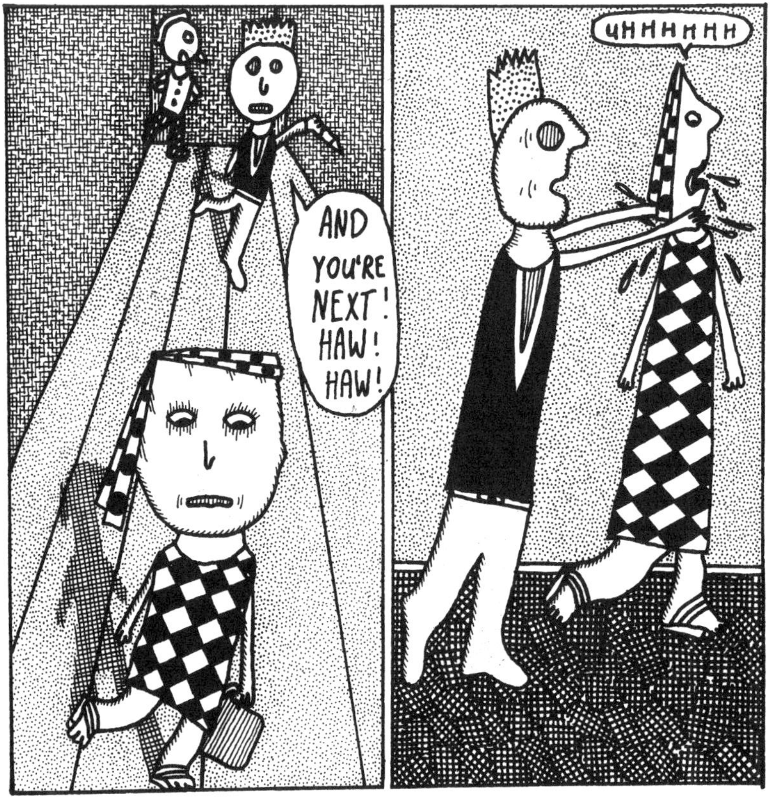
AND YOU'RE NEXT! HAW! HAW!
UHHHHHHH

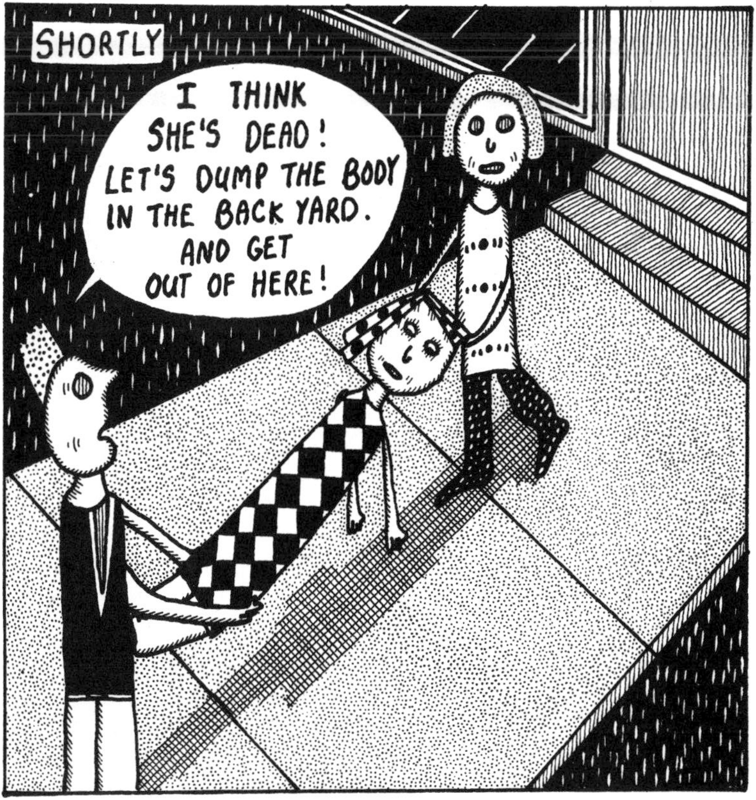
SHORTLY
I THINK SHE'S DEAD! LET'S DUMP THE BODY IN THE BACK YARD. AND GET OUT OF HERE!

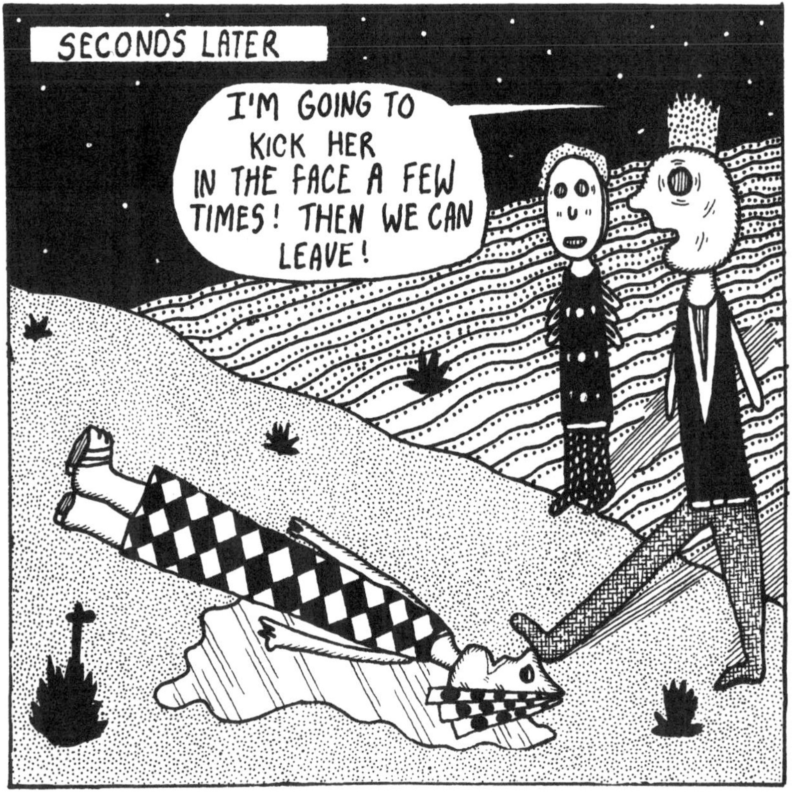
SECONDS LATER
I'M GOING TO KICK HER IN THE FACE A FEW TIMES! THEN WE CAN LEAVE!

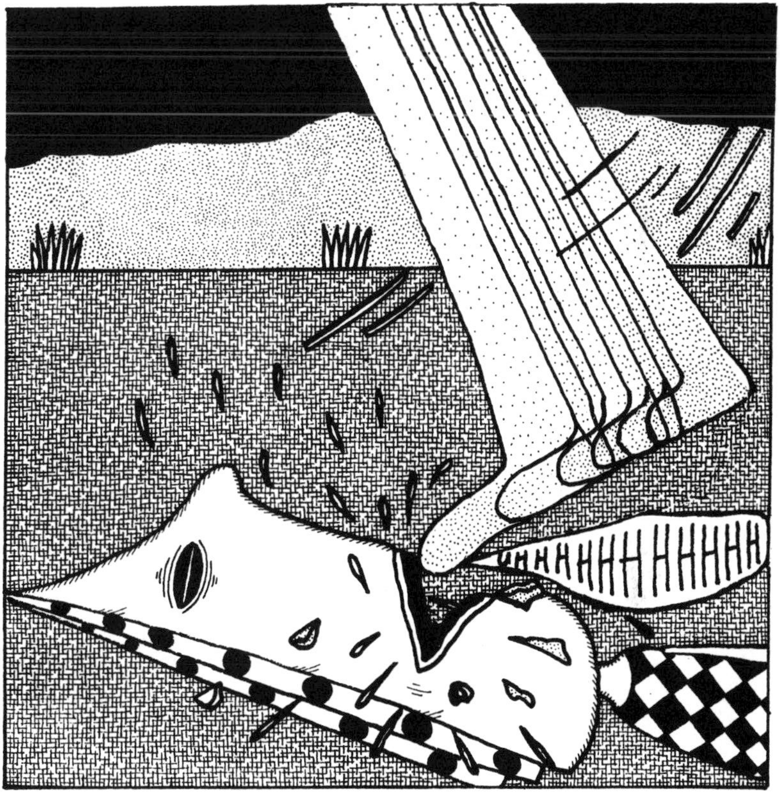

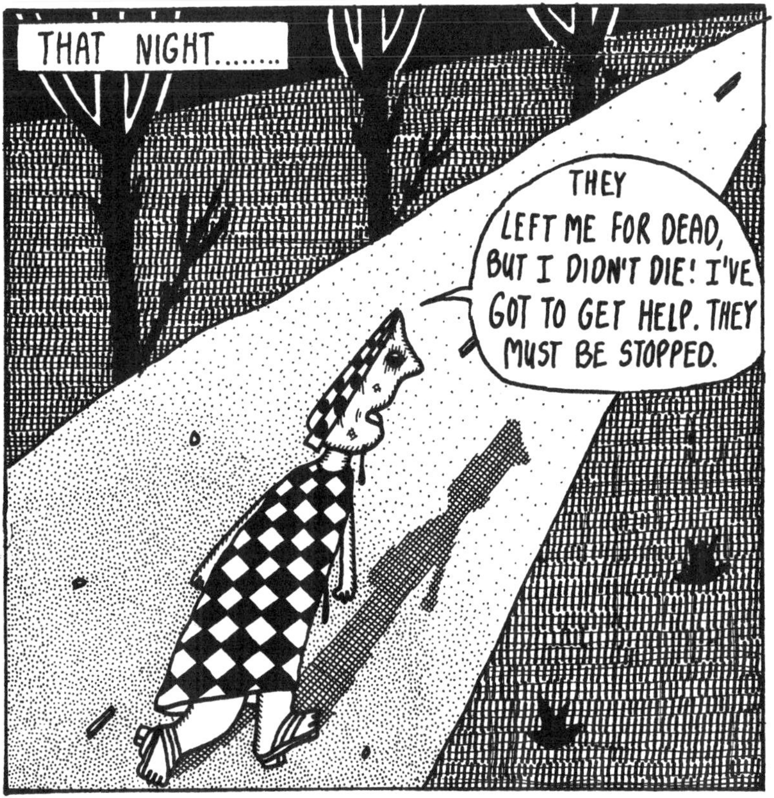
THAT NIGHT........
THEY LEFT ME FOR DEAD, BUT I DIDN'T DIE! I'VE GOT TO GET HELP. THEY MUST BE STOPPED.

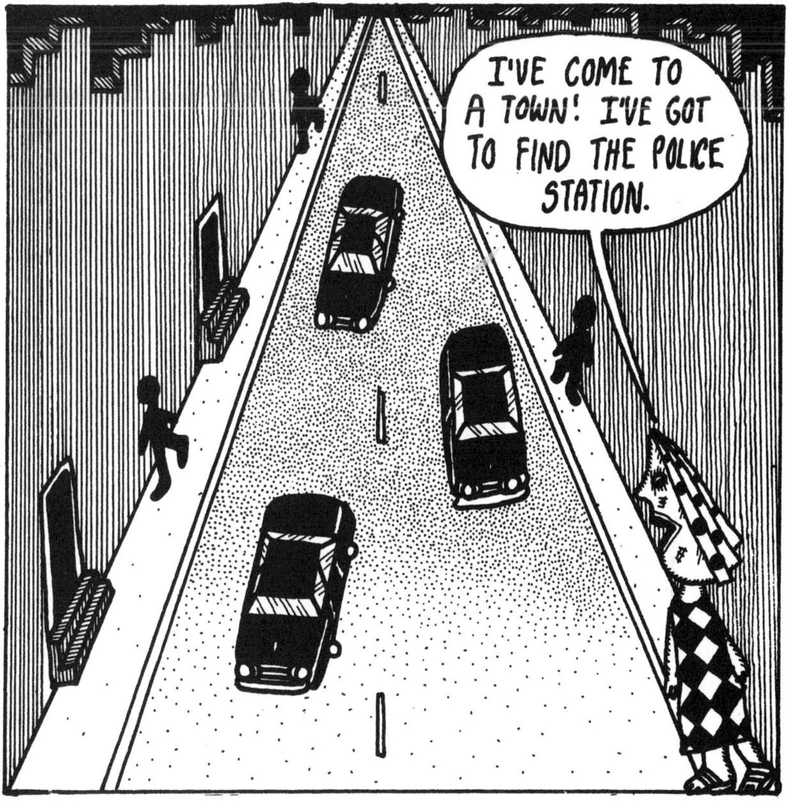
I'VE COME TO A TOWN! I'VE GOT TO FIND THE POLICE STATION.

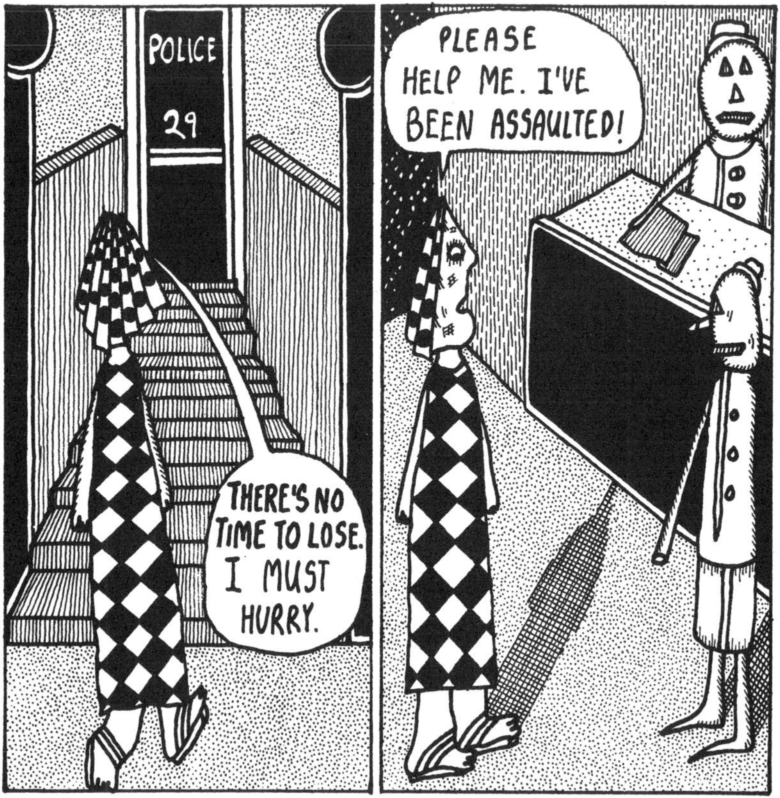
POLICE
29
THERE'S NO TIME TO LOSE. I MUST HURRY.
PLEASE HELP ME. I'VE BEEN ASSAULTED!

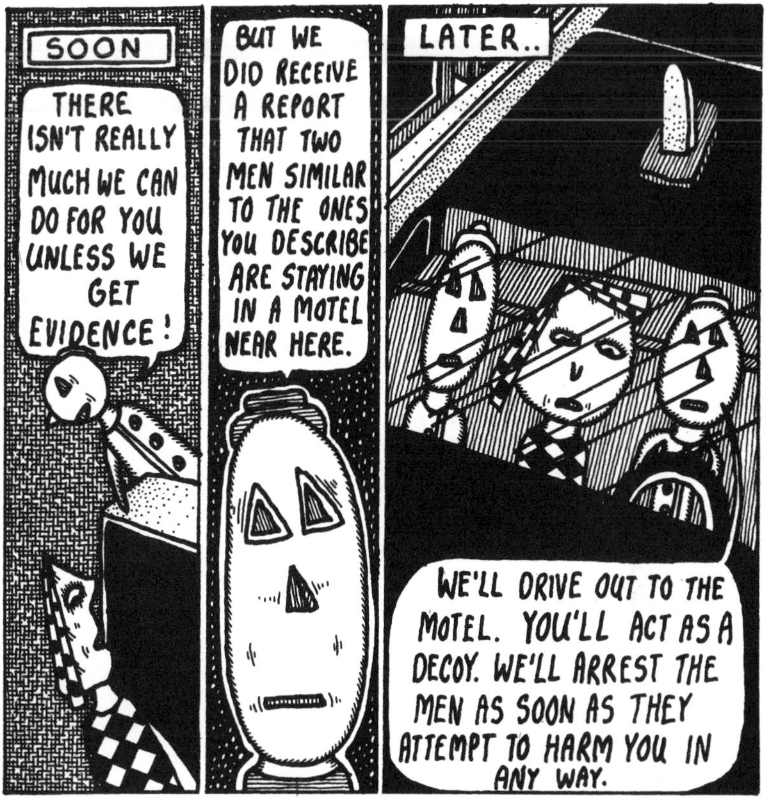
SOON
THERE ISN'T REALLY MUCH WE CAN DO FOR YOU UNLESS WE GET EVIDENCE!
BUT WE DID RECEIVE A REPORT THAT TWO MEN SIMILAR TO THE ONES YOU DESCRIBE ARE STAYING IN A MOTEL NEAR HERE.
LATER..
WE'LL DRIVE OUT TO THE MOTEL. YOU'LL ACT AS A DECOY. WE'LL ARREST THE MEN AS SOON AS THEY ATTEMPT TO HARM YOU IN ANY WAY.

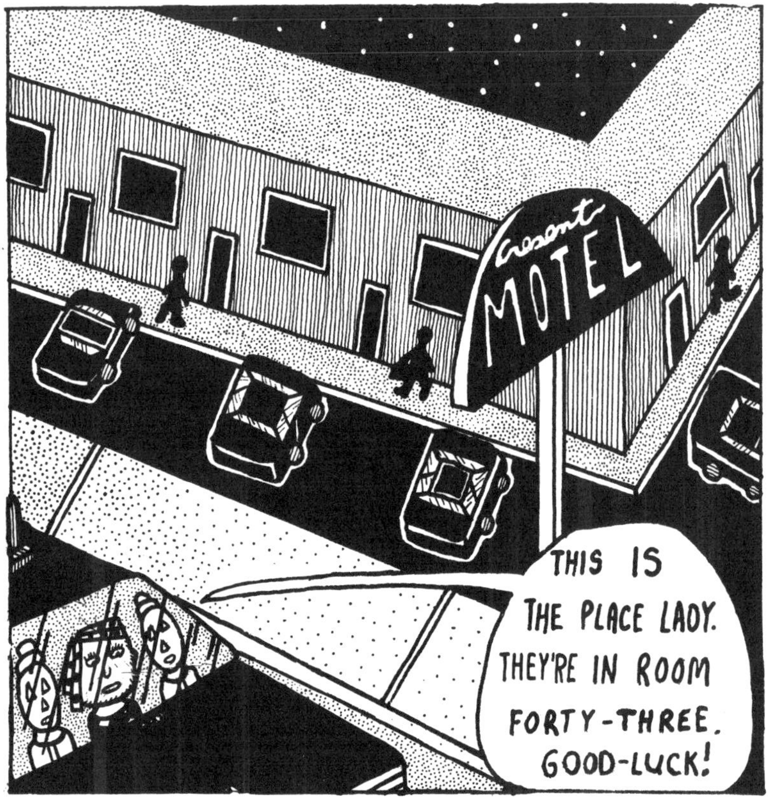
Cresent
MOTEL
THIS IS THE PLACE LADY. THEY'RE IN ROOM FORTY-THREE. GOOD-LUCK!

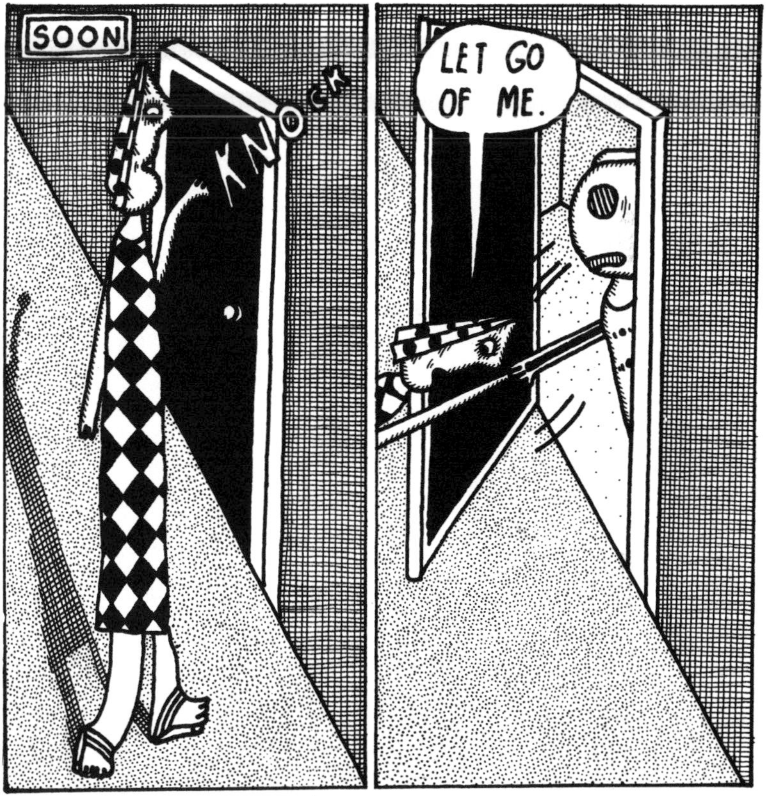
SOON
KNOCK
LET GO OF ME.

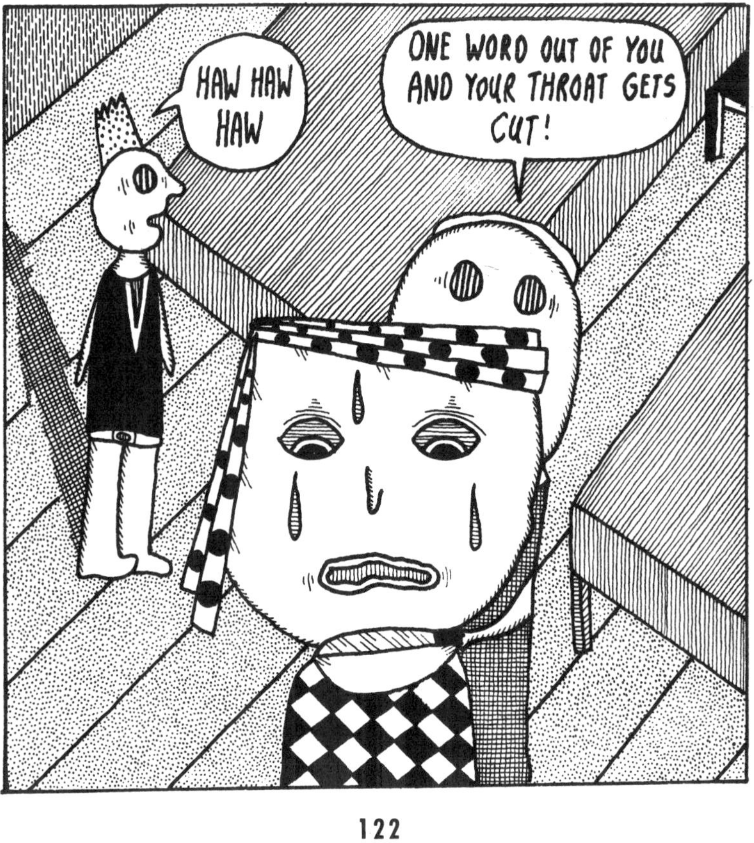
HAW HAW HAW
ONE WORD OUT OF YOU AND YOUR THROAT GETS CUT!

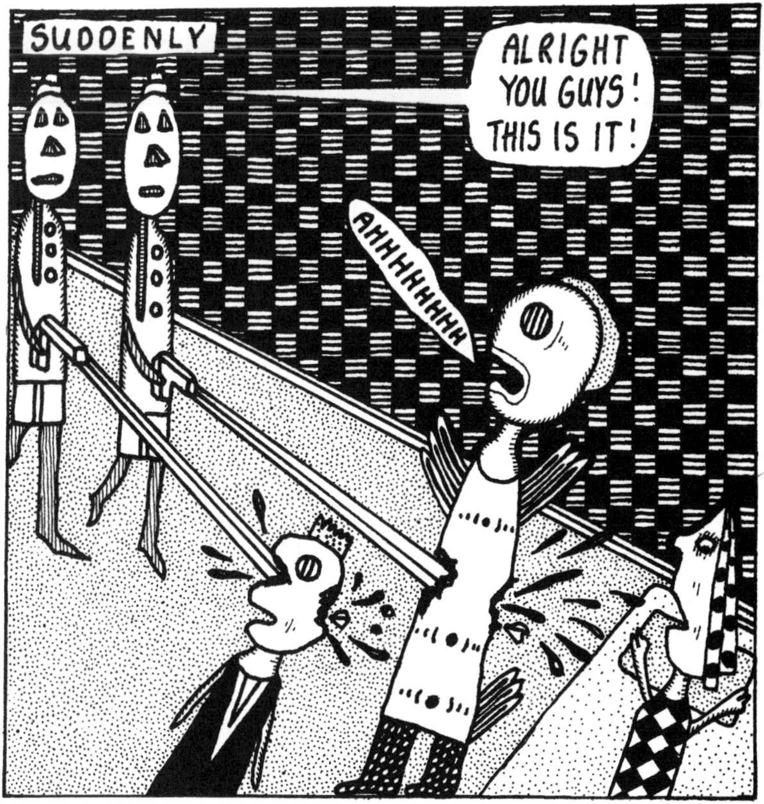
SUDDENLY
ALRIGHT YOU GUYS! THIS IS IT!
AHHHHHHHHH

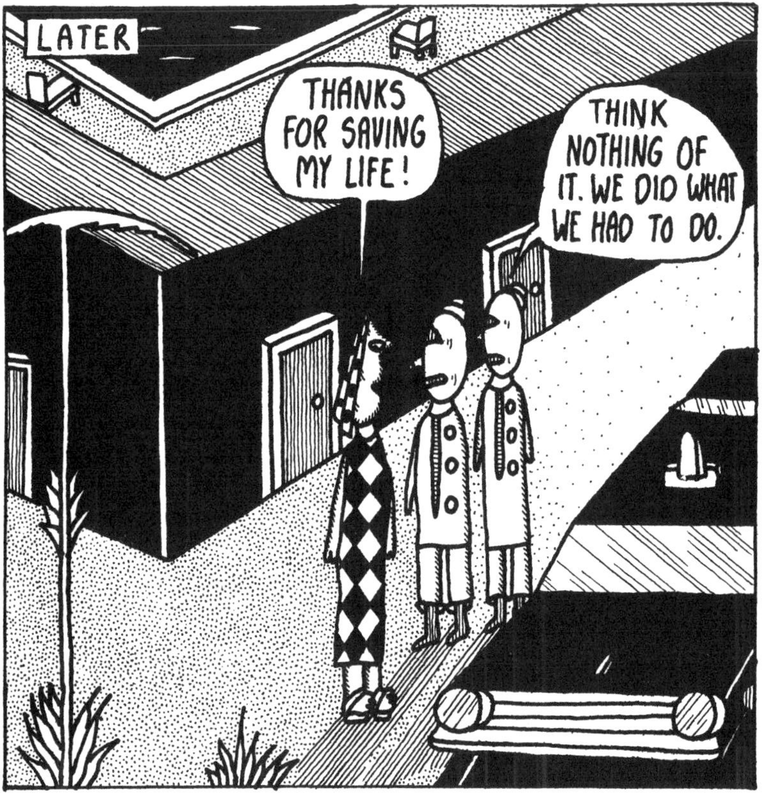
LATER
THANKS FOR SAVING MY LIFE!
THINK NOTHING OF IT. WE DID WHAT WE HAD TO DO.

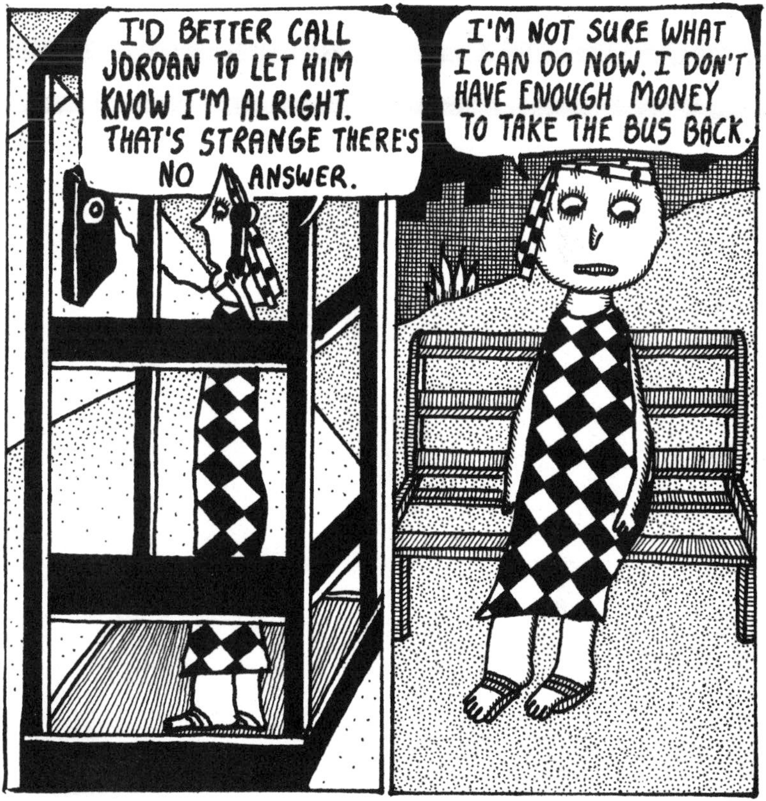
I'D BETTER CALL JORDAN TO LET HIM KNOW I'M ALRIGHT. THAT'S STRANGE THERE'S NO ANSWER.
I'M NOT SURE WHAT I CAN DO NOW. I DON'T HAVE ENOUGH MONEY TO TAKE THE BUS BACK.

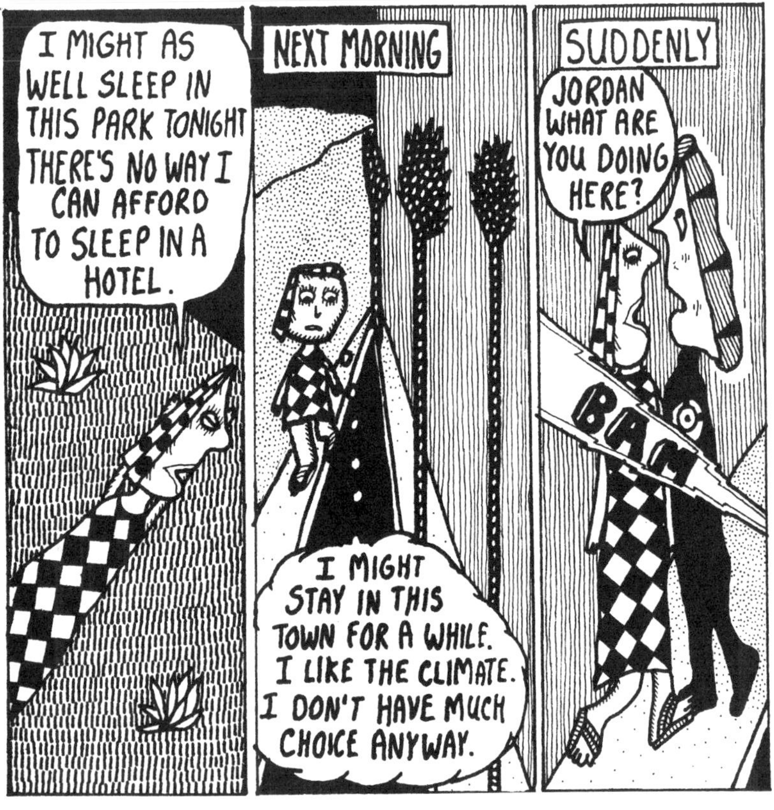
I MIGHT AS WELL SLEEP IN THIS PARK TONIGHT THERE'S NO WAY I CAN AFFORD TO SLEEP IN A HOTEL.
NEXT MORNING
I MIGHT STAY IN THIS TOWN FOR A WHILE. I LIKE THE CLIMATE. I DON'T HAVE MUCH CHOICE ANYWAY.
SUDDENLY
JORDAN WHAT ARE YOU DOING HERE?
BAM

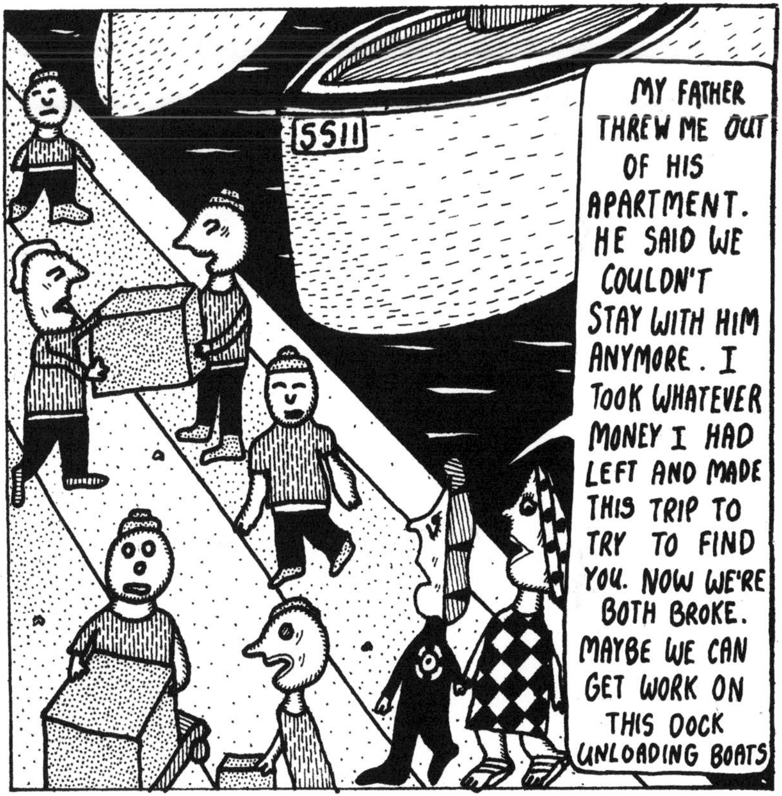
5511
MY FATHER THREW ME OUT OF HIS APARTMENT. HE SAID WE COULDN'T STAY WITH HIM ANYMORE. I TOOK WHATEVER MONEY I HAD LEFT AND MADE THIS TRIP TO TRY TO FIND YOU. NOW WE'RE BOTH BROKE. MAYBE WE CAN GET WORK ON THIS DOCK UNLOADING BOATS

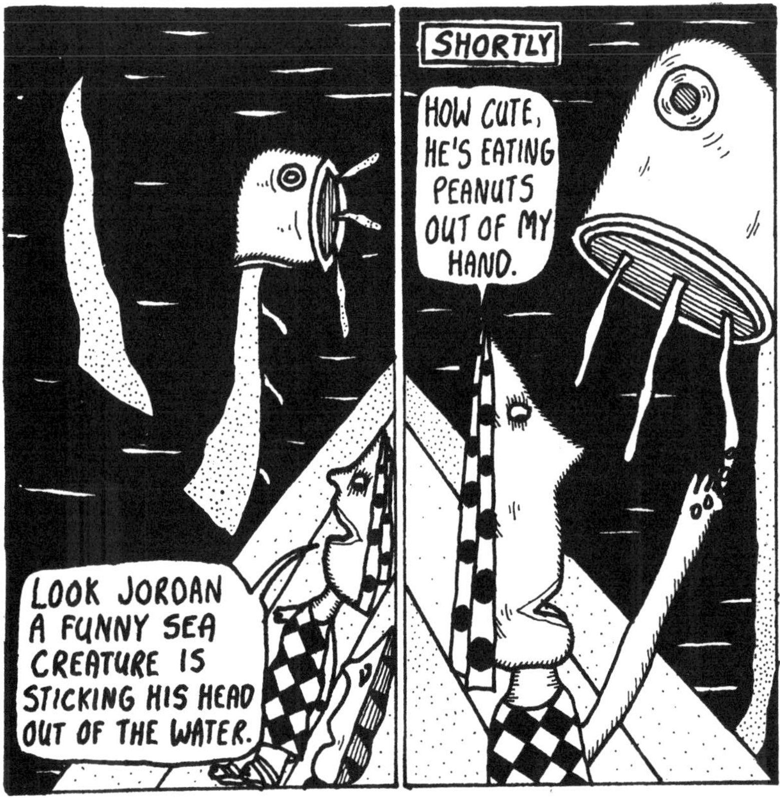
LOOK JORDAN A FUNNY SEA CREATURE IS STICKING HIS HEAD OUT OF THE WATER.
SHORTLY
HOW CUTE, HE'S EATING PEANUTS OUT OF MY HAND.

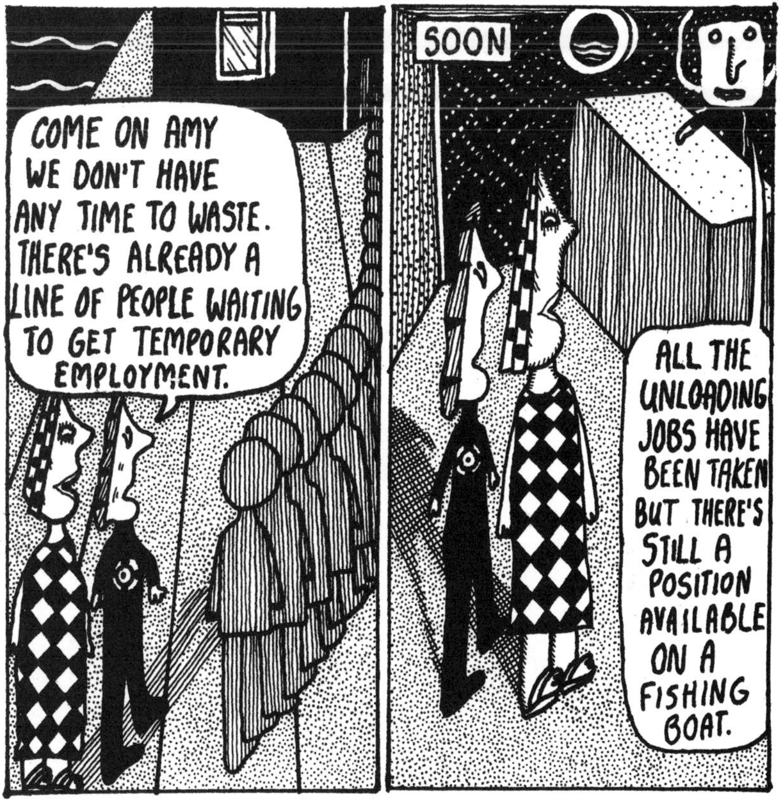
COME ON AMY WE DON'T HAVE ANY TIME TO WASTE. THERE'S ALREADY A LINE OF PEOPLE WAITING TO GET TEMPORARY EMPLOYMENT.
SOON
ALL THE UNLOADING JOBS HAVE BEEN TAKEN BUT THERE'S STILL A POSITION AVAILABLE ON A FISHING BOAT.

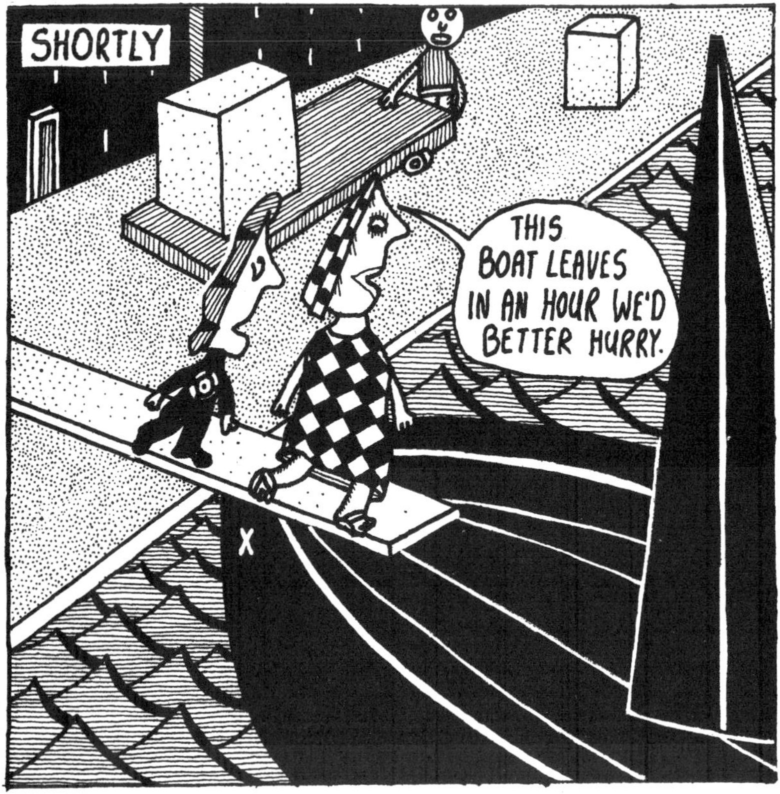
SHORTLY
THIS BOAT LEAVES IN AN HOUR WE'D BETTER HURRY.

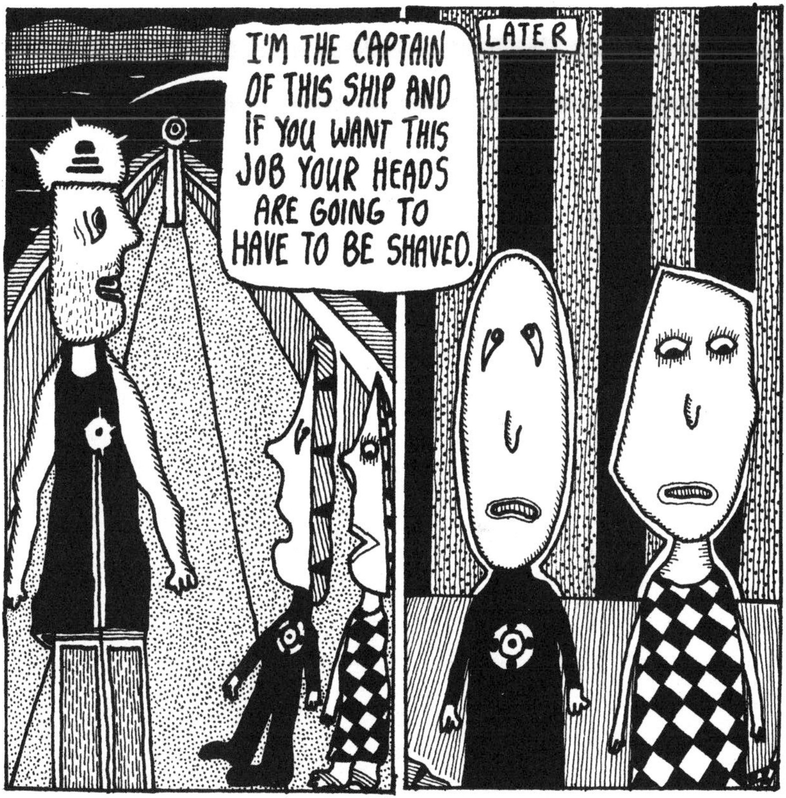
I'M THE CAPTAIN OF THIS SHIP AND IF YOU WANT THIS JOB YOUR HEADS ARE GOING TO HAVE TO BE SHAVED.
LATER

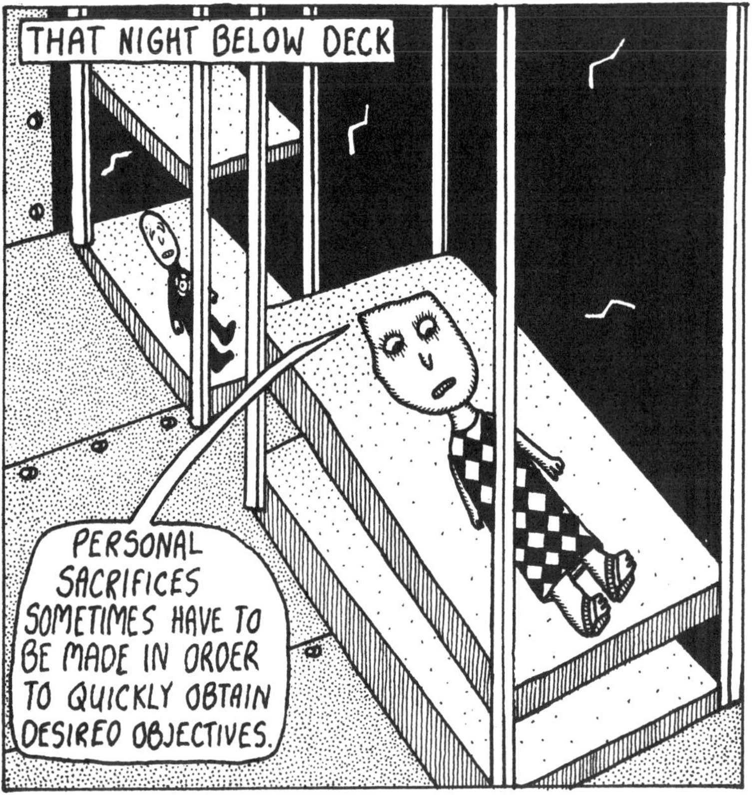
THAT NIGHT BELOW DECK
PERSONAL SACRIFICES SOMETIMES HAVE TO BE MADE IN ORDER TO QUICKLY OBTAIN DESIRED OBJECTIVES.

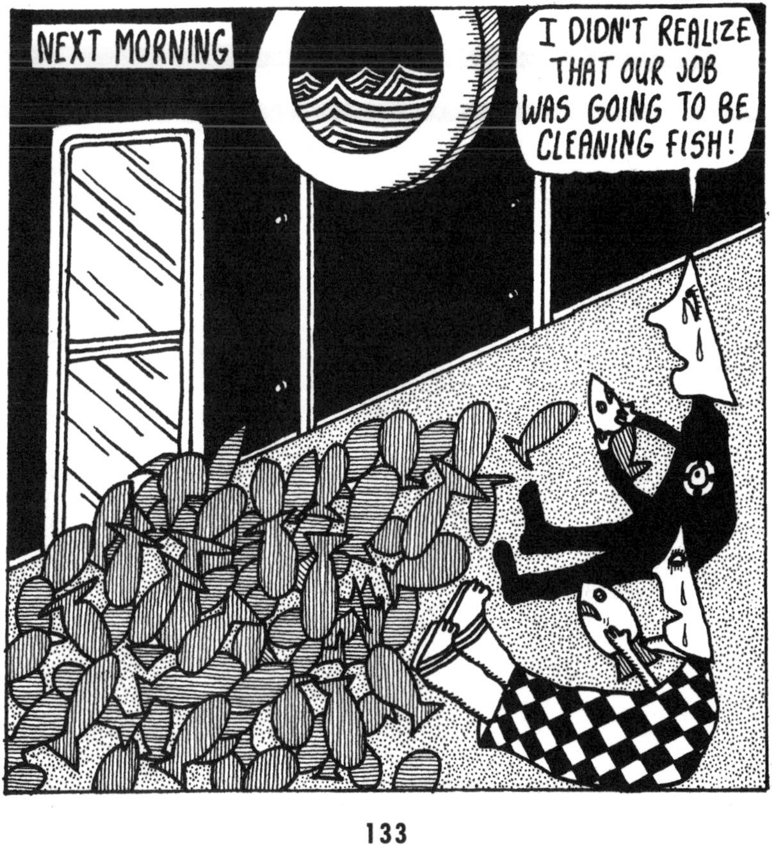
NEXT MORNING
I DIDN'T REALIZE THAT OUR JOB WAS GOING TO BE CLEANING FISH!

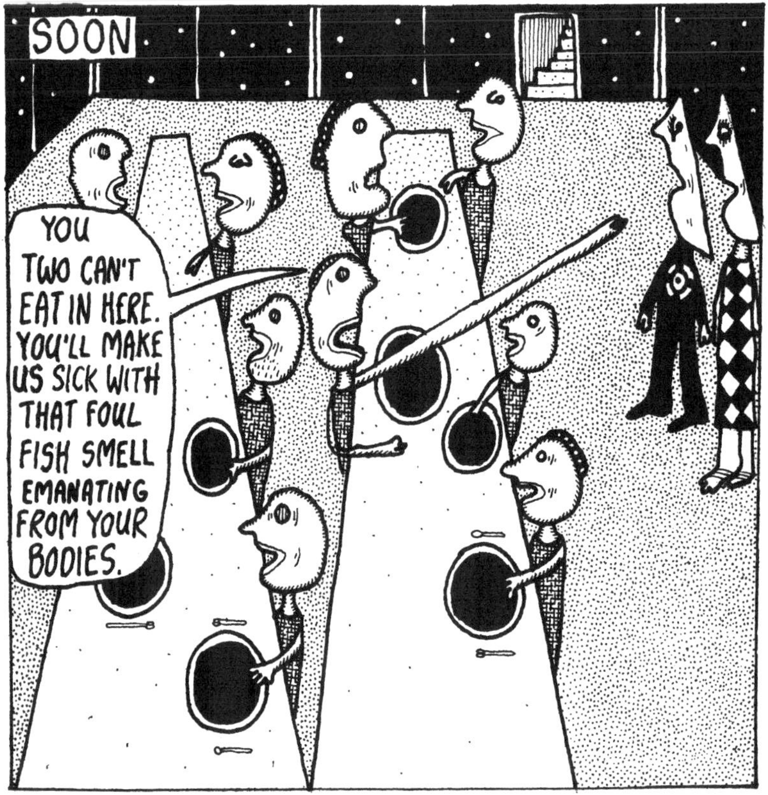
SOON
YOU TWO CAN'T EAT IN HERE. YOU'LL MAKE US SICK WITH THAT FOUL FISH SMELL EMANATING FROM YOUR BODIES.

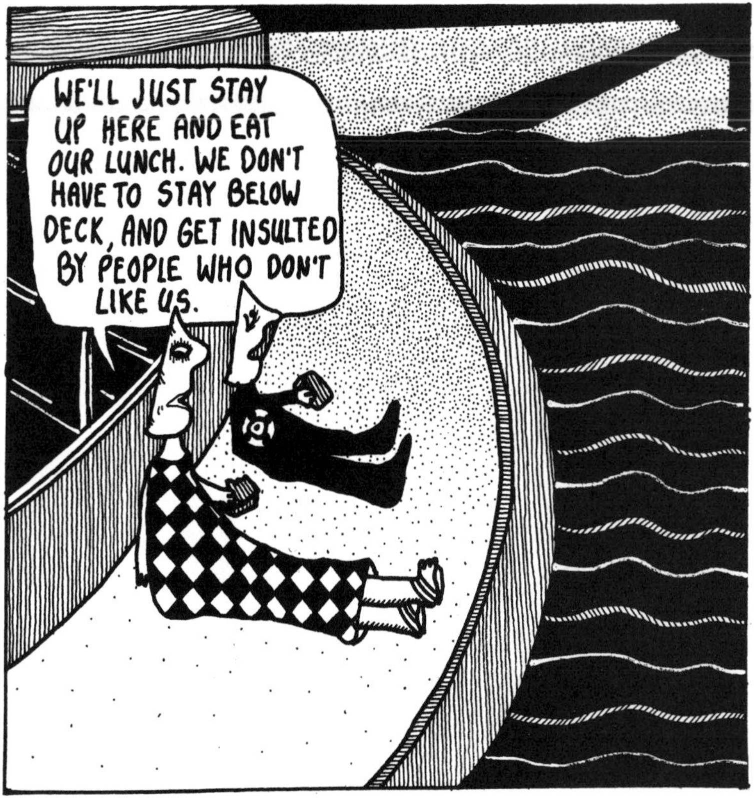
WE'LL JUST STAY UP HERE AND EAT OUR LUNCH. WE DON'T HAVE TO STAY BELOW DECK, AND GET INSULTED BY PEOPLE WHO DON'T LIKE US.

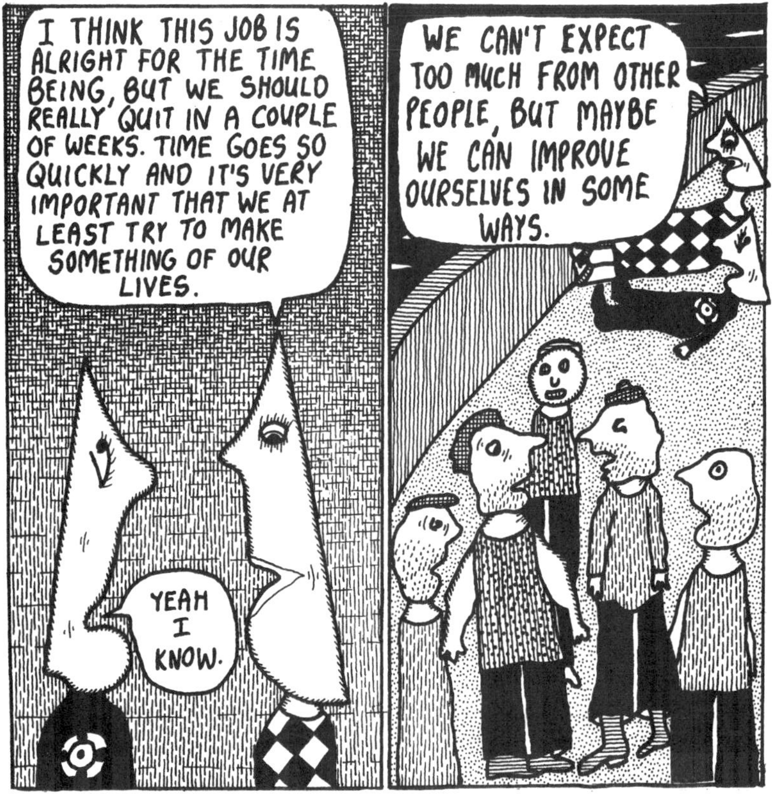
I THINK THIS JOB IS ALRIGHT FOR THE TIME BEING, BUT WE SHOULD REALLY QUIT IN A COUPLE OF WEEKS. TIME GOES SO QUICKLY AND IT'S VERY IMPORTANT THAT WE AT LEAST TRY TO MAKE SOMETHING OF OUR LIVES.
YEAH I KNOW.
WE CAN'T EXPECT TOO MUCH FROM OTHER PEOPLE, BUT MAYBE WE CAN IMPROVE OURSELVES IN SOME WAYS.

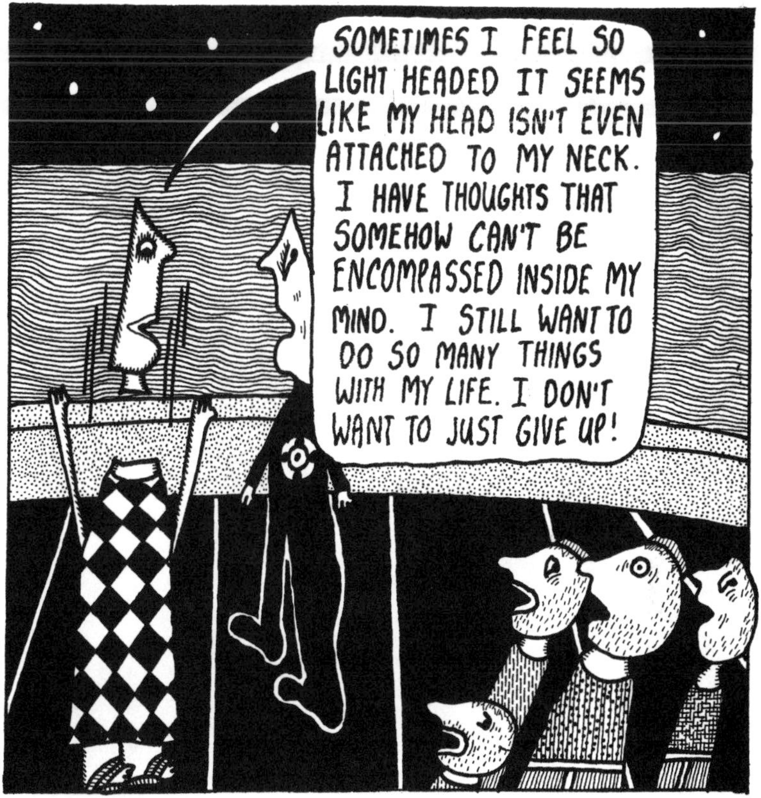
SOMETIMES I FEEL SO LIGHT HEADED IT SEEMS LIKE MY HEAD ISN'T EVEN ATTACHED TO MY NECK. I HAVE THOUGHTS THAT SOMEHOW CAN'T BE ENCOMPASSED INSIDE MY MIND. I STILL WANT TO DO SO MANY THINGS WITH MY LIFE. I DON'T WANT TO JUST GIVE UP!

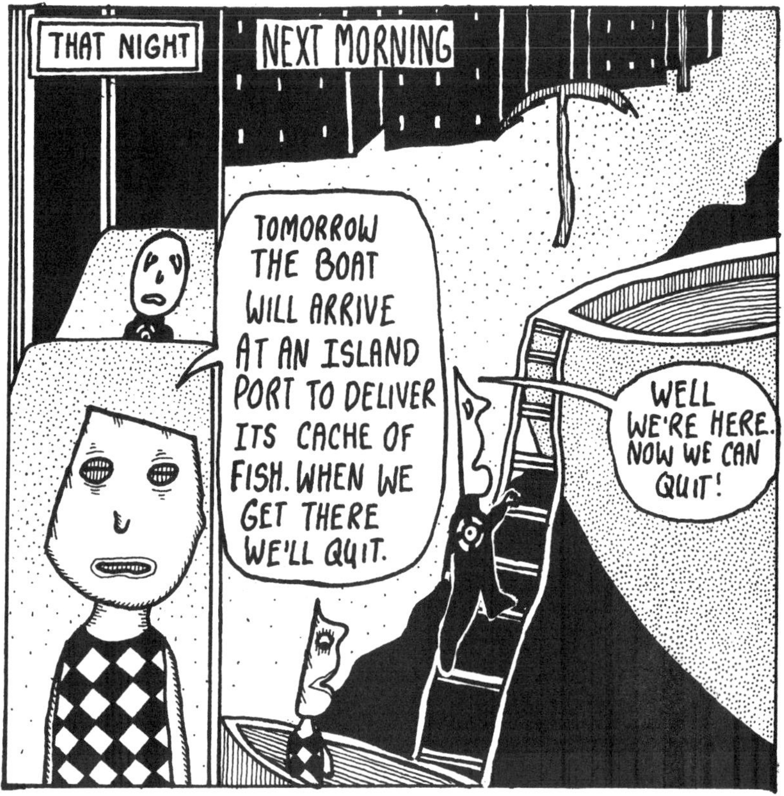
THAT NIGHT
NEXT MORNING
TOMORROW THE BOAT WILL ARRIVE AT AN ISLAND PORT TO DELIVER ITS CACHE OF FISH. WHEN WE GET THERE WE'LL QUIT.
WELL WE'RE HERE. NOW WE CAN QUIT!

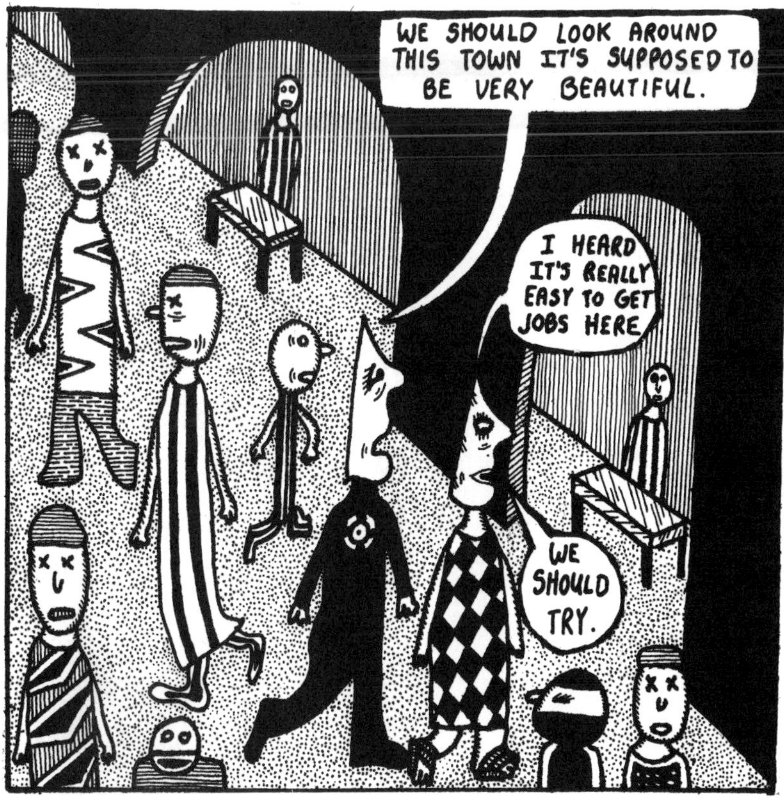
WE SHOULD LOOK AROUND THIS TOWN IT'S SUPPOSED TO BE VERY BEAUTIFUL.
I HEARD IT'S REALLY EASY TO GET JOBS HERE
WE SHOULD TRY.

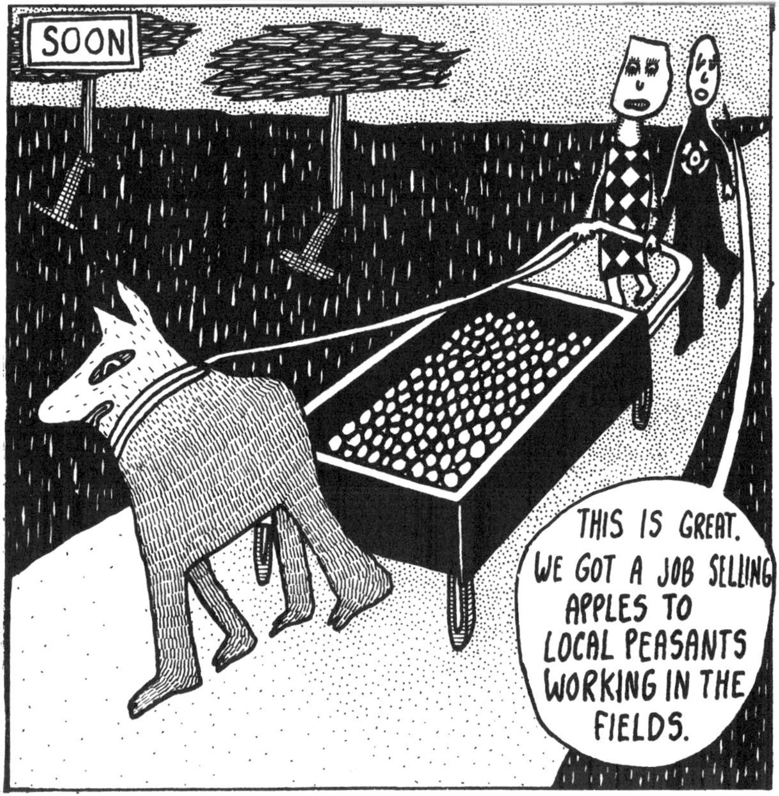
SOON
THIS IS GREAT. WE GOT A JOB SELLING APPLES TO LOCAL PEASANTS WORKING IN THE FIELDS.

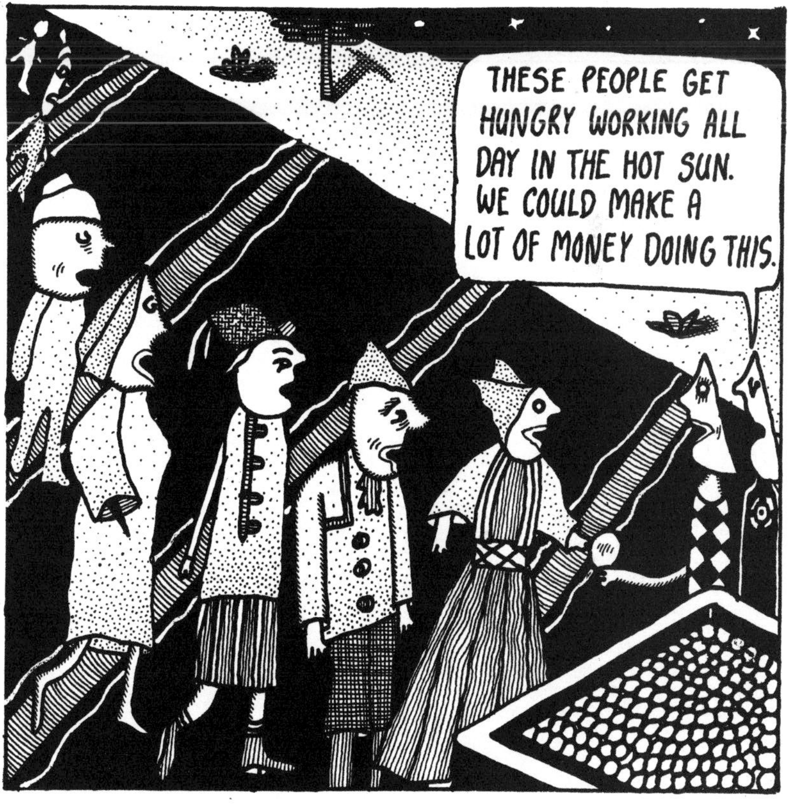
THESE PEOPLE GET HUNGRY WORKING ALL DAY IN THE HOT SUN. WE COULD MAKE A LOT OF MONEY DOING THIS.

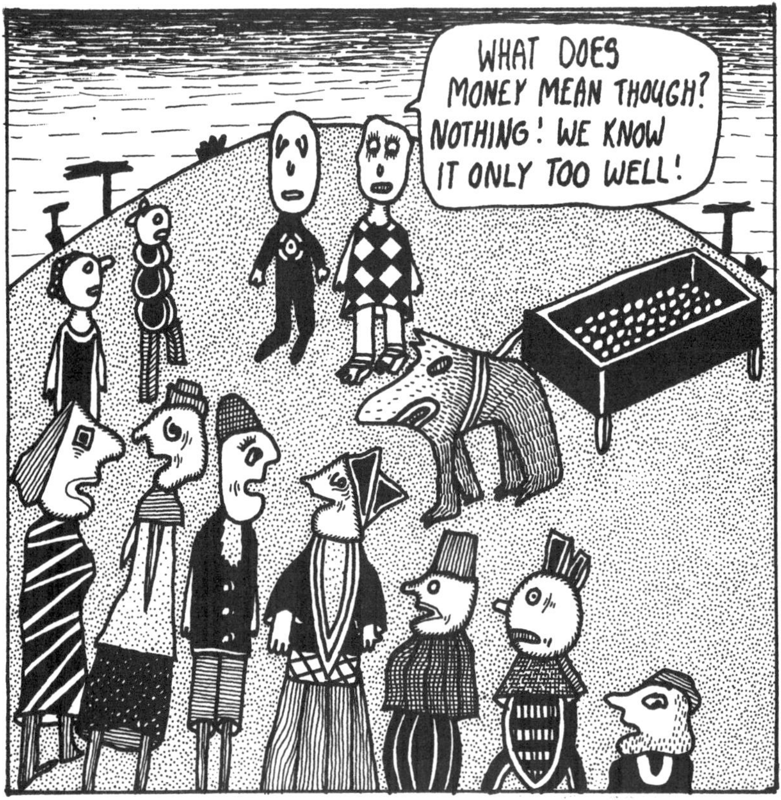
WHAT DOES MONEY MEAN THOUGH? NOTHING! WE KNOW IT ONLY TOO WELL!

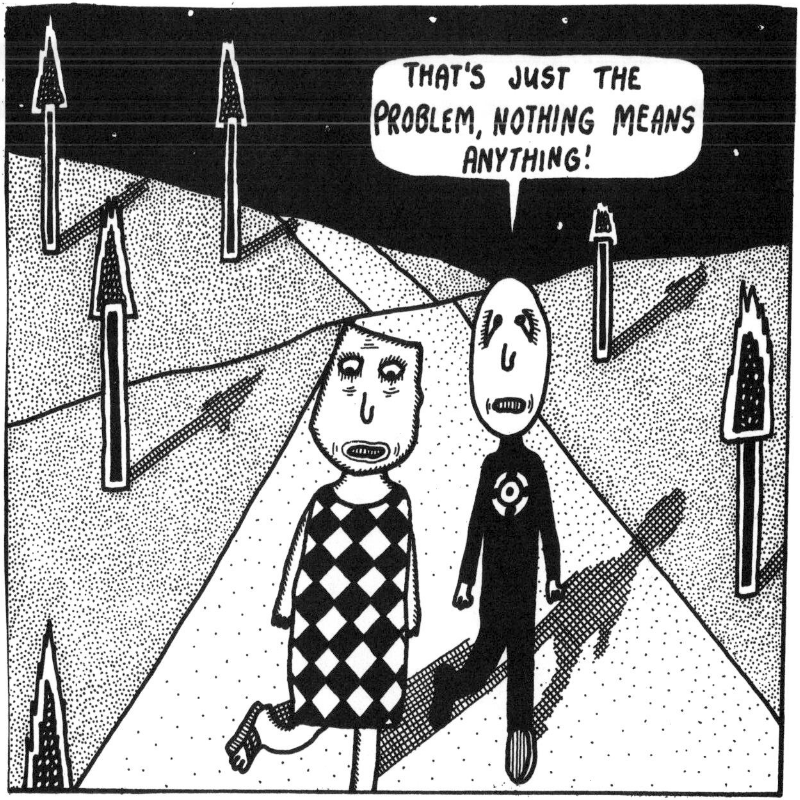
THAT'S JUST THE PROBLEM, NOTHING MEANS ANYTHING!

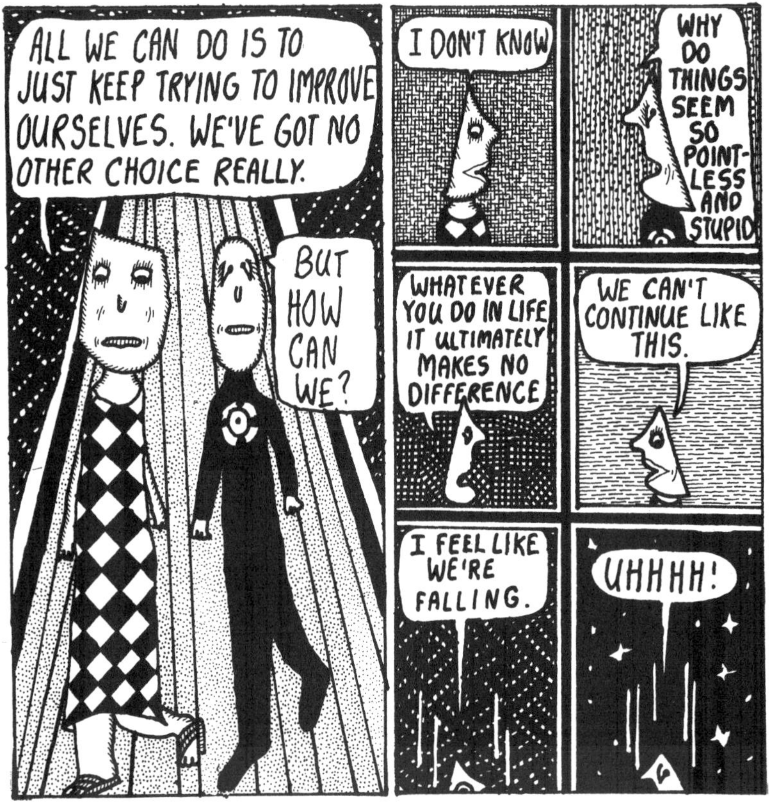
ALL WE CAN DO IS TO JUST KEEP TRYING TO IMPROVE OURSELVES. WE'VE GOT NO OTHER CHOICE REALLY.
BUT HOW CAN WE?
I DON'T KNOW
WHY DO THINGS SEEM SO POINTLESS AND STUPID
WHATEVER YOU DO IN LIFE IT ULTIMATELY MAKES NO DIFFERENCE
WE CAN'T CONTINUE LIKE THIS.
I FEEL LIKE WE'RE FALLING.
UHHHH!

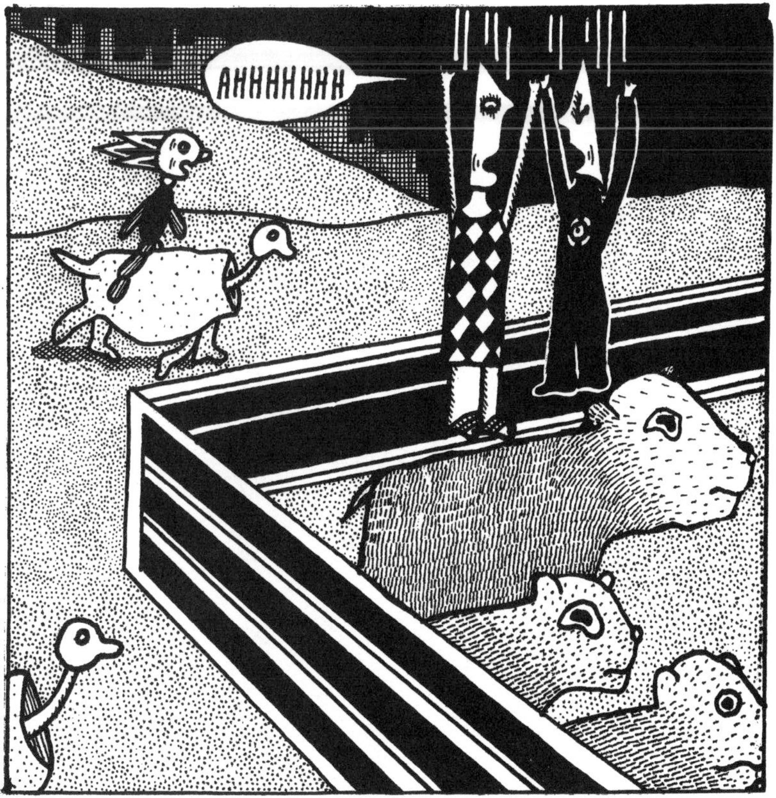
AHHHHHHH

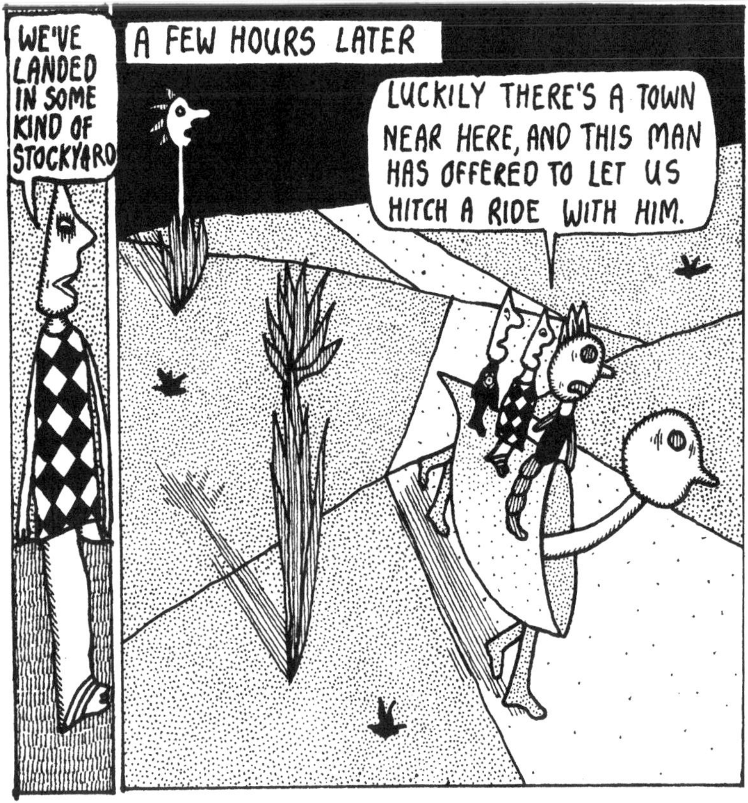
WE'VE LANDED IN SOME KIND OF STOCKYARD
A FEW HOURS LATER
LUCKILY THERE'S A TOWN NEAR HERE, AND THIS MAN HAS OFFERED TO LET US HITCH A RIDE WITH HIM.

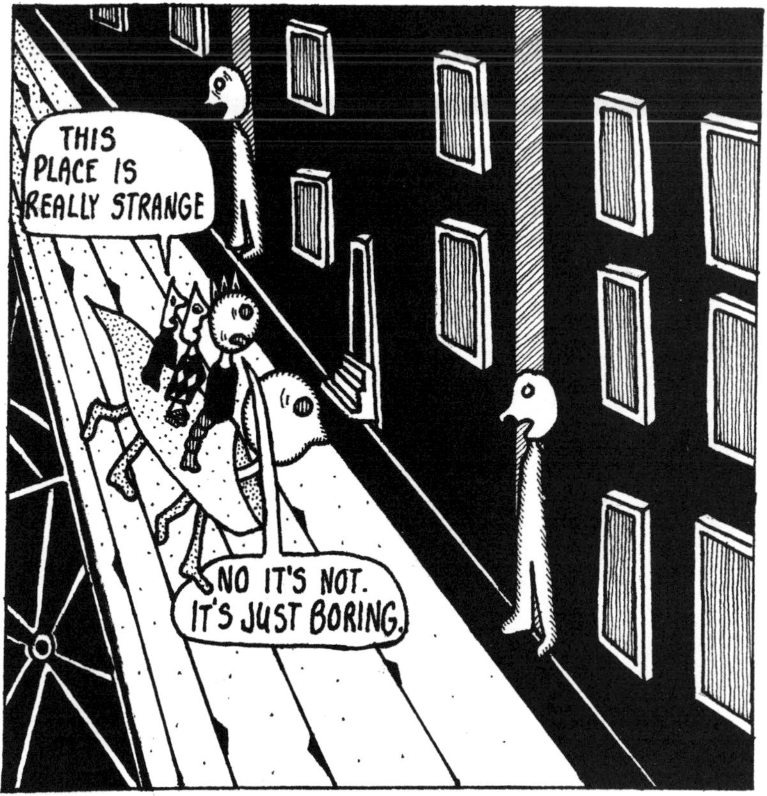
THIS PLACE IS REALLY STRANGE
NO IT'S NOT. IT'S JUST BORING.

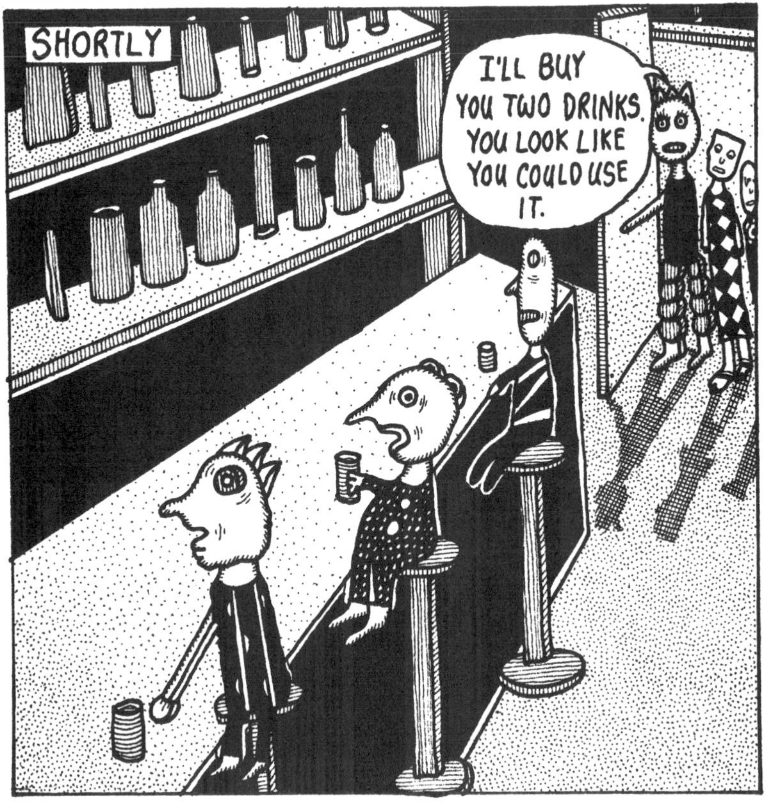
SHORTLY
I'LL BUY YOU TWO DRINKS. YOU LOOK LIKE YOU COULD USE IT.

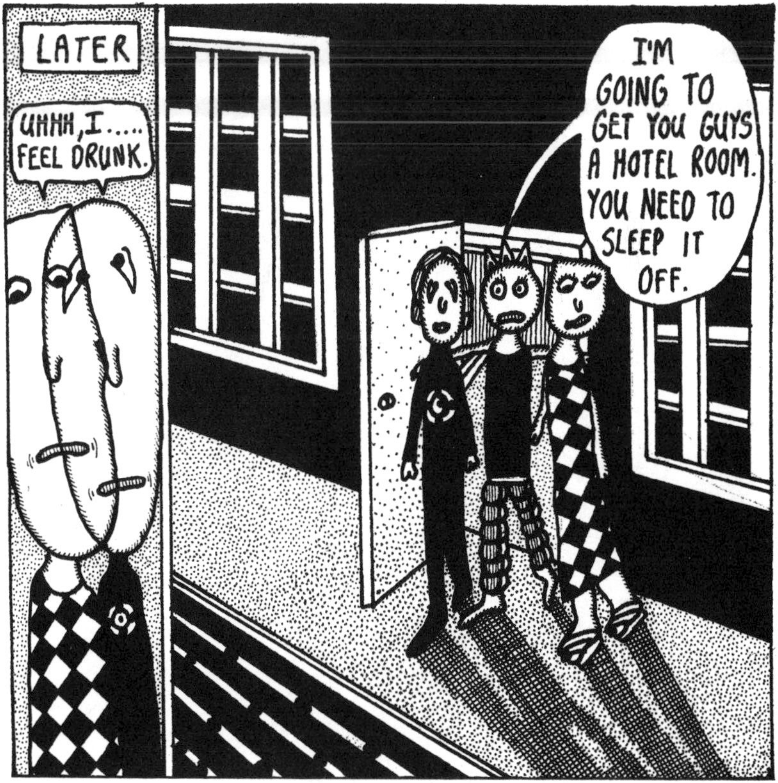
LATER
UHHH, I..... FEEL DRUNK.
I'M GOING TO GET YOU GUYS A HOTEL ROOM. YOU NEED TO SLEEP IT OFF.

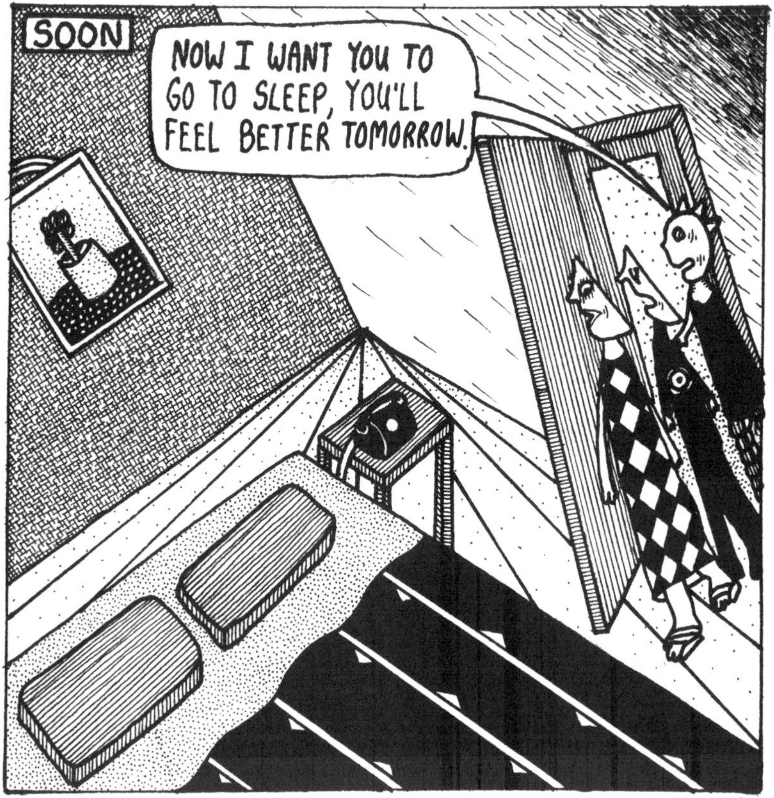
SOON
NOW I WANT YOU TO GO TO SLEEP, YOU'LL FEEL BETTER TOMORROW.

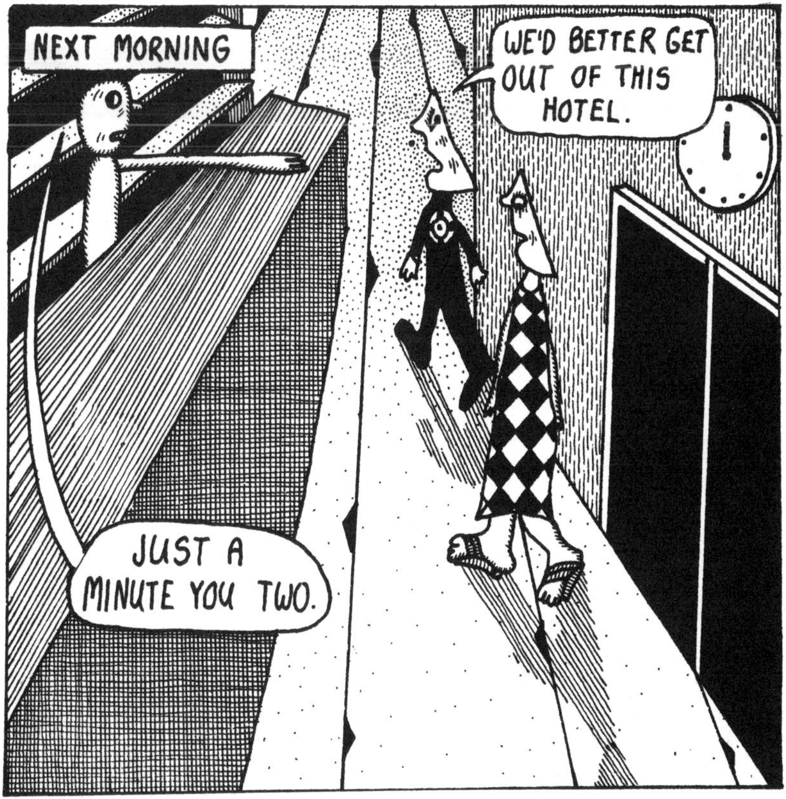
NEXT MORNING
WE'D BETTER GET OUT OF THIS HOTEL.
JUST A MINUTE YOU TWO.

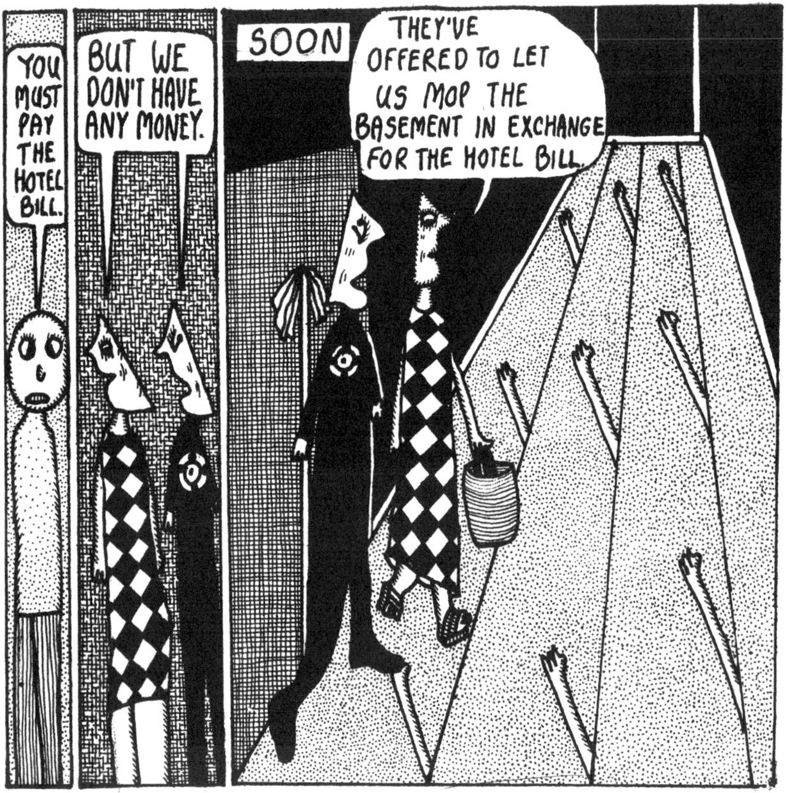
YOU MUST PAY THE HOTEL BILL.
BUT WE DON'T HAVE ANY MONEY.
SOON
THEY'VE OFFERED TO LET US MOP THE BASEMENT IN EXCHANGE FOR THE HOTEL BILL.

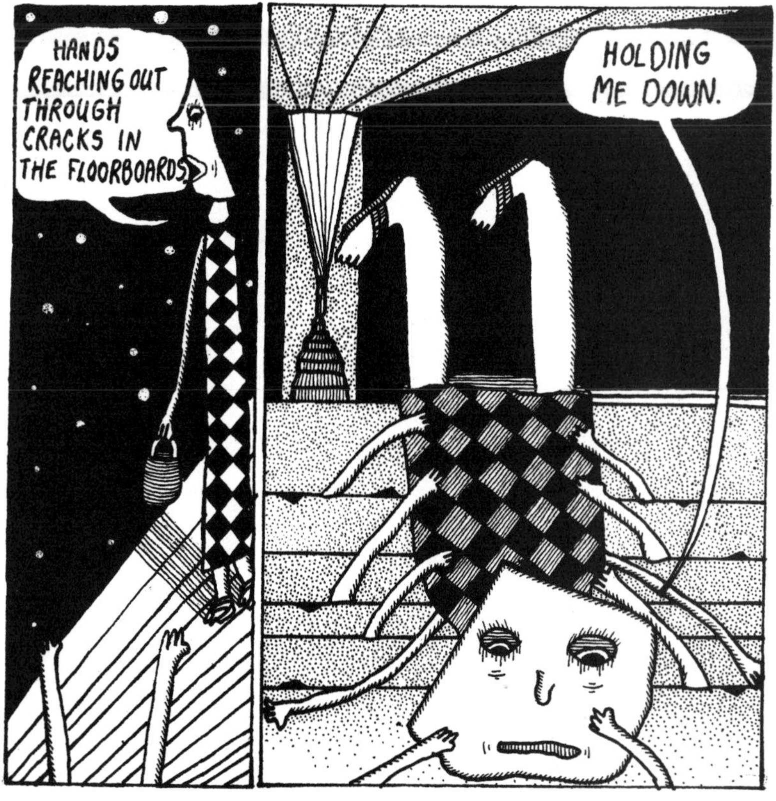
HANDS REACHING OUT THROUGH CRACKS IN THE FLOORBOARDS
HOLDING ME DOWN.

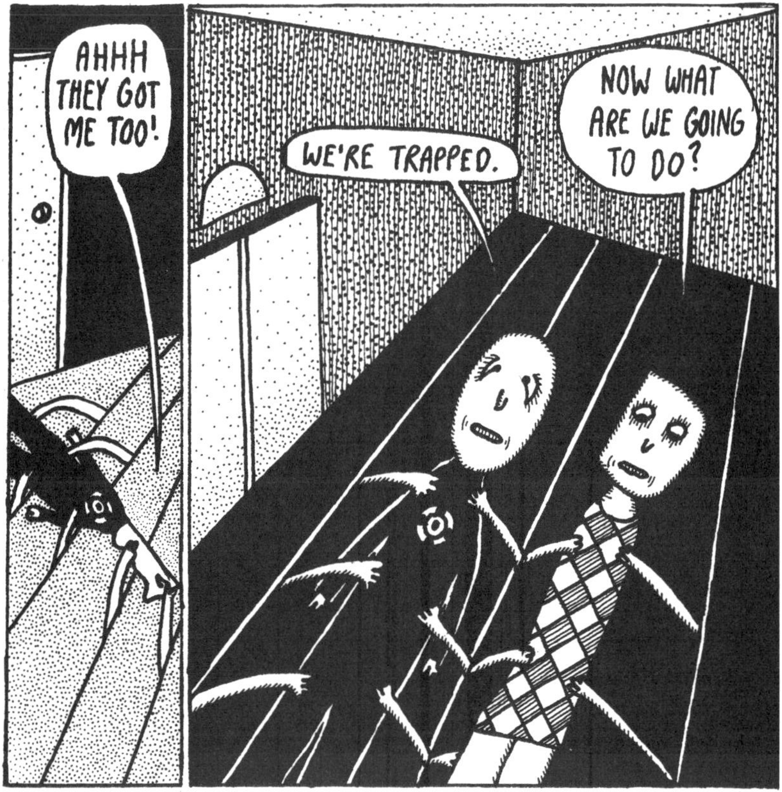
AHHH THEY GOT ME TOO!
WE'RE TRAPPED.
NOW WHAT ARE WE GOING TO DO?

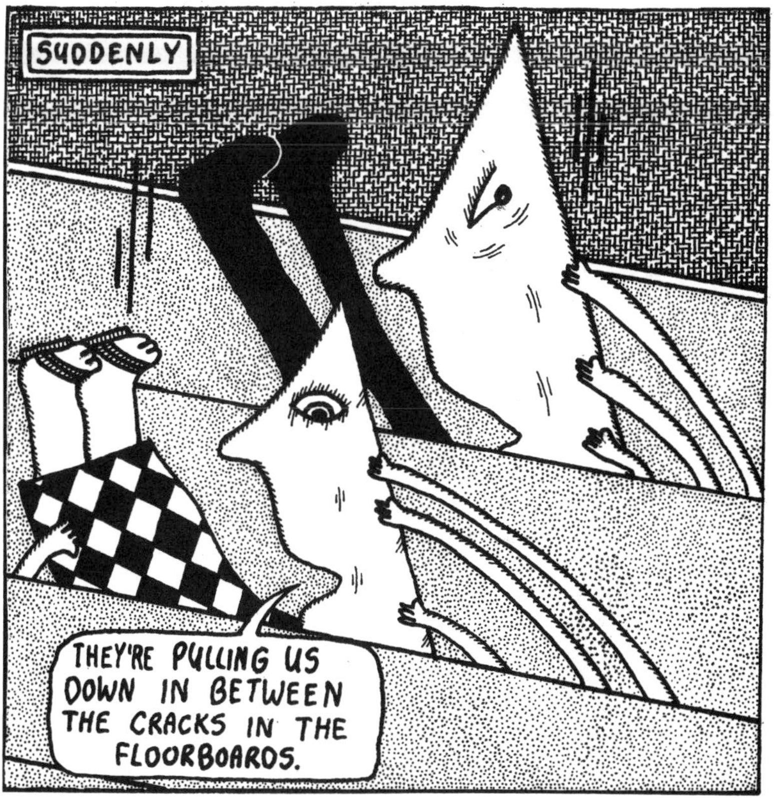
SUDDENLY
THEY'RE PULLING US DOWN IN BETWEEN THE CRACKS IN THE FLOORBOARDS.

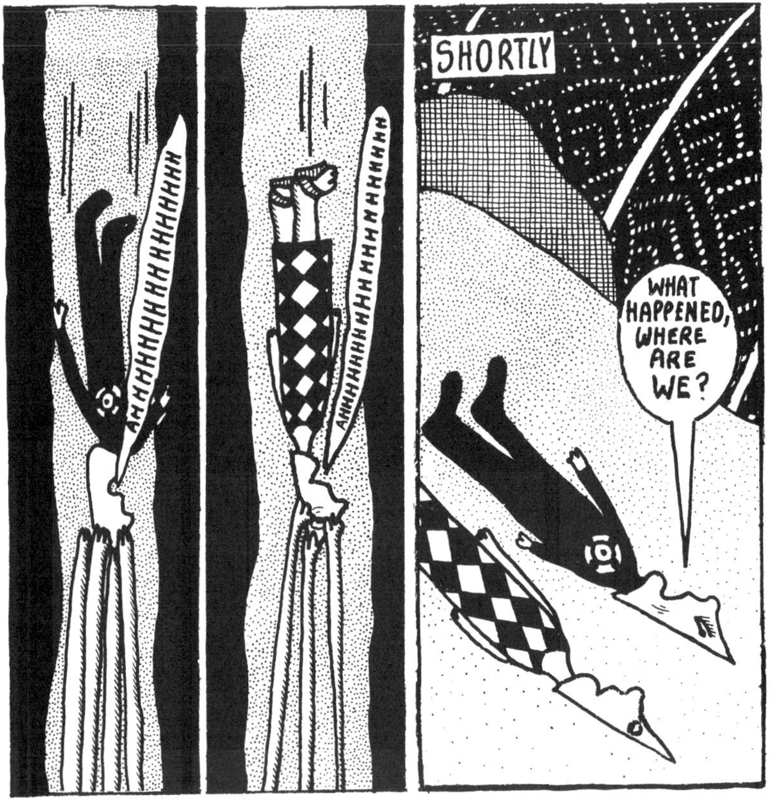
AHHHHHHHHHHHHHHHH
AHHHHHHHHHHHHHHHHHHHHHHH
SHORTLY
WHAT HAPPENED, WHERE ARE WE?

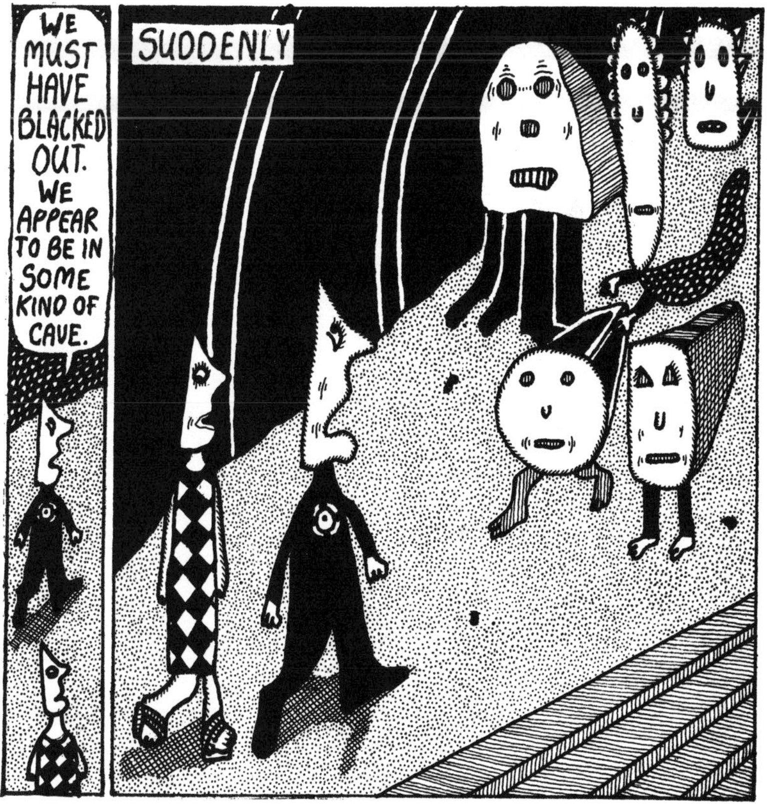
WE MUST HAVE BLACKED OUT. WE APPEAR TO BE IN SOME KIND OF CAVE.
SUDDENLY

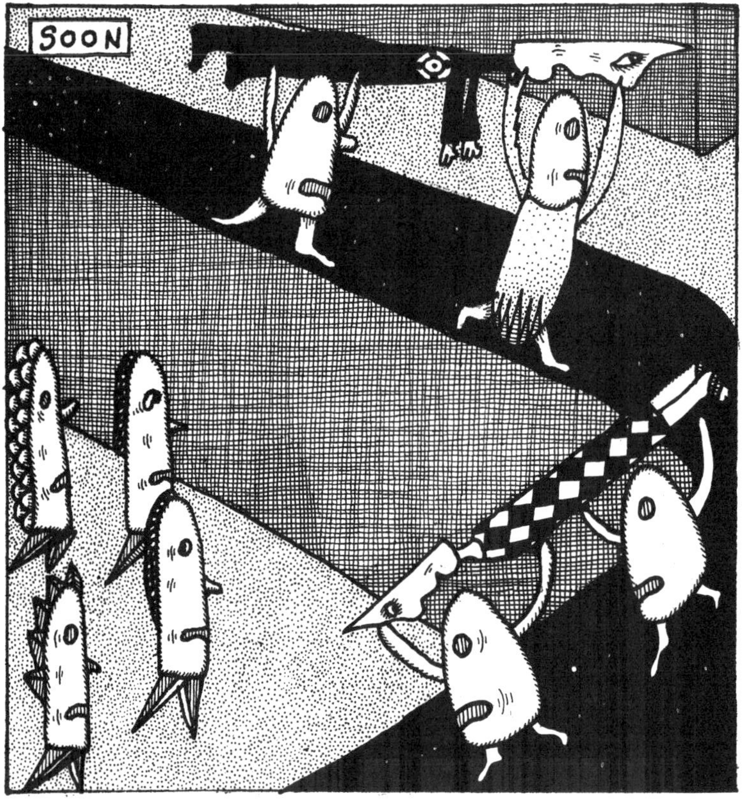
SOON

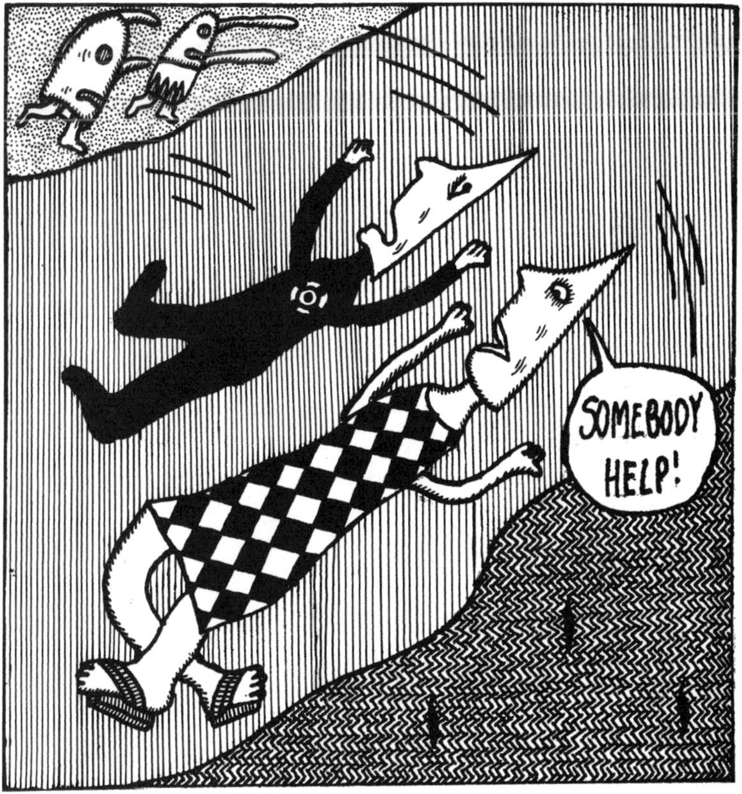
SOMEBODY HELP!

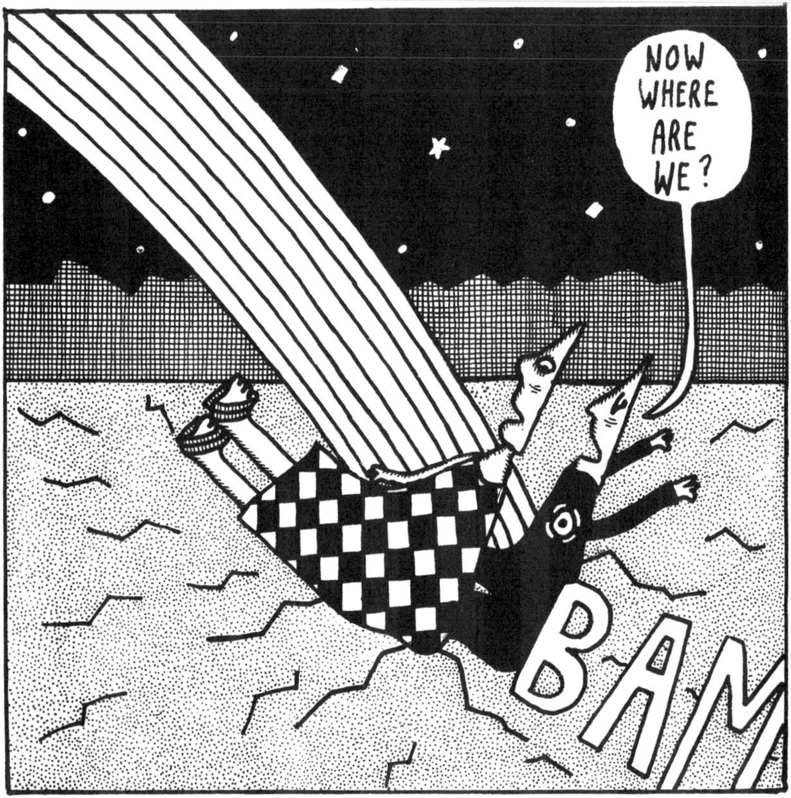
NOW WHERE ARE WE?
BAM

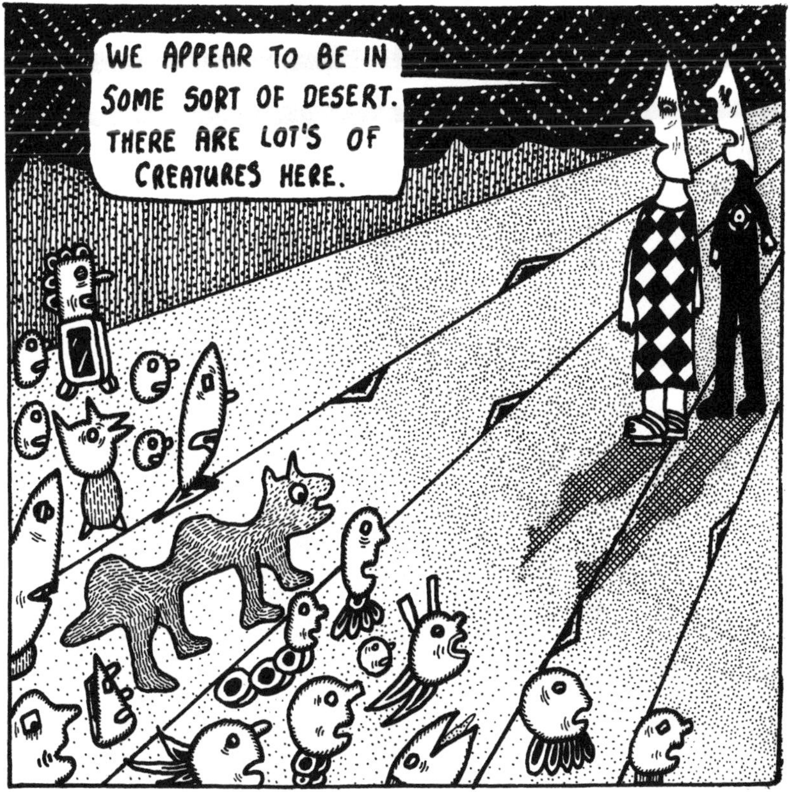
WE APPEAR TO BE IN SOME SORT OF DESERT. THERE ARE LOT'S OF CREATURES HERE.

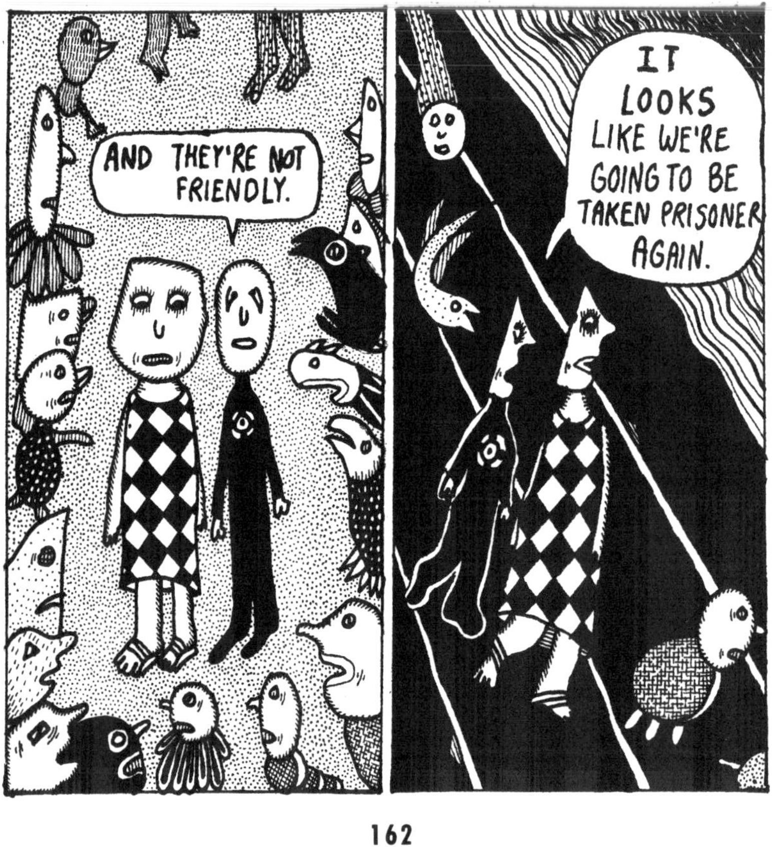
AND THEY'RE NOT FRIENDLY.
IT LOOKS LIKE WE'RE GOING TO BE TAKEN PRISONER AGAIN.

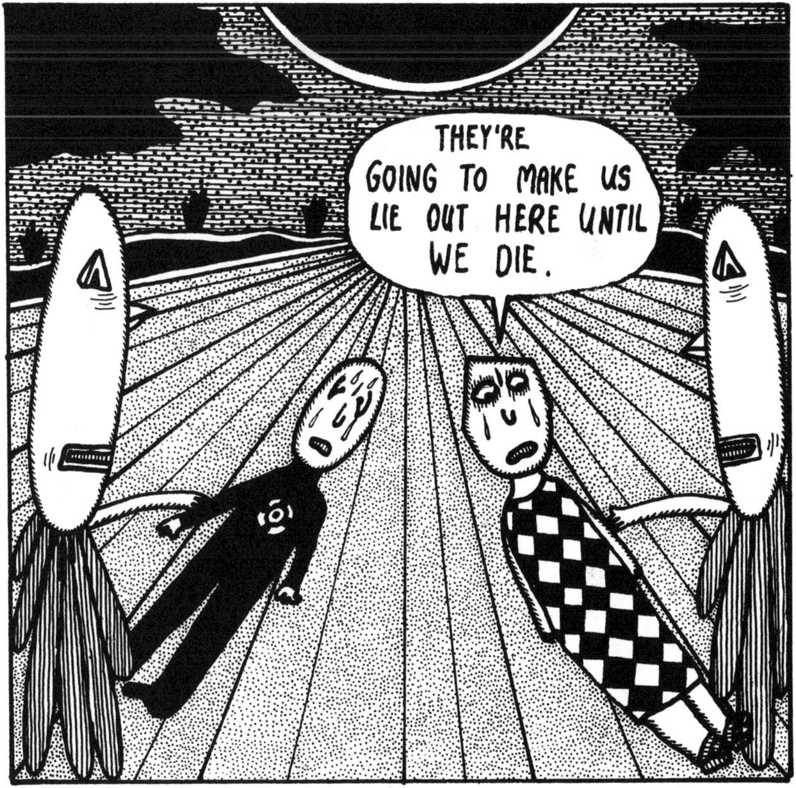
THEY'RE GOING TO MAKE US LIE OUT HERE UNTIL WE DIE.

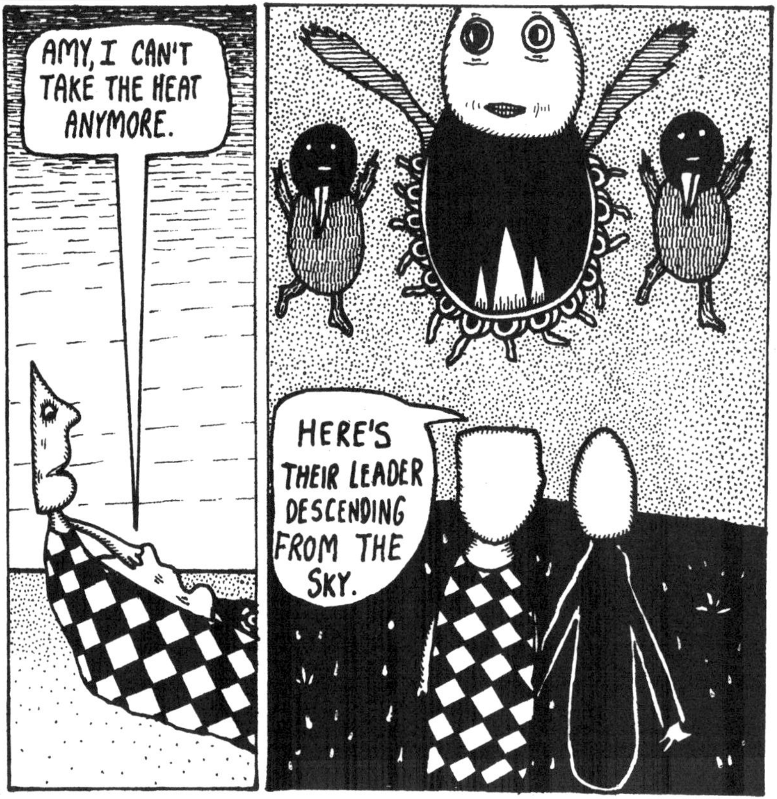
AMY, I CAN'T TAKE THE HEAT ANYMORE.
HERE'S THEIR LEADER DESCENDING FROM THE SKY.

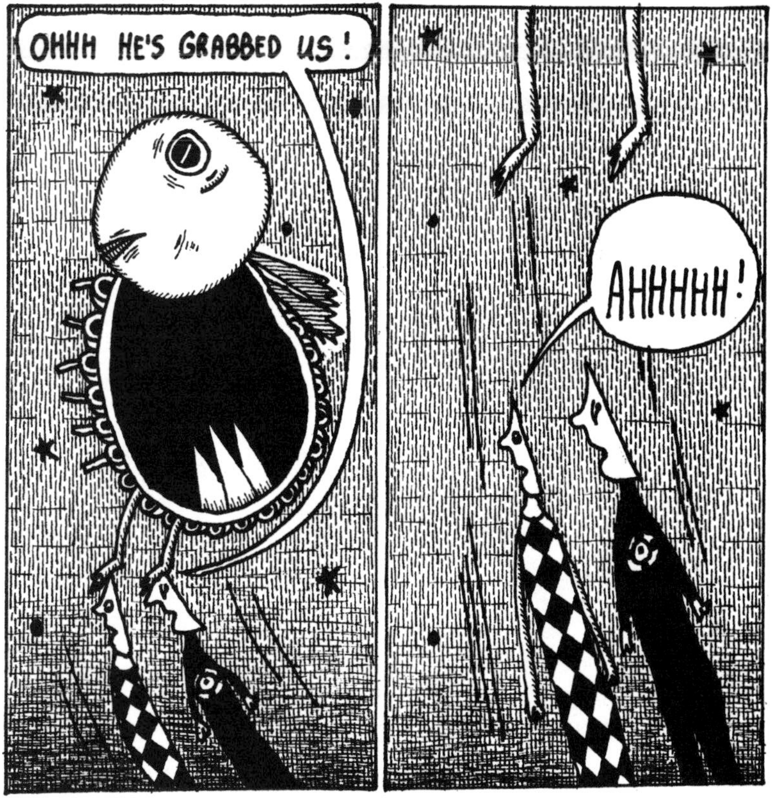
OHHH HE'S GRABBED US!
AHHHHH!

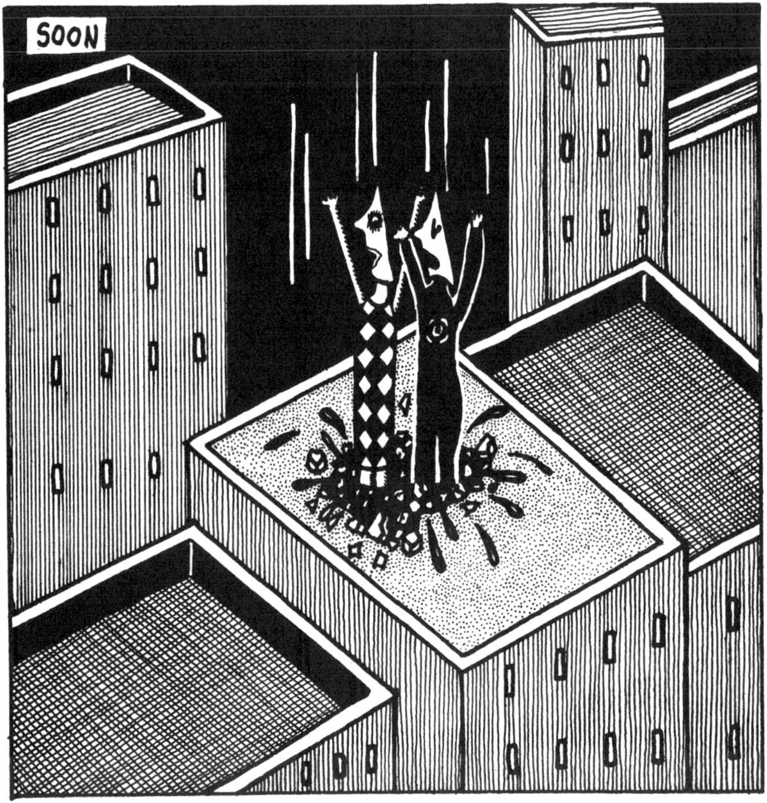
SOON

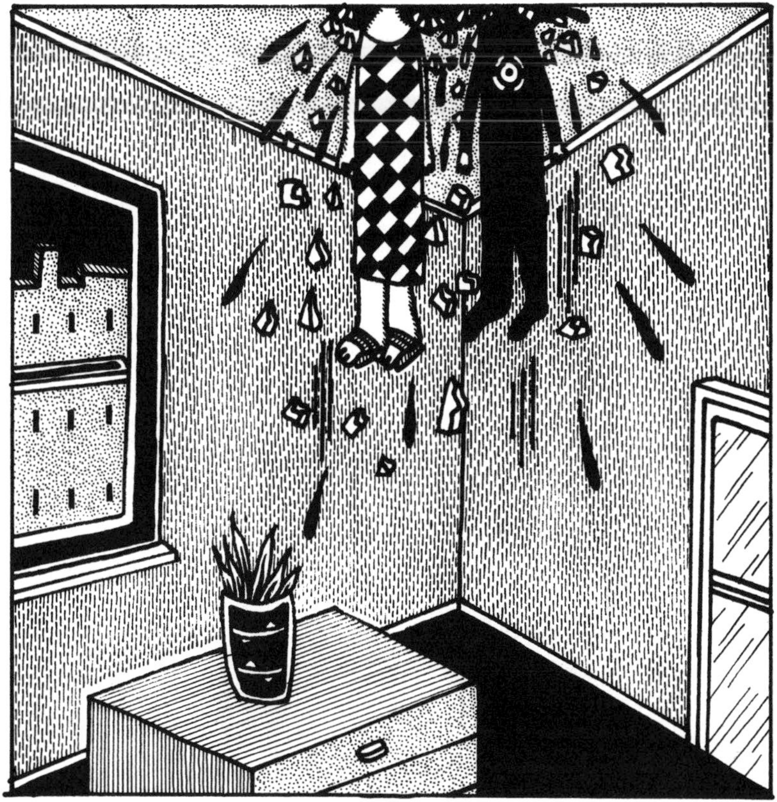

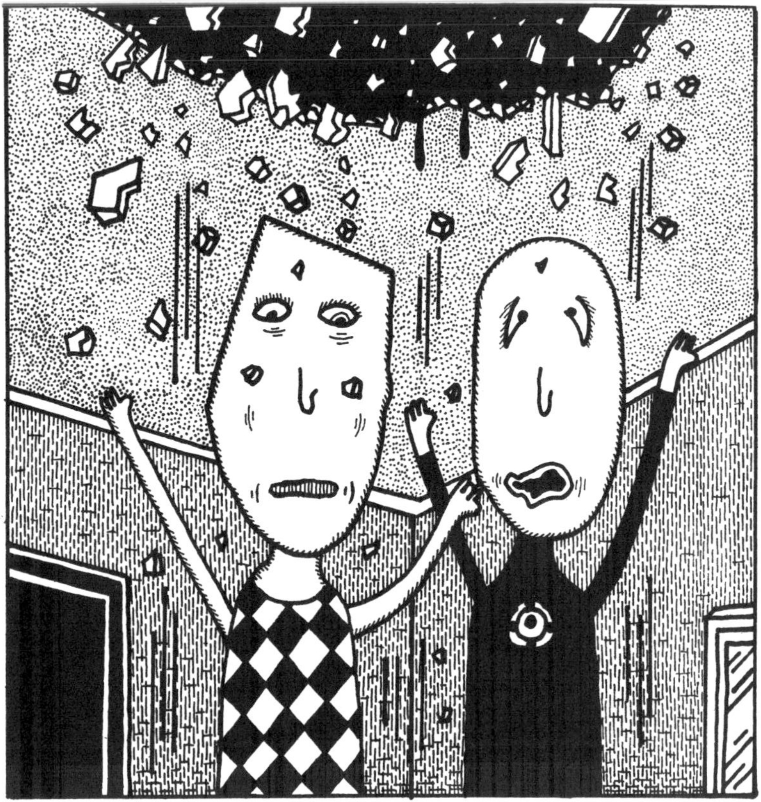

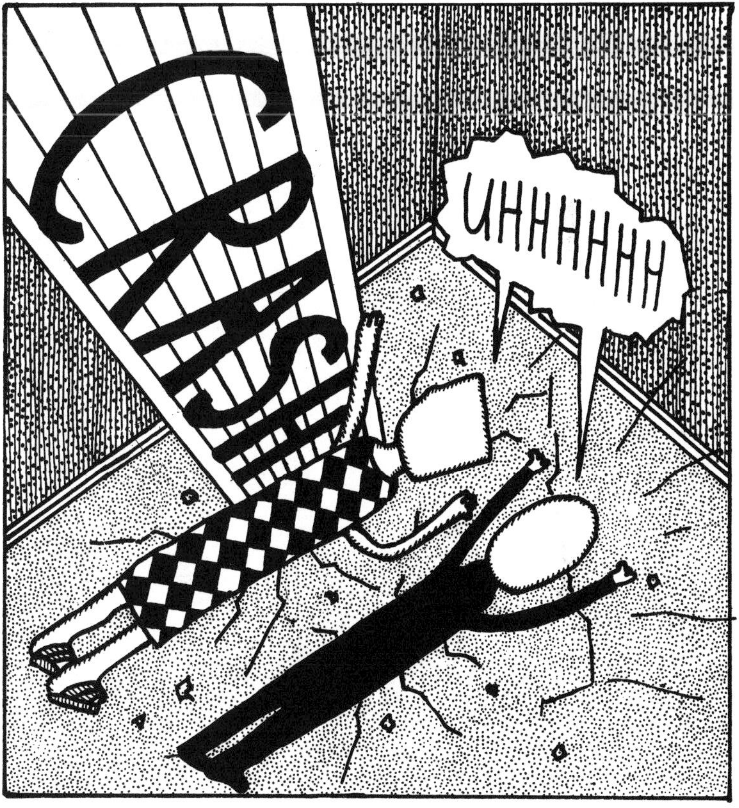
CRASH
UHHHHHH

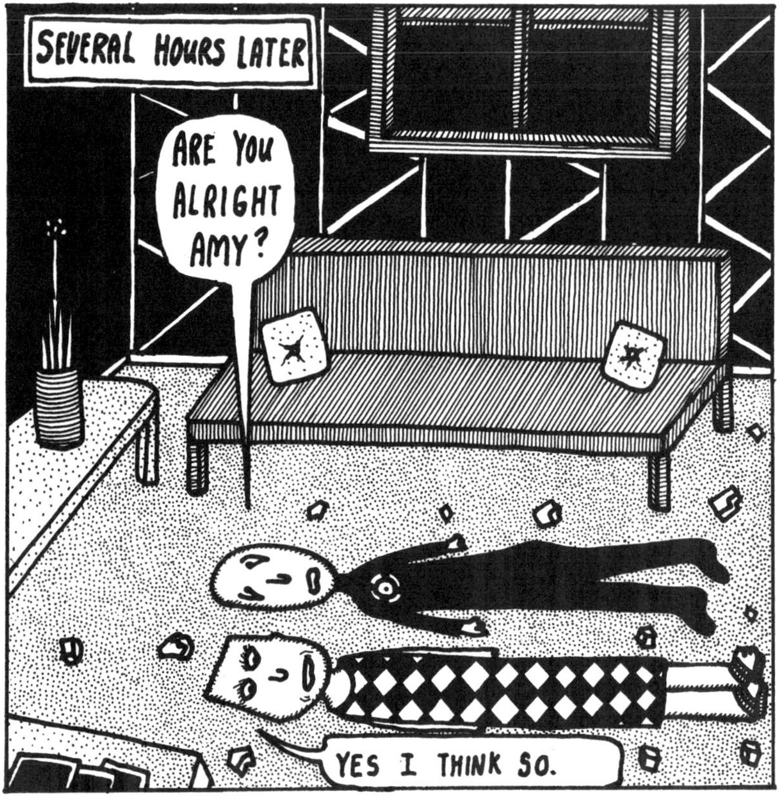
SEVERAL HOURS LATER
ARE YOU ALRIGHT AMY?
YES I THINK SO.

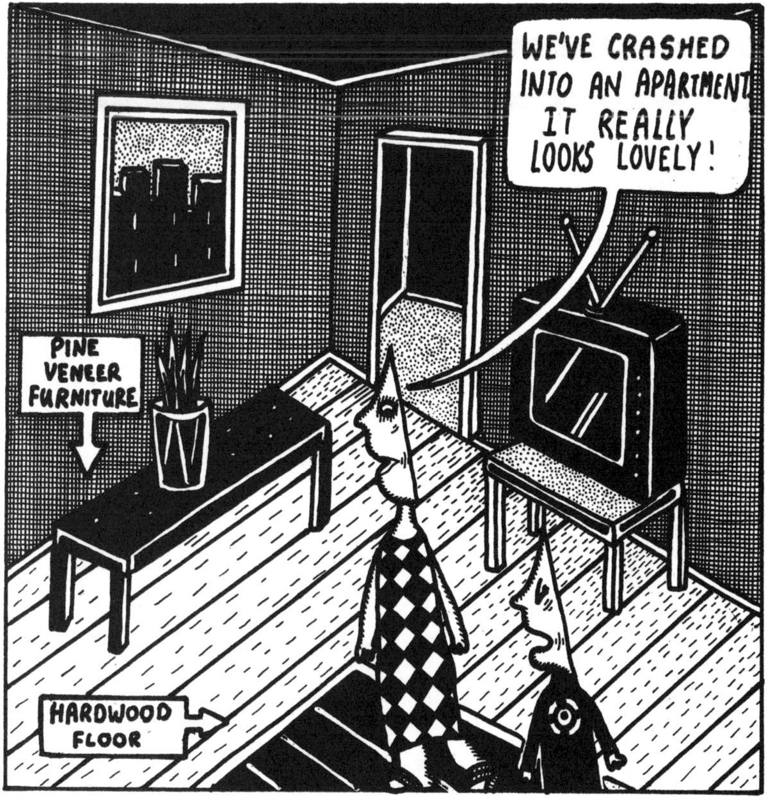
WE'VE CRASHED INTO AN APARTMENT. IT REALLY LOOKS LOVELY!
PINE VENEER FURNITURE
HARDWOOD FLOOR

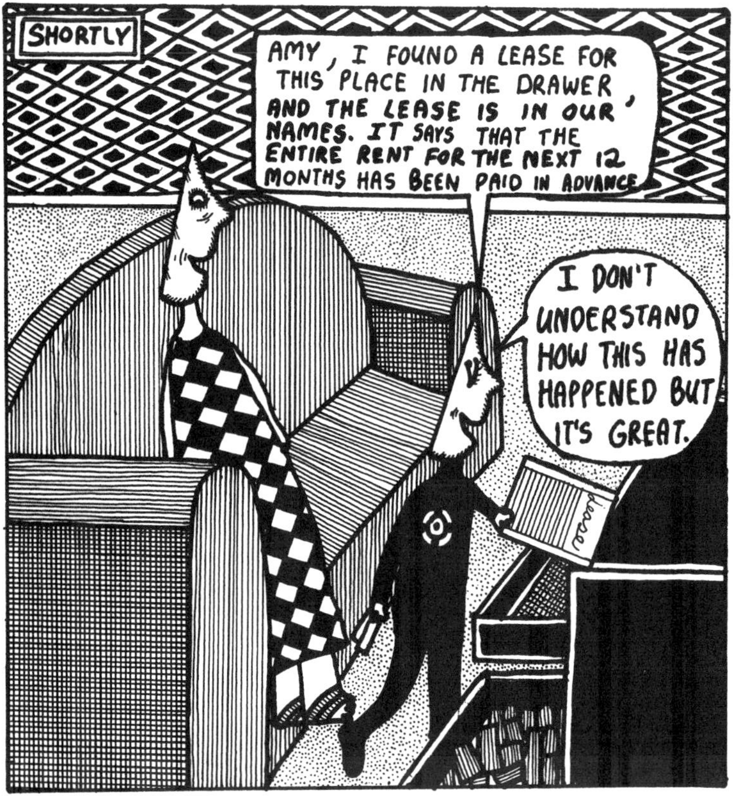
SHORTLY
AMY, I FOUND A LEASE FOR THIS PLACE IN THE DRAWER, AND THE LEASE IS IN OUR NAMES. IT SAYS THAT THE ENTIRE RENT FOR THE NEXT 12 MONTHS HAS BEEN PAID IN ADVANCE
I DON'T UNDERSTAND HOW THIS HAS HAPPENED BUT IT'S GREAT.
lease

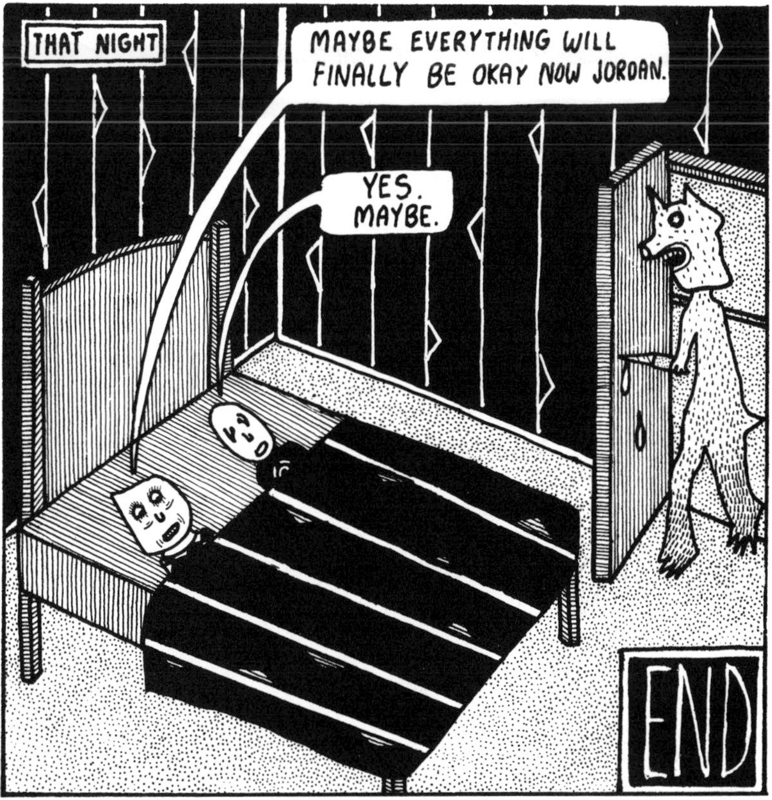
THAT NIGHT
MAYBE EVERYTHING WILL FINALLY BE OKAY NOW JORDAN.
YES. MAYBE.
END

MARK BEYER, 1987

NEW AND FORTHCOMING TITLES
FROM NEW YORK REVIEW COMICS

PEPLUM
Blutch

ALMOST COMPLETELY BAXTER
Glen Baxter

SOFT CITY
Pushwagner

PRETENDING IS LYING
Dominique Goblet

WHAT AM I DOING HERE?
Abner Dean

NYRC